For my Nanny and in loving memory of my Grandad, who made me believe in soul mates.

'I see when men love women. They give them but a little of their lives. But women when they love give everything.'

-Oscar Wilde

CHAPTER ONE

Dorothea

The air in her bedroom was crisp in the early hours of the morning. With walls as thin as paper, little else could be expected. There was a chill during the winter but the meagre walls pleasantly ensured the cottage was not too stuffy throughout the summer months. It was often refreshing, to feel cool air caressing the surface of her skin, especially when the girl who inhabited the room had been haunted with the terror of her weekly, bordering on nightly bad dreams. But how could she not be fearful in the lonesome darkness of her bedroom, when her life had become a living nightmare itself?

The truth was Thea would often wake up with sheets damp with sweat and tears. She'd suffered with nightmares since she was a girl, stories of war keeping her awake. She'd been a sensitive youngster but often hid that part of herself with her stubborn nature. Unfortunately, the anxiety didn't fade as she'd grown older, and the slightest thing seemed admissible during the day but when the night came, she could not sleep thanks to her constant overthinking. Yet nothing could prevent the nightmares, as her mother constantly told her. Thea would scowl because that was not at all true. Thea's father could prevent them, always. He would stroke her hair and hum a lullaby about vast oceans and Mediterranean shores. But that comfort was gone. He wasn't in his room at night, sleeping soundly beside her mother, snoring louder than anything. He wasn't sat at the table at breakfast, reading the paper and going on about lazy, fat politicians, whilst gracing the rest of the table with his awful coffee-scented morning breath. And her brother was not sat beside him, still half asleep with red eyes, dark curls like a mop on his head, sticking out in different directions, yawning every time their father finished a sentence.

The only sound Thea heard now as she sat at the wooden dining table was a deafening silence. It wasn't that Thea and her mother didn't get on; it was simply that their different opinions often resulted in uncomfortable silences anyway, so there wasn't much point in conversing.

It had been a week since the men of the family had left. Looking at her mother now, Thea could still recall her expression when the two men had stepped onto the train, coated from head to toe in military uniform. Her mother had said they looked handsome, but seeing them like that reminded Thea of the military officers pointing at men like her brother and father and stripping them of their lives whilst they sat at desks, ordering people around. Perhaps it was an unfair assumption, considering she knew little about the war, and the only information she had was from her father, who had strong political beliefs.

As a rule, Thea tried desperately not to think about her brother and father; whether it was considering the trauma they faced or facing the possibility that they may never return home. She had to remind herself that worrying wouldn't help anybody. All she needed to know was that it was her responsibility and duty to look after the life her father had left behind.

It just so happened that the Millers lived on a farm; one that had been in the family for generations. Thea knew it was more than just work to her father. It was a duty to produce food, and farming was a business that never stopped. It was a labour of love. Thea had been told there had been joy throughout the village when Mrs Miller gave birth to James, her older brother, the Miller name would continue when the boy took over the family farm. It had never occurred to Thea's parents that James would not have the same passion for it his father did and that, on the contrary, Thea would be the one who cherished the farm and be willing to wake up as soon as the cockerels crowed.

Thea and her father were practically inseparable. They spent early mornings together when the sun had not quite risen and the air had a strong scent, like damp grass and flowers. The pair shared a pot of tea each day before heading across the muddy Welsh fields to attend to the daily chores that came with growing up on a farm. Work on the farm was never scarce but working the land had been tough for Thea when she was a younger. Consequently, she would sit on a fence, watching her father tend to the crops with care, a grey flat-cap atop his head. They'd talk about everything and nothing. Her father never bored of her ramblings about flowers and the bugs and creatures that would shelter themselves under their petals. As she grew older, receiving a pair of overalls as a gift for her birthday, she began working on the fields with enthusiasm like her father's.

As time passed, Thea became more confident in farm work, taking on more demanding jobs such as using new machinery to harvest the crops. Her mother hadn't been too happy about that, already greatly upset by the fact her daughter was now wearing trousers and doing what she'd called a 'man's job'. Her father would smile at her when her mother scorned her ways. He would always defend her, claiming he needed the help and that James was not willing to assist, since he was far too busy wooing local women. At first, it was obvious to Thea that her father was lying for her benefit because he had many men helping in the fields. But eventually, when war was declared and food became scarcer, it reached a point where her assistance was essential.

Farming was declared a reserved occupation; a replacement had to be found if a man left his job as a farmer to join the armed forces. And it was extremely difficult to find men for the job. Those who were not yet at war were either very young boys or too elderly and frail, so Thea took on some of the most physically demanding jobs, previously only taken up by the strongest of men. She had expected some harsh words in the village about her working out on the fields, but the hardships of rationing made them more generous towards her. More food was required and people were getting scared, so if it meant women had to do 'a man's job', there wasn't much room for complaint. Eventually her father and brother left too, and Thea had never felt loneliness quite like it. She'd been holding on tightly to the hope that her father would not be sent away due to the importance of his job. But necessity meant that he had been sent to war along with her brother James. Something was missing from her life and everything was different.

The girl snapped out of her daydream, glancing up at her mother. She had her greying hair set up in pin-curls. It really did baffle Thea that her mother was still putting effort in to having nice hair. It was probably comforting for her, providing her with a sense of normality in this strange, solitary time.

"Isn't it chilly this morning?"

The weather or the current temperature were typical conversation starters for her mother. Thea shrugged.

"I've told you to stop doing that," the woman huffed, getting plates out of one of the kitchen cabinets. "It's rude to shrug Dorothea. You aren't mute. Use words."

Sometimes Thea wished she was mute if it meant she didn't have to be involved in pointless conversations.

"It's always cold in February, Mother." Thea tried not to sound bored and uncaring, but that was virtually impossible when her mother's reactions were always so humorous, the way her cheeks burned red with frustration.

"Do not use that tone with me young lady." Thea cringed.

She sat in silence, listening to the sound of the kettle squealing, only glancing up when her mother set some toast on the table. Unbuttered... that usually meant she was having a bad day. Thea reached to retrieve the remains of the homemade marmalade from across the table, spreading it clumsily. Two weeks ago Thea had made this marmalade with her father. She wished she'd savoured it, knowing it wouldn't taste the same when she made a new batch without him there to help. After using as little as possible, she screwed the lid on and ate the toast, glancing up at her mother when she leant over to switch on the radio. A few minutes passed by and Thea interrupted the man speaking,

"Do we have to listen to this? It is the same information we get most days."

Her mother looked up at her, mouth falling open in surprise at her little outburst.

"You do know there is a war going on." Her tone was slow, concentrated. "Your father… your brother—"

"Yes. I know..." Thea swallowed, feeling a little guilt, "but they aren't exactly giving us detailed updates on where they are. It's just those stupid politicians."

Much to Thea's surprise, her mother only laughed sadly, shaking her head with a melancholy smile.

"You sound just like your father."

Thea frowned. The way she spoke about him, as if he wasn't alive anymore. Soldiers did come back from war. She knew plenty of ex-soldiers in the village. Granted, many had missing limbs and talked total nonsense for most of the day, wasting their time in local pubs, but they still *returned*.

Thea finished her toast without another word, downing a cup of tea that was so hot it burnt her tongue, she didn't care. She went upstairs, pulling on a pair of trousers and her father's old jumper to spite her mother, who still hated it when she wore it. She tied up her boots by the front door, laces still muddy from spending hours outside working. She tugged on her father's old flat-cap and held her head up high. Her father and brother were coming back, she did not doubt it. They were brave, courageous men. She knew of much weaker that had survived war, like the sobbing drunken men at the bars in the village who spoke so quickly in Welsh that Thea, who had heard the language since she was a baby, couldn't even understand what they were saying. But that didn't matter because her father wasn't like that. He was strong.

The important thing was that she took care of the crops, the animals and everything her father loved. That probably also included her mother. Other than some disagreements, she was certain that job wouldn't be too difficult. She'd do anything for them to return to a happy home.

CHAPTER TWO

<u>Angeline</u>

The whole ordeal of hiding under the stairs in the shelter was by far the most atrocious part of Angie's week– and they were living in wartime, so that was saying something. The darkness was unbearable, and the smell of damp wood combined with sweaty bodies created a distasteful odour. She was pressed up against her mother– Angie knew this because the Carter household was full of boys, and her mother was the only one that didn't stink like dirt. Focusing on the smell of dirt in such an enclosed place was not a good idea, daydreaming herself away would be better.

Before hiding had become a regular occurrence, the space had been filled with sobs from her family members who were undoubtedly visualising the streets of London– the very ground on which they had taken their first steps and ridden their first bikes on– being demolished and turned to ash. Now, the family huddled in a silent and knowing acceptance. This was life now, and they simply had to follow orders, ration food and look after one another.

Angie had had a privileged childhood. The girl had been raised just short of royalty throughout her first few years of life– even the maids had begun calling her 'little princess' from a young age, especially when she tugged on their skirts and begged for the prettiest and most expensive dolls from Hamley's. But that was the past, things were different now.

The Great Depression was the most severe worldwide economic crisis, known as the Great Slump in the United Kingdom. Beginning in the United States in the 1930s, Angie's father had firmly believed it would have no effect on his trading business. However it became more difficult, employment rates decreased rapidly and the cities were hardest hit. Living in the capital city meant the Carters were at a disadvantage. The effects weren't sudden; the Carters had kept their house and belongings but their savings had almost gone, so after Angie's father was sent away her mother had to work. Unlike many of Angie's friends' families, they couldn't afford to move the entire family to the countryside. If the bombing continued at the current severity, Angie knew it wouldn't be long until her and her brothers were evacuated.

"It's quieter, now."

The sound of her mother's voice broke through the silence. Of course it was her mother. Nobody else was brave enough to speak when they were in their shelter under the stairs. It wasn't like the Germans could hear the slightest noise and know where to drop a bomb– it was mainly because the children were too scared to form a single word. Angie responded,

"May we light a candle now?"

She looked in what she believed to be the general direction of her mother.

"Just a little longer, sweetheart. I can hear them in the distance," her mother replied, voice shaking. It couldn't be true that her mother could hear the German planes in the distance. The room was soundproofed, and the planes were only audible when they were very close.

Despite this, Angie did not reply, only nodding, even though nobody could see it.

Angie was not sure how much time had passed when her mother finally lit up the room with a dull orange glow from the candle she held with shaky hands. She spoke quietly still, "We can head out now. William?"

"Yes, Ma?"

The eldest of Angie's younger brothers replied. Angie could see in the dimly lit room that he was puffing his chest out, standing tall and prepared to listen to whatever their mother had to say.

"Stay here with your brothers for a moment. Angie and I will be back."

Normally, the entire family left the shelter at the same time, because the Carters always stuck together. Apparently, that was not the case today. Her mother led her out, holding her hand, clammy with fear. The woman unlocked the door with the rusted key. Once they exited the shelter, the pair made their way down the corridor. It was uncomfortably silent. The grandfather clock seemed to be ticking a few octaves lower than usual, and there was no hustle and bustle on the street outside, no dogs barking or children laughing.

When Angie gulped, and it felt like it was the only sound in the world. Her mother even heard it, squeezing her hand.

"Don't be scared, my darling."

Her soothing voice, one which had comforted Angie when she had trapped her fingers in the grand piano at the age of eight, or quietened her as her mother patched her up after falling off her rocking horse, or had sung a lullaby to her when a fever had prevented her from singing her solo in the church choir on Christmas Eve. The voice that usually calmed her, no matter what now seemed entirely ineffective. Angie knew what was going to happen. She lowered her voice, unable to stop the tears from forming in her eyes,

"Mother, I won't leave you."

Her mother sat down on the bottom step, placing her hands in her lap. Angie sat beside her without hesitation.

"Listen to me, Angeline. I need you to take care—"

"No!" Angie interrupted her, her face red with fury. Not at her mother, but at this war. Everything kept getting worse. It felt as if she could not have one good thing anymore.

It all started with her father having to leave to protect his country. It was not right. He should be sat at his desk, as usual, pipe in hand, his office smelling like strong tobacco. What made Angie even more furious was the fact she would now not only be miles away from her father, but soon would also be miles away from her mother.

"Lower your voice, Angeline; you may worry your brothers."

Angie could not help the outburst.

"They should be scared!" she said, tears streaming down her freckled cheeks. "They should be terrified! Terrified of leaving you here all alone to go to some ghastly house in the middle of the countryside! To be taken in by some old codger..."

"Watch your language, young lady!"

Oh, how Angie despised being called that.

"Evacuating the city is the safest thing I can do for you. In this case, staying alive is more important than staying with me. If I must send you and your brothers away on a train, so be it."

Angie stood up from the bottom step, shaking her head frantically.

"I will not go!"

"You will. Lower your voice, dear."

Angie sank down beside her mother again, defeated. She kept her head low, despite years of deportment training telling her to keep her head up when she spoke.

"I don't want to leave, Mother,"

Angie let out a wistful sob. Feeling those familiar, comforting arms around her, she tilted her head to rest on her mother's shoulder. She smelt like lavender; it was a hint of calm that Angie needed badly in that moment.

"I know, my darling."

That was all she said. Her mother stroked her hand through her blonde locks– she had not had time to pin them up– resulting in what Angie would call a frizzy mess. Not that her appearance was her top priority right now. It was not like Albert was there to see it. Angie felt a little guilty that she had barely thought about the young man who had been courting her since summer the previous year. It wasn't that she did not adore him, she did. He had regularly walked with her, kissed her hand when he greeted her, and he had written her many

19

letters that summer when he had gone away to the north, for a family holiday.

Angie couldn't think about the future right now. Peculiarly, this was not due to war. Angie had always struggled to picture the future. When she'd looked at her mother nursing her brothers as infants, it made her grimace in disgust. Was that all a young girl had to look forward to? Getting married to a rich man? Changing her family name? Going through painful childbirth to bring children into the world, only to raise them and go through the stresses of watching them leave the nest?

"We should get your brothers. I just wanted to tell you first."

Angie looked up at her mother. She dabbed away the last of her tears as her mother held her face, stroking her cheeks softly with the pads of her thumbs.

"I am so proud of you, darling. I know you will keep your brothers safe."

Angie let out a deep breath.

"We won't be split apart, will we?"

Her mother shook her head, but Angie was good at reading people and could tell that it was a hesitant gesture.

The two stood, her mother squeezing her hand one last time and heading to the shelter under the stairs where the boys were now play fighting, as children do. William, being only nine, was standing with a red face, looking as if he was on the verge of tears.

"Mother, I did tell them to stop being childish! They wouldn't listen–"

Angie smiled at him, kneeling to kiss his forehead.

"You did a good job, don't you worry."

He grinned, reassured.

The boys left the shelter, continuing to argue like cats and dogs in the living room instead, whilst Angie's mother flipped through the newspaper at an alarming rate, searching for news for when the next train to the countryside would depart from Waterloo station. Angie sat on the piano stool, looking away from her mother's frantic searching. The melody of the music transported her to an entirely different time and place; somewhere peaceful and safe. Her piano playing served as a comfort to the entire family and evenings had been spent in the living room with Angie playing for them. If Angie closed her eyes, letting herself relax into the melody of the music, it could all feel normal, just for a moment. But to ignore fear was a coward's way. She had a duty to protect her brothers, for the sake of her mother.

"Alright, Charles and Peter, stop fighting and listen." Her mother's voice of authority broke through the sound of squabbling. "We have talked about what might happen, haven't we?"

The boys nodded in perfect synchronization, taking a seat on the soft mat that carpeted the living room floor. Little Charles spoke up excitedly,

"We get sent on a train!"

Angie pouted at his childhood innocence. Looking to her mother, her expression one of sadness as she tried desperately not to cry at how oblivious her son was.

"Yes. Do you remember what I said about who is going with you?"

Peter and the boys looked at each other, faces blank with confusion. William spoke up then, voice knowing and mournful,

"You aren't coming with us, are you? You were telling Angie she had to look after us."

William was the most intelligent by far and insightful beyond his years.

"That's right, William. Now, Maria will assist you in packing your cases for tomorrow. I advise you to also bring a satchel with books and pencils to keep you entertained on the journey. There's a list in the paper of what you must pack."

She sounded adamant as she retreated out of the room. Angie glanced at her brothers' blank faces.

It was not discussed for the entirety of the evening. Her mother had headed off to bed early and Angie had stayed downstairs, lying on her stomach on the floor, re-reading the same sentence in her book over and over, her mind was racing. She could not bring herself to concentrate. After a while, Maria came in, jumping a little when she saw Angie sprawled out on the floor.

"Oh, Miss! You gave me a fright." Maria exclaimed in surprise.

She was one of the only members of the Carter's staff that remained; Angie knew it was because they couldn't afford any others. It wasn't as bad as Angie had expected, having no personal maid prepared to help her whenever she requested. It just meant that their food was not quite as luxurious as it normally was, with no cooks. However, there was the effect of rationing to consider. Angie wondered if the food would be better out in the countryside. It would be fresher, surely.

Angie turned to respond to the maid, sitting up politely.

"I'm sorry. I know it's late, but I don't think I can sleep."

Maria nodded understandingly, drawing the large curtains and casting the living room into darkness, other than the glow of the fire. She eventually let out a sigh.

"It won't be that terrible, Miss. I grew up in the countryside."

Angie raised her eyebrows in shock, despite the fact it was not actually that much of a surprise. It was just that Angie didn't ask about the maids' lives and, selfishly, it had never even crossed her mind.

"You did?" Angie asked.

"Why, yes Miss. I did a lot of dairy work," she responded. Angie's nose scrunched up in distaste. She'd never even been near a cow.

"Well, that sounds rather... intriguing?"

Maria laughed, shaking her head, "Don't worry, Miss. I highly doubt you will be expected to do hard work of any kind– perhaps just some chores."

Angie nodded, sighing thankfully.

"You should head off to bed, Miss." Maria smiled sadly, and Angie nodded in agreement.

Angie looked around the living room, one last time. Was this it? Would she ever return to this house, the place she had been brought up? Or would it simply have been turned to rubble, by the time she returned? It was unhelpful to think like that, but it was practically inevitable. Angie slipped off to bed.

The girl put on a nightie, glancing at her case and satchel by the door, packed and ready for the journey tomorrow. Partly, she was excited to explore a new place, fields of green and flowers growing wild and free instead of the flowers she would see when she cycled past the shop, already dead and ready to sell. These would be alive and brightly coloured.

Angie had expected a terrible night of tossing and turning, but it had not been too difficult with the thought of wildflowers, spacious green fields and air that wasn't contaminated with pollution from the abundance of factories in the city. After a short while she managed to drift into a soothing slumber, where the realities of war simply did not exist.

CHAPTER THREE

Dorothea

In Thea's opinion, the greatest innovation in farming over the past few years had been the tractor. Her father had been delighted when it was finally introduced to their farm; the cumbersome chunk of metal had proven most helpful as it gradually replaced the work of the horse up and down the country. It was more economical, easier to handle and did not require feeding, unlike the many horses Thea cared for. Despite the usefulness of the tractor, the horses were not forgotten.

One of Thea's favourite jobs, without a doubt, was grooming her beloved companions, whom she'd treasured since she was a girl. The stables were hidden now. War had been declared on a warm, sunny day that had felt so normal at sunrise and Thea demanded, with her usual stubbornness, that the horses be protected as well. She wanted them closer and more sheltered, rather than being in an open stable that was many yards away from their cottage. Her father had agreed to her request and the pair spent weeks clearing out the old shed, making it suitable for the horses.

As well as the horses, Thea enjoyed ploughing the fields on her father's tractor. The machine was not all that fast, just fast enough to ensure the wind blew into her face, waking her up on days that she wanted to do nothing but sleep. Normally, Thea would tie her hair back for most jobs in the fields, but for riding the horses or the tractor she would always leave it loose so as to feel the wind in her wavy, brown locks.

After the job was complete, she switched the vehicle off and hopped down with ease. Thea jumped in surprise as she saw Margaret, one of the Land Army volunteers out of the corner of her eye. She spoke up,

"Good morning, Miss Miller! I was wondering if you needed any assistance?"

Thea laughed, a hand on her heart.

"I might need a hospital bed! You gave me a fright, Margaret!"

Margaret blushed. She was new, probably still not convinced the job and accommodation was permanent, and wanting to do everything right. The woman stumbled over her words,

"Oh, Miss, I am sorry. I woke early this morning and saw you leave, and I just thought–"

"Don't worry," Thea said with a smile, leaning against the tractor with her arms folded. "I was going to head over to the stables. Horses don't make you sneeze, do they?"

Margaret shook her head slowly. Thea doubted her hesitation was due to the question. She probably was not used to tending to animals at all. Thea continued,

"Well, the stables are near the cottage now. I don't like them being too far away, you see. You can help out, unless you rather work on the fields?"

Margaret opened and closed her mouth. Thea had to stifle a laugh because she looked like a fish blowing bubbles. Thea leant off the tractor and walked over to the fences, holding the heavy wooden gate open and beckoning Margaret with a wave of her grubby hand.

"Coming?"

The woman finally followed. It baffled Thea how she managed to walk in wellington boots like she expected them to grow high heels. Thea supposed Margaret had spent years working at a desk, on a typewriter or sorting files, only ever wearing pretty, girly shoes. It wasn't an unfair assumption– most of the Women's Land Army had worked in such a manner before they volunteered. But Thea was still trying not to laugh, because Margaret kept tripping over stones on the bumpy terrain. Her mother would call her rude, lecturing her that not everyone had been brought up on a farm and was totally comfortable walking across uneven ground in bulky wellington boots.

When they reached the stables, Thea unlocked the door to reveal the back room where the horse's food had been stored. There were also some reins, bridles, and saddles hung up on the wall. Thea rooted in the basket she kept which was filled with mints she and her father purchased from the sweets store in the village long before rationing began, they'd be too clumpy and hard for a human to eat now. She turned to Margaret, who was looking around with an expression of confusion.

"You should give them a mint when you first stroke them."

Margaret tilted her head and her perfectly painted red lips pulled into a pout, she must have been confused Thea was giving the horses such a luxury.

"A mint? I thought mints were for… well, humans,"

"Well, yes, but my father has been feeding them mints for years and they seem as healthy as… as horses. I'd eat the mints myself or offer them to you and the land girls, but we bought them ages ago and I don't imagine they'd be all that pleasant."

Thea pulled down some equipment, stuffing some of the mints in the right pocket of her trousers. She shut the door behind them and walked around the front of the stable to tend to the horses. They were neighing and huffing already, probably having heard movement in the back room.

"Now, I think you can stroke Edward first. He's the youngest," Thea lowered her voice, opening the latch.

Margaret walked closer with hesitation, still not entirely convinced by the concept of doing work with the horses. Her face seemed to change entirely when she caught a glimpse of Edward, who was sticking his head out at Thea.

"Hello, you! Missed me, pal?" Thea said,

He huffed a reply, nudging his nose into Thea's hand and Margaret's mouth parted in awe. Thea felt pride that her horses were so affectionate. Margaret spoke up,

"I think he definitely missed you."

Thea stroked him gently. She really did adore the horses, often getting distracted when she was meant to be doing some other job. Her father had never complained, but she tried to stop the habit when her father and many of the other farmers had been sent away. Thea realised she was distracted at that very moment, when she still had a list of other things to be doing. She turned her attention back to Margaret.

"How about I show you the ropes? We can treat today as a trial run. Just brush him through and check if his coat is matted. It's rather painful if he gets all knotted up," Thea explained.

Margaret nodded enthusiastically. They opened the stable door, leading Edward out. Thea would be sure to give the other horses some attention when she fed them, in a short while. Much to Thea's surprise, Margaret was an extremely fast learner. It only took one mint before Edward seemed comfortable being stroked by her, and one more until he was relaxed enough to let her put a brush through his coat. Margaret gasped joyfully,

"He isn't bucking up! Does that mean he likes me?!"

Thea smiled.

"Sure, he does. See? I told you he was friendly."

Margaret sat on the wooden stool Thea had provided for her as she combed through the horse's tail with total concentration. Thea, much to her own surprise, felt quite comfortable leaving the woman while she fed the other horses. They were huffing excitedly as she poured grain into buckets. She brought Edward's over, causing him to flick his tail in Margaret's face in his excitement. She held onto the stool and planted her feet on the ground, thankfully managing to stay upright and keep her balance. Thea exclaimed,

"I am so sorry! He didn't mean to. He does that when he's happy–"

Astonishingly, Margaret just laughed uproariously.

"Don't be silly, Miss. I didn't hurt myself." She patted Edward and shook her head.

"You're good with horses," Thea commented.

"Not as good as you, Miss. You're only young, and it seems as if you run the place."

Thea looked down at her boots, speckled with dirt. That was not true. Her father ran the place, and would continue to do so, as soon as he returned home. And he *would* return home.

"I'm only running the place at the moment, until my father comes home."

Margaret smiled, sympathetically. It felt like an insult to Thea– like she didn't think her father would return, like Thea was dreaming of something that would never happen. It wasn't fair to assume Margaret meant harm, she'd only smiled, it was just Thea's mind blowing things out of proportion.

"Oh, another thing— my name is Dorothea. You don't have to call me 'Miss'."

 "Well, in that case, I go by Peggy."

Thea was grateful. She didn't bring up her own nickname, mainly because it was only really her father who called her that. It was special to her, only for people she truly loved. A short list. But the fact Peggy was being so nice lightened her mood. It felt good to have a friend– if that was what this was. Thea had never had many, wasn't too sure when somebody stopped being a stranger and started being a friend.

"Well, thank you for the help. I'm heading in to get something to eat, will you be alright for a moment?"

Peggy nodded confidently, and Thea felt at ease leaving her with Edward as she retreated inside. Her mother was sat in the same position she'd been in since earlier that morning. Her head was right beside the radio, listening intently. The only difference was she was now in her daytime dress, pins taken out of her hair and eyes and lips darker with makeup. It was a sorry sight.

"Hello, Mother," Thea spoke as she took a reddening apple from the fruit bowl, taking a large bite.

"I do wish you would cut them up. It is far more ladylike," her mother said. Thea couldn't help but roll her eyes.

"And being ladylike really does matter, at a time like this?" she responded sarcastically. Her mother switched off the radio in a hurried movement.

"Can you at least attempt to be polite with me?"

"Me, be polite?" Thea laughed, setting the apple on the counter, hoping to antagonise her mother further. "You're the one who criticises everything I do."

"Oh, don't be so dramatic, Dorothea!"

She'd never heard her mother bellow so loudly. How was she being dramatic? She was getting out and doing chores, not sat sobbing by the radio like a widow and childless mother. Her mother lowered her head,

"I'm sorry. I'm just anxious about making room."

Making room?

"For what?" Thea replied, short and simple, to show she was still angry.

"Why, the children. They're coming in their thousands now, Dorothea."

Thea stared at her mother, who turned up the radio. The man on it was talking about the evacuees. Thea had heard about them; she was extremely thankful she lived in the country and didn't have to move away from her home. Thea was baffled as to why her mother was listening to a report on evacuated children.

"I reckon we can probably fit around four. Possibly five..."

Thea's heart dropped, the furrow of her brow deepening. They were taking in evacuees? Children from the city, in their tiny little cottage house, with barely enough room for four family members?

"We're taking in children?" Thea asked with a voice much quieter than before. Her mother was now nodding.

"We'll go to the station tomorrow morning. That's when the next train comes in."

Thea stared at her mother with a blank expression. Everything truly was changing. Thea feared it may not be for the better.

CHAPTER FOUR

<u>Angeline</u>

The first thing Angie felt, as she woke from her pleasant slumber, was instant dread. Finally, the day that she had feared for months was upon her. She could hear movement across the landing as well as cupboards and drawers opening and closing, checking for any last minute items that had been forgotten and would be essential for their trip. In this context, the word trip was to be used lightly, as it implied that they would only be away for a short while and that was, undoubtedly, not true.

The unusual predicament left an uneasy feeling in Angie's chest. Her heart felt heavy as she glanced around her room. It was the same room she'd woken up in her entire life but it felt strange now. The light seeping through her curtains seemed a little greyer and the temperature had altered to a chill. An abundance of unanswered questions, circulating constantly in the forefront of her mind, left an essence of uncertainty.

"Miss?" Maria called; her voice familiar behind the wood of Angeline's door.

"I'm awake Maria, I'll just be a moment," she replied, sitting up out of the comfortable cocoon of her cotton sheets.

"Miss, I have run you a bath, your clothes are laid out and I have some buttered toast here for you," the maid said, voice as chirpy as ever. Angie imagined her mother had told her to stay positive, to lighten the mood.

"Thank you," she replied, standing up to walk over to the door. She took the tray of food and placed it on the cabinet beside her bed. There was a glass of water on it, which she instantly gulped down, thankful for the refreshment. Angie let out a gasp at the cold floor beneath her feet; it served as a well-needed reminder that this was not just a bad dream. It stopped her from feeling as if she was falling into a nightmare, without clear plans for her future and being forced to follow an unpredictable path. Before the girl became caught up in her daydreams, she finished her breakfast and headed to the bathroom.

The bath was not enjoyable in the slightest. It had the sweet scent of lavender– the oils had been added by Maria, to calm Angie's stressed mind. It did not provide any sense of comfort. The smell reminded her of the previous day, when her mother had held her close. It made her sorrowful; the warmth of her mother's hugs was soon to be unreachable.

In addition to the lavender, Angie was also disrupted by her youngest brother who was throwing a tantrum on the stairs. It had probably taken the little boy a longer time to process moving away and Angie assumed he had begun to figure it out. The cries broke her heart. All Angie wanted to do was fall to the ground and sob beside him but that was not an option for her. She had a duty to care for her brothers. Being the first born really was awful. Of course Angie would never even dream of saying that out loud, but it was a thought that had frequently crossed her mind.

Perhaps it was not just being the first born that was so unpleasant, but being a girl too. From when William was born, Angie had been given the responsibility of caring for him. Most jobs were taken over by Maria or another maid, but there were times when Angie was still expected to often bottle feed him and help him get to sleep. It wasn't that Angie had hated caring for her brothers. After all, without those experiences she doubted that they would have become as close as they were now, but truthfully, it was tiring. Friends from the church choir, or from around the neighbourhood envied her but Angie couldn't understand what all the fuss was about, dolls were far more entertaining and they didn't cry.

After a while of soaking, the bath water had become lukewarm and the scent of lavender had gradually faded. Angie stood, wrapping a soft towel under her arms. Would the towels in the country be as nice?

"Not relevant, Angie," she whispered to herself under her breath.

She padded her feet carefully along the tiles of the bathroom, ensuring she did not slip. The girl looked at the outfit that had been selected; a blue dress with an open collar, buttons down the centre and a wrap around the waist. It was a pretty item, one that Angie hadn't seen before. She slipped it on and headed to the mirror to carefully unpin her curls. After a short while, there was a knock at her door,

"Are you decent, Angeline?" her mother called.

"Yes, Mother," she turned just as the woman entered. She had subtle eye makeup and her signature red-painted lips, which curled into a smile when she saw her daughter.

"Oh, my darling you look beautiful," her voice was a little shaky. Angie prayed she wouldn't start crying.

"Thank you, Ma. I haven't seen this dress before," she faced the mirror again, continuing to unpin her blonde hair.

"It's one of my old ones. I was waiting for the perfect time to give it to you."

This? This was the 'perfect time'?

Her mother sighed, putting a hand on her daughter's shoulder, "I'll finish your hair."

Angie didn't speak, knowing that if she tried to form words she would cry. Her mother moved with ease, gently brushing through her hair. Angie glanced at herself in the mirror, her hair growing now just past her shoulders. Her eyes looked redder than usual as well. None of that mattered though. Angie had no one to impress. Which was an unfamiliar concept, looking beautiful had been a necessity from a young age, going hand in hand with the idea that it was a woman's most important trait.

"I could stay," Angie blurted, "there's not a single reason why I couldn't help with war efforts here. After all..."

"Slow down," her mother spoke, placing her hands onto Angie's shoulders, "we aren't having this discussion."

Angie spun around, staring right into the green of her mother's eyes.

"Why not? Give me a reason."

Angie never normally requested anything from her mother without adding a 'please' to the end of it. But this was different. Angie needed an answer. She couldn't bear this.

"Angeline, you have had a good education. You should be clever enough to understand that it's the safest option for you," she replied, her tone wasn't angry, it just seemed as if she was exhausted from repeating herself.

"I'm sixteen, Mother. I'm not a child," she protested.

"You are a child, Angeline," she lowered her voice, "But you are also the most mature, responsible girl I have ever met, which is why I trust you to take care of our family."

She couldn't argue when her mother was expressing her thoughts so sincerely. Angie stood and reached up to hug her mother, whose mouth was close enough to whisper in her ear, "I'll be here, always."

Angie buried her face further into the material of her mother's dress, still afraid she would cry. What if her mother was not always there? What if she returned home and—

"I love you."

"It's going to be perfectly alright, Angeline," she stroked her hand over the back of Angie's head, holding her face as she leant away.

Taking her mother's hand, the pair headed downstairs to see Maria putting the final cases by the front door. The boys were all standing, dressed in shirts and jumpers and their best, polished black shoes. They seemed mostly comfortable leaving the house. It was absurd they weren't as distraught as Angie; this was the house she'd feared they'd lose when the Carter's financial issues grew worse, she'd prayed she could live here until she married and now her entire life was to be put on hold. Angie turned to glance at it, one last time taking in the familiarity of the front porch on which she had sat for many summers with her friends, playing with dolls or talking about love, silly things that faded into insignificance now. She looked to the bay window at the front of the house, from which the grand piano in the centre of the room could clearly be seen. Angie could not prevent herself from thinking of the many memories made in that house, as she prayed she could return home, to relive them again.

The journey to the station was a short one; however it felt much longer when one had to listen to a five-year-old's constant blabbering. Angie took in the demolished buildings as they walked past what her father called 'the wrong side of the tracks'. Past the cramped together houses that only had two rooms, past the cobbled streets where the children, who were skinny even before the war, used to play. They'd mostly been sent away now, and though Angie and her friends always teased the children who only had one pair of holey shoes and clothes filthy with grime, she missed their laughter now. She made brief eye contact with an old man with teary eyes as he rocked with his head in his hands, suddenly feeling overwhelmingly thankful for the privilege she had.

Other than her brothers talking, the background noise was unfamiliar. There were no people laughing or chatting, only occasional sobs. In what world could Angie ever feel happy about leaving her mother in a place like this?

As they approached the station Angie's eyes widened. The train was huge. Angie didn't know what else she should have expected really, but the girl did not think she had ever seen so many carriages attached to the same train.

"Now, do you all have your tags?" their mother asked.

They all nodded. Each child had a luggage label pinned to their coat with their name, school and evacuation authority. Her mother began passing each one of them a brown paper bag.

"This is your lunch. Peter?" Her brother glanced up, a cheeky grin plastered on his face, "Do not eat it all before midday."

The platform grew more crowded after a few minutes. Angie knew logically that they should be on the train looking for a seat, but their mother had her gloved hands on Angie's and William's shoulders, as if she were an animal protecting her young.

"Mother," Angie spoke loudly, so her mother could hear her over the noise of the frenzied platform, "I think it's time."

The woman seemed to be staring at a spot in the distance and she only snapped out of it when a whistle was blown from the front of the train. She knelt; all the children forced into an uncomfortable group hug as she peppered kisses across their foreheads. Angie gave her a reassuring nod, before leading her brothers onto the train. The Carter children didn't even bother going to look for a seat, not when the windows of the carriage were open so they could lean out and wave to their mother. There was uproar as the train began to move. Angie waved until her wrist ached,

"Goodbye Mother!" Charles spoke up, still sounding obliviously excited, "the train is moving now!"

She laughed in between sobs, jogging a little to catch up with the train as it sped up until it left the station. Angie watched as her childhood home passed out of sight.

Her mother was gone.

CHAPTER FIVE

<u>Dorothea</u>

"We'll go to the station tomorrow morning. That's when the next train comes in."

Thea stared blankly at her mother, entirely distracted with thoughts of the hazy future. It wasn't that she minded having to share the farm with other people. In fact, the assistance of the Women's Land Army had proven that the help of others was needed, now that her father was away. Their work on the fields was necessary, and Peggy accompanying Thea to the stable work took some of the work load off her shoulders. But the women did not stay in the cottage, which meant that Thea still had her own space. They stayed in the guest house, across the courtyard– far from Thea when she was tired at the end of the day. When the evacuated children from the city arrived, her privacy would be invaded by four, or possibly more, self-obsessed snobs.

Thea had never actually been to the city, she listened to the radio and her father expressing his political beliefs, usually in Welsh and under his breath but Thea heard enough to know that he had a dislike for city folk. And Thea always agreed with what her father said. She imagined they would have no respect for the lush green grass that had once also graced the land on which their grotesque, polluting city now sat. They had no knowledge of the peace one could feel, alone with one's self, surrounded by the beauty of a vast cornfield, or the gentle whisperings of the breeze as it rustled through the yellow-green leaves of a forest. Thea imagined they would have no patience to sit and listen to the birds when the early morning light came over the rolling hills, casting the world below into a pleasant orange glow. To simply sit and enjoy the sounds of nature, in the absence of any voice coming from a radio.

"Dorothea?" Her mother spoke, snapping her out of her daze.

"Yes?"

"You were daydreaming," she replied. "We were talking about the children."

"I know. What about them?"

"I just wanted your thoughts."

Thea furrowed her brow.

"Why do my thoughts matter? You aren't going to reject the children, just because of what I say."

"Dorothea!" she said, indignantly.

"What?" Thea just shrugged, baffled by her mother's outrage. "I'm not wrong."

"I just wanted to *communicate* with you." Her mother stood, brushing her dress down, with a bitter expression on her face. "We are still a family."

Thea scrunched her nose up in distaste. She hated sentiment, especially coming from her stuck-up mother.

"Well, I think it's fine," she said. Her mother looked surprised at her polite response. "It'll be the highlight of my year! Some young stiffnecks in the cottage, treating us with no respect."

"Oh, for goodness sake!" her mother yelled at her. "You can't go calling people names when you haven't even met them!"

"And you have? You know exactly what they will be like, Mother. They'll treat us like maids," she scoffed with disdain.

Her mother switched off the radio. Without the voices as background noise, the awkward tension in the room was palpable.

"You know, I was around your age when I met your father." The woman looked down at the ground, smiling to herself at the distant memory.

"What does that have to do with the children?" Thea asked, sarcastic tone subsiding at the mention of her father.

"It has nothing to do with the children, but it has everything to do with your attitude."

"What does my 'attitude' have anything to do with...?"

"How do you expect to meet someone when your first instinct is to judge them?" her mother asked.

Thea could feel her blood boiling as it did every time her mother mentioned her lack of courting.

"Are you really bringing this up now?" she spat. "In case you hadn't noticed, most of the men we know are currently fighting a war."

"It won't be long. And when they return, you'll be ready to take the first step into womanhood–"

"How can you say it won't be long?" Thea ignored the last statement; it had made her cringe far too much to respond.

"It won't."

"Oh, Mother," she laughed, her disbelief evident in her tone, "they thought the troops shipped out to France would return home by Christmas, and they are still out there."

"That's beside the point. It's about time you grew up."

Her response seemed final and Thea was under the impression her mother did not want to continue with the conversation, which was fine by her. Thea slipped out the back door, letting it slam to further annoy her mother. She walked across the courtyard to the stables, realising she was still projecting her rage judging by Peggy's hesitant glance at her, still tending to Edward with gentle care. Thea released a long, frustrated sigh, deciding the only way to relax herself would be to continue with her day and her chores as she plastered a fake smile on her face.

"How are you getting on, Peggy?"

Peggy's eyes were gleaming. It was as if she was exuding happiness.

"I can't believe I've lived for twenty five years and never brushed a horse!"

That made Thea smile, temporarily forgetting her disagreement with her mother.

"I'm glad you're enjoying it."

"Just wait until the other girls wake up!" Her cheeks were rosy with excitement. "Oh… sorry, could the others meet him?"

Thea nodded, a small smile on her lips.

"You don't have to be so polite. If you enjoy working with the horses, I could give you a key to the stables."

"Oh, please!" she squealed.

Thea was glad Peggy was so jubilant, even if she was in a bad mood herself.

"Where are the others?" Thea narrowed her eyes with curiosity. Normally the Land Army women were up bright and early.

"Oh. Well, it's a Saturday, you see. They're probably used to sleeping in. But I could always…"

"Don't wake them up," Thea interrupted. "They've been working hard. They deserve a rest, as do you."

"Oh, well, thank you," Peggy said, stroking the greying mane of the horse, "but I'm happy here."

Thea looked into the stable to check on the horses, who all seemed content.

"Just put him back in the stable when you're done," she concluded, deciding it would be good for her to go for a walk to clear her head. "I'm just heading out for a little while to pick up some groceries in the village. Need anything?"

"Your mother stocks up the guest house with food every few days. We're doing just fine."

Thea nodded, stroking Edward on the nose one last time before heading back to the cottage. She changed out of her muddy boots on the porch and slipped on shoes, kneeling to do the buckles up. She disliked the shoes, finding them highly uncomfortable. She favoured a different pair that she had upstairs in her wardrobe but suffered the temporary discomfort so as not to encounter her mother as she passed through the kitchen.

Thea enjoyed a gentle stroll past the cottage and guesthouse, through the courtyard, toward the damp, cobbled street that led to the village. It was a walk that Thea had frequently taken on Sundays with her family to go to church, or to the butcher's to pick up the meat for their Sunday roast. However, Thea preferred the company of her own thoughts, rather than the sound of her brother James and her father, arguing about whether they would prefer pork or beef. Thea missed them. She clenched her fists, taking a deep breath in through her nose. This was a technique her father had taught her in order to calm herself down when she grew angry at the world. It had consistently proven to be successful, even though she often felt frustration at... *everything*. It was an uncomfortable feeling– one that felt as if her stomach was being tied into knots.

Eventually, she reached the greengrocers, and saw the old man that owned it smiling through the glass of the front window. Thea opened the door, taking a basket.

"Good morning, Henry."

The man smiled, the wrinkles around his eyes crinkling further.

"How are you today, Miss Miller?" His voice was a little shaky and rough– unpractised. The man lived alone, so Thea imagined he didn't have many people to speak to.

"I've had better days, in all honesty," she replied.

"Well, we've seen better times." The man looked a little melancholic. Part of Thea wished she'd said something positive so the grey-haired man would have a reason to keep smiling.

"That is, sadly, true," Thea replied, picking up a few red onions and a cabbage, before placing the basket on the counter.

"Anything else you need today?" The man asked as he put the vegetables into paper bags.

"That's all." She retrieved a few coins from the front pocket of her overalls, counting them out in her palm before placing them in Henry's wrinkled hand. She hesitated before turning away.

"Actually, that isn't all," she continued, looking at the man who appeared to be over the moon as she chose to continue the conversation. "I was wondering... how old were you? During the first war, that is."

Henry tensed up.

"I fought, if that is what you were wondering."

Thea let out a sigh of relief. This man provided a glimpse of hope– hope that her father and James would return home to continue with the pleasant domesticity of life in the village.

"Thank you."

"Have a good day, Miss," he replied as she picked up the vegetables, holding them in her arms and pushing the door handle down with her elbow.

Thea walked down the street, smiling at anyone who smiled at her. Quite a few would smile when any of the Millers walked down a street, since they were well known for the farm and people were grateful for their fresh produce, especially when food was becoming scarcer due to rationing. The comfort of having a farm nearby was reassuring to the village folk.

After a short while, Thea's mind quietened down. It was not yet peaceful, especially when the train station came into view, and she was struck with the reminder that the children that would be arriving soon. It was out of her control; she'd always been told not to worry about things that couldn't be changed. That was an illogical piece of advice– just as pointless as being told 'don't be afraid'. Her mother was probably the one who'd said that. Her father's advice was always well-thought out and practical.

The girl glanced at the train station, a resentful look in her eye as she picked up her pace, returning home swiftly. She vowed to try not to get frustrated at her mother again which, without her father there to relax her and offer his advice, would be an impossible task.

CHAPTER SIX

<u>Angeline</u>

Angie didn't look back once the train had started moving. The painful sound of cries coming from almost every person on the train, as well as those standing on the platform, was far too much for her to bear. Angie knew that if she had seen her mother's tear-stained face, she would have attempted to stop the train and run back into the security of her mother's arms. That luxury was out of reach though Angie reminded herself, her new aim was to find something else that would provide the same sense of safety and comfort.

There were vast meadows coming into view as the land outside the train window matured from the tedious sight of dull buildings into what appeared to be boundless fields of green. Angie could see the wonder in her four brothers' eyes as the boys gawked in awe at the rolling hills. Despite the sorrow of their situation, it was warming to see that the young boys enjoyed the pleasant sight. The persistent chatter of many other children was now waning as they too stared in admiration at the country landscape. Angie imagined her mother would appreciate the view. She'd always spoken of the poems she'd read, describing the beauty of nature and love and all the things Angie had yet to experience. Angie hadn't given nature much thought throughout her life, she had been far too caught up in her studies. Writing melodies at the piano or simply dealing with normal, daily occurrences and household chores.

"Michael, stop putting your hands all over the glass," Angie reprimanded her brother, who was pressed against the glass, watching the world go by.

The boy rolled his eyes dismissively, leaning away from the window and sitting down with a huff. Angie noted that he would never have behaved in such a way had he been in the presence of their mother. As if to deliberately disobey his sister, Charles, the youngest of the five repeated Michael's actions, his hands creating prints on the cool glass.

"Now look what you've done, Michael!" Angie shouted, the pressure of her role as caregiver becoming stressful already.

The boy held up his hands defensively. "Not my fault he copies *everything* I do!"

"For goodness sake," Angie muttered, trying to keep her voice down so as not to draw attention to herself.

She continued, "Charles is only little. He copies you because he looks up to you."

Angie pulled her little brother away from the glass, settling Charles on her lap. The boy tried to squirm away.

"I'm not *that* little," he mumbled folding his arms.

"You should treat Angie with more respect, Michael," William spoke then, chocolate-brown eyes fixed on his younger brother. "She could have stayed in London and helped Mother with the war effort, but she came with us."

Michael just shrugged. He didn't appreciate Angie's commitment yet, but when he had spent a week in an unknown bed, Angie was sure she'd be the one to help him overcome his homesickness.

"Some children are with their mothers, though," Peter whispered, glancing at other children who were beside older women.

Peter, along with William, was wise beyond his years. He was alert, always paying attention to detail, but above all he was sensitive. He'd barely spoken for weeks when their father had left for war.

"That's because their mothers aren't doing jobs," Angie explained. "In the city, mother has duties at the Post Office. She's vital to the war effort."

"So, these mothers are all bone idle?" Michael asked, *far* too loud, whilst pointing directly at a mother who was sat beside her young daughter, who was smiling eagerly at a picture book. The woman looked up at Michael.

Angie grabbed his hand to stop him from pointing. Her cheeks were burning red with humiliation.

"Michael!" she whispered furiously. "Don't point!"

Angie mouthed an apology to the woman, who responded with a nasty scowl.

"They aren't bone idle," Peter explained, demonstrating far more calm in the light of Michael's outburst than Angie had the self-control for. "I think some of them have to travel with their children."

Peter gestured over at a mother, who had a very young child resting in her lap, nuzzled into her chest. The woman was smiling down at the baby in her arms, her face one of total tenderness and love, the child her very reason for existing.

"Mothers who have little babies can't let them go alone," Peter explained.

Charles leaned over to look at the woman, before placing his head on Angie's arm, seeking comfort. Seeing the motherly love probably made him miss home. She ran her fingers through her little brother's golden hair.

She looked back over to the young mother nursing her baby. She was pretty, lips painted with a light pink rather than the typical red that was currently in fashion. Her hair fell elegantly just below her shoulders, appearing shorter due to the curl of her light brown locks. Angie estimated she was in her early twenties, probably in love with some soldier– the baby's father– who was fighting overseas. Angie enjoyed making up scenarios of strangers, but she felt somewhat envious of this mystery man. He had a beautiful wife and child and she probably wrote him letters in elegant, cursive writing, in which she told him how she longed for his warmth. How she longed to kiss him with her soft, pink lips–

"Angie?" The sound of Michael's voice snapped her out of her fantasy. "I asked if we could get a bar of chocolate."

Angie looked at him in confusion, realising a member of staff was pushing the cart of food towards them. She managed an awkward smile, as she searched in her satchel to retrieve her purse. There were only a few coins in there, since she had left most of her savings at home, a measure to keep her hopeful that she *would* return.

"Milk chocolate, please," Angie requested, as she handed the woman a few coins, taking the bar as it was passed to her.

Charles sat up, no longer leaning on Angie's arm. At the mention of chocolate, he bounced in his seat eagerly. The boys were all licking their lips as if they had never been fed before.

As the woman wheeled the cart away, Angie flipped open her pocket watch: a quarter to one.

"Shouldn't we eat our sandwiches, first?" Angie asked, realising she should not have phrased it as a question, as that gave them room to disagree.

"No!" They all argued, practically in synchronisation.

Angie couldn't help but smile. The Carter children had many disagreements, but the one thing they all had in common was their undying love for anything chocolate. Angie split up the bar as evenly as possible to avoid arguments. Normally, the girl would have given herself a square or two more, but she had to be mature now, as she took on a maternal role.

Thankfully, the boys all ate their lunch even after the chocolate treat. Angie hadn't doubted that they would. Her father had always joked about the boys having hollow legs to fit in everything they ate. Angie savoured every bite of the sandwiches. She knew it hadn't been her mother who had made them– it would have been Maria. It may have been the same bread, ham, cheese and margarine that Angie had eaten practically every day for almost the entirety of her life, but this time it tasted like home.

After reading a few chapters of *The Wizard of Oz* to the boys, Angie doing the same silly voices for the Munchkins as her mother always had, Charles had dozed off. Angeline found herself alternating between dozing on the glass of the train window, which vibrated as it chugged along the tracks and telling Peter and Michael to stop squabbling in case they woke their brother up. This seemed to make time pass as Angie soon felt the train slowly grind to a halt.

She looked outside, lips parting as she tried to concentrate on the sight of the station, which was dimly lit as the sun was beginning to disappear behind the countryside hills. From what Angie could see in the poor light, the station was decorated in an unfamiliar way. No stations in London had flowerpots beside the station sign, or old gas lamps that cast an orange glow onto the ground. She nudged the sleeping form beside her. Charles let out a sleepy yawn, which was followed by the yawning of her other brothers. Angie smiled at them. They were quite sweet, when they weren't arguing.

"Charles?" Angie nudged him again.

He smiled at her sleepily, his eyes glazed over.

"Yeah?"

"Don't let go of my hand." She squeezed his hand to enforce the message. Angie looked at her brothers. "You better stay right by me."

It was chaotic. The Carters had been rushed into a hall by billeting officers, who organised them into groups. The hall felt empty and cold and the only warmth for Angie was the comfort of having her brothers beside her. Charles was hiding behind her, clutching his suitcase.

"May I see your tags?" an officer asked, his voice deep and gravelly, which was out of place after a day on a train with only the soft voices of women and children.

William was the one to hold up his tag to the man, who hummed. He turned away as he heard a child screaming.

"I want to go home!" the little girl shrieked.

She appeared to be shaking, face red from the exhaustion of crying and shouting. Her dark hair was in two messy braids and she looked so tiny next too all these people, far too young and innocent to be there all alone. She was escorted elsewhere. Angie, noticing the empathetic glances her brothers had shared, knelt to them.

"She's only little, see. You're braver than that. You have me. We have each other."

The boys nodded but didn't look entirely convinced. Angie stood up, as if guarding her brothers the way her mother had at the station. Her arms wrapped protectively around them, unwilling to let her children go, she would protect her brothers to ensure they would not be taken away from her and placed into different households.

And Angie would fulfil her duty, for her mother's sake.

CHAPTER SEVEN

<u>Dorothea</u>

When Thea returned from the village the sun was high in the sky, shining bright with its glorious, golden glow. She admired the cornfields as she passed them, proud of how healthy and rich the crops looked. It provided a beacon of hope for her– that in the midst of this terrible war, the corn still grew.

Climbing over the wooden gate to reach the cottage proved difficult with an armful of vegetables, but finding the correct key to unlock the padlock would have been far too much of a hassle. After a few attempts, she managed to stumble over the obstacle. The sound of women giggling reached her before the stables came into view. It was then that she saw the four members of the Land Army, finally awake and dressed, petting Edward with gleeful expressions.

"Hello, ladies," Thea said as she struggled to open the door to the cottage.

"Oh! Let me help you, Miss," Heather exclaimed, stepping away from a grey horse. "I can put these away for you."

She gestured to the paper bag in Dorothea's arms.

"It's quite alright," Thea said.

"Give it a rest, Heather!" Florence said, calling over from the stables. She was stood beside Peggy, petting Edward, "She's only offering to help inside because she hates working on the fields!"

Peggy and Mary laughed in response. Mary was another Land Army member; Thea was a little scared of her dark, calculating gaze and fervent devotion to Catholicism. It wasn't that Thea and her family weren't religious– they were, they attended church weekly. It seemed to Thea that Mary was able to include Jesus and scripture in practically every conversation.

"Shouldn't have become a Land Girl if you don't like the outdoors," Peggy chuckled.

"I like the outdoors just fine," Heather protested with a pout.

The other girls exchanged glances, not entirely convinced. Thea felt a little bad for the redheaded girl so spoke up.

"You can help put the groceries away Heather," Thea said, finally getting the door open. Heather practically leapt in excitement at the offer, quickly following Thea inside.

"Oh, thank you Miss! If you ever need assistance in the kitchen I am an excellent cook. Not to sound boastful but I used to make wonderful dinners for my entire family back in London," she said as she reached to put away some of the vegetables.

Thea wasn't listening. She was just looking at her mother's empty spot at the kitchen table, and the radio beside it.

"I'm also great at making beds, and cleaning. Well I think I'm good at cleaning. Peggy always says my room is the messiest room in the guest house. I personally think Florence's is the messiest. I mean the entire space is filled with bits and bobs. Mostly pictures– which I understand. Pictures are important, aren't they? A nice reminder. I noticed you don't have many pictures around the house. Where does your mother keep them all?" Heather rambled.

Thea stared at her, eyes wide with shock. She did not know it was physically possible for a person to speak so much with just one breath.

"Uhm…" Thea trailed off as she leaned against the counter, "I think she has them in a photo album."

That was not the truth but saying that was easier than explaining that her mother behaved like her son and husband were dead, taking down all the photographs so she didn't get upset.

"Oh, that's very… modern," Heather said.

Thea smiled at her, she wasn't used to people talking to her. Young girls around Thea's age never seemed to like her and it was strange to be surrounded by all this feminine beauty. And she was a pretty woman; it seemed all the Land Army women were. Heather was undoubtedly the most beautiful, with long ginger hair pulled out of her face in elegant twists, and freckles scattered across her nose. Dorothea was always jealous of girls with freckles, wishing she had been blessed with them. They would provide a distraction from the sickly paleness of her skin. It was frustrating to be the only one in the family with skin as pale as snow; especially considering she was outdoors far more than her brother and mother. It also served as another reason for people to tease her.

"Can I help with anything else, Miss?" Heather asked.

"Uh, no. That is all," she said. "Would you like me to explain the jobs again–?"

"No, Flossie has a good memory," the redhead said. "If anybody forgets something– most likely that will be me– Florence can explain."

"That's perfect. Did my mother mention the children?"

Heather had to think for a moment. Despite being the most beautiful of the Land Girls, she wasn't the brightest of them. It seemed that she took much longer to process information and respond to a question.

"Ah. The evacuees," Heather nodded, grinning wide, "I was expecting that in all honesty. I was surprised they weren't already here. Most people around here already have evacuees."

Thea realised that she really should have expected the evacuees arrival as well, but it had come as a shock to her and she certainly didn't share in Heather's excitement. Thea valued her privacy and the pleasant tranquillity of her home, soon to be a thing of the past.

"I think my mother and I needed time to adjust first before taking in any children," Thea explained.

Heather blushed bright red.

"Oh, of course! I wasn't dismissing how awful it was that Mr Miller left! I must sound so rude! I simply meant…"

Thea laughed at her flood of apologies.

"It's perfectly alright! I know you meant no harm by it."

The redhead kept her head low. Thea imagined Heather's cheeks were still warm.

"I'll be off now, Miss," Heather murmured as she turned away to exit the kitchen.

Thea argued with herself about whether to go and talk to her mother and make up with her before the children arrived in the evening. She should, in order to make a good impression– to convey that the two were close and hadn't been fighting like cat and dog constantly since the other members of the family had left. However, Thea decided against it, because if there was one thing she loved more than her father, the horses and the farm, it was annoying her mother until her face went red and she was grinding her teeth. Perhaps it made Thea immature that she could never be the bigger person, but she could not care less.

Consequently, Thea left the house, slamming the door once again for good measure, just to disturb her mother who would probably be reading in the living room. She headed to the stables and set out to complete all the chores regarding the horses, and begin work on the fields in the late afternoon, when the sun had gone down. That way she did not risk another case of severe sunburn– a side effect of her pale complexion. Which was frustrating, as someone who spent most of her days outside.

The first time Thea had been burnt was after the Millers had visited the seaside. It was so terrible that the doctor from the village had to come in order to ensure it was just sunburn, as the girl was screaming in pain, her skin peeling. Her father was convinced something else was wrong, demanding the doctor come at once. He'd always been so protective of his only daughter. Sometimes Thea questioned whether he would have loved her as much if her mother had had more children. Thea glanced at the huddle of women who were now fussing over a different horse. She wondered whether they had any siblings themselves.

"Peggy?" she asked.

"Yes, Dorothea?" the dark haired woman smiled.

"I was just wondering," she said, tossing a few bales of hay closer to the stalls, "if..."

Scary Mary, a new name Thea had recently started calling her in her head, cut her off before she could finish her sentence.

"We'll get to work soon," the woman snapped. "God did not create the Earth in one day, you know. The jobs have been tough and hard work requires rest."

Surprised at how quickly Mary had been to jump down her throat, Thea held up her hands defensively. The feeling was too familiar; years of people disagreeing with whatever Thea said, or just ignoring her entirely just because they didn't like that she wore trousers and not dresses, and she spent her time talking about farm

77

work, not love and boys. Thea could spot when a person hated her from a mile off, she couldn't help but feel frustrated because Mary had no reason to hate her at all.

"I was actually talking to Peggy," Thea remarked, proud of her own confidence. "Do you have any siblings, back at home?"

Peggy's brown eyes seemed to twinkle with delight.

"Why, yes," she replied. "My sister works for the post, my brother was…" She swallowed then. The twinkle seemed to fade away from Peggy's chocolate brown eyes. Heather, Florence and Scary Mary were all glaring at Thea who felt guilty, knowing she must have misspoken. "He was killed in a bombing," she finished.

Oh dear, thought Thea, realising now why she should not have brought it up. Peggy looked down. Racer, the other horse the women were petting, nudged her nose at her hand as if to comfort her. Peggy stroked her, managing a weak smile.

"I am terribly sorry," Thea spoke up after a few uncomfortable moments of silence. She clumsily dropped the bale of hay, further emphasising the awkwardness of the situation.

"You couldn't have known," Peggy replied.

The woman led Racer back into the stable.

"I suppose we should get back to work then," Scary Mary snapped, glaring daggers at Thea, as though it were Thea's fault Peggy's brother had died in a bombing incident.

Thea watched the women leave the stables, a horrible feeling of guilt settling in her stomach. Setting off on the wrong foot with Scary Mary and reminding Peggy of her dead brother had not been on her list of things to do that day.

"One last thing!" Thea practically squeaked, "Could one of you pick up the children from the station?"

"Me!" Florence squealed excitedly.

The rest of the day passed agonisingly slowly. Thea couldn't stop feeling guilty about Peggy, and anxious that Scary Mary wasn't just a little strange but a possible bully that had an issue with Thea for some unknown reason. That on top of the arrival of the evacuees resulted in feeling like she had rocks in her belly and an uncomfortable ache in her chest. It did not make sense to Thea; the day always passed slowly when someone was excited about something, but it also passed slowly when someone was dreading something. Time made little sense. Thea felt that nothing made much sense anymore.

CHAPTER EIGHT

<u>Angeline</u>

An hour must have passed by now, possibly more, Angie thought. She did not want to voice her concern in fear of distressing her brothers, who were already sat on their cases biting their nails out of worry or boredom. She prayed it was the latter.

"It won't be long now," Angie reassured them, infusing as much positivity in her tone as she could, as yet another group of children were shown out of the hall.

"You said that half an hour ago," Michael groaned impatiently.

"Stop your complaining, Michael," William snapped, "It isn't Angie's fault."

"Whose fault is it then?" Michael stood up, chest puffed out and chin up, ready to start a fight, "Mother's? You think it's Mother's fault?"

"It isn't her fault!" Peter said defensively.

Charles buried his face in Angie's side, thumb in his mouth, his face slack with exhaustion.

"Quit the arguing," Angie snapped, "Charles is tired."

"We're all tired," Michael argued, sitting on his suitcase again, "In case you hadn't noticed, we've been waiting for over an hour in a freezing cold hall in the middle of nowhere!"

Angie ignored her younger brother, distracting herself by threading her fingers through Charles's hair, a habit that seemed it give as much comfort to Angie as it did to Charles. She looked around absentmindedly, and noticed one of the scary billeting officers making a beeline toward them. Angie was certain he'd change direction at any moment and go to another group. But he didn't.

"May I see your numbers?" the man asked.

The children all held their tags up eagerly.

The man nodded, "Follow me, please."

Angeline nudged Charles, who reached up to his big sister to be carried. She sighed and, much to her surprise, Michael picked up her case as well as Charles', carrying them for her so she could keep the boy on her hip. The Carter children followed the officer outside where they were met with the sight of a long queue of adults. They all clutched paperwork, waiting to meet their evacuees.

They were led to a woman who was sat on a sandstone wall, smiling widely. She had blonde hair, much like Angie's but a little shorter. Her blue eyes were also rather captivating, like the colour of the sky but with a ring of darker blue around them. She seemed very motherly, which reassured Angie enormously.

"Hello. I'm Florence," the woman greeted them as the officer read the paperwork she had passed to him. Her accent was unlike the billeting officers, she didn't sound Welsh in the slightest.

Angie waved awkwardly, still holding Charles.

"I'm Angeline. This is Charles, William, Peter and Michael."

"Angeline," Florence smiled. "That's a pretty name."

"It appears as if everything is in order here," the billeting officer nodded as he passed the paperwork back to Florence, "the telephone number is written on the leaflet, which Mrs Miller should have from when she applied. Please let her know she can call if there are any issues."

Florence smiled, "Thank you for your help, sir."

The man's cheeks reddened at that. Perhaps he was not used to polite thanks from a beautiful woman. Angie wondered whether she'd be confident enough to smile flirtatiously at men when she was older.

Soon after the billeting officer went back into the town hall, Angie and Florence left; the children followed them, their curious eyes taking in the unfamiliar surroundings.

"I'm new here too, that's why I was a little late. I got lost." Florence sighed as she debated which turn to make next.

That explained the hesitation in her movements as they ventured through the town and the hint of a cockney accent.

"I'm from London too," Florence explained, "I'm part of the Women's Land Army."

"Army?" Charles spoke, "girls can't be in the army."

Florence chuckled at that, taking a turn down a country path. It was a little muddy and Angie could feel her pumps getting wet.

"It is a different kind of army."

"I've read about it," William spoke.

"Have you?" the woman turned back to look at William.

"Yes, it was founded in 1917, re-established in 1939. You help farmers," William tilted his head, seeking confirmation.

"You've got a smart brother there, Angeline," Florence smiled at her.

"He takes after our father."

"He's in the army!" Peter expressed proudly.

Florence smiled sympathetically, "I'm sure it won't be long until he returns."

"Good," Michael muttered under his breath, but they could all clearly hear him, "I don't want to be here for long. It smells."

"Michael!" Angie admonished.

"I like you," Florence laughed, pointing at Michael, "you're funny."

That wasn't really true, Angie thought. Before their father had left and war had been announced, Peter had always been the funny one. Yet now he was reserved and silent most of the time and the only 'humour' came from Michael being rude and abrupt.

"What are the owners of the farm like?" Angie asked politely, still cringing as her shoes strode closer to ruin with every new muddy puddle she walked through.

"They're nice enough. It's just Mrs Miller and her daughter. But don't get too excited boys!" Florence joked. "She's far too old for you."

William blushed at that. He was as awkward as Angeline.

"Right…" Florence mumbled to herself, "or maybe it's left? This would be far easier if the houses hadn't been blacked out."

That saddened Angie. One thing she had been looking forward to about the countryside was the fact there wouldn't be a blackout but it seemed nowhere had escaped the war entirely.

"Why do you block the windows? We're in the countryside. Surely we're safe here?" Peter asked, sounding anxious. It was the first time he'd spoken since they'd got off the train.

"Oh, sweetheart," Florence pouted sympathetically, "it doesn't quite work like that. We still have to take precautionary measures."

The woman must have noticed Peter's defeated expression.

"But you can go out whenever you like for walks to the village. There are no restrictions," Florence added.

Michael suddenly groaned impatiently, "What have you got in this case, Angie?! It's so heavy!"

Angie was thankful for the change of subject and was quite surprised at Michael again for being the one to initiate it.

"The same as all of you, everything that was on the required list," she chuckled softly so she wouldn't jolt Charles as he rested comfortably on her shoulder.

"You definitely packed some extra shoes," Michael said suspiciously.

"I should have offered to carry a case," Florence halted and held her hand out to Michael.

"It's really…" Michael was cut off by Florence,

"Please. I work on a farm."

She carried the 'heavy' case for the rest of the walk with ease.

Angie liked her. She had an easy confidence that reminded her of her mother, which made her wonder whether Florence did have children herself and if she did, where were they now?

After reaching the cottage, it dawned on Angie that she'd had no clue how to react to it. It was small and not to her taste at all. She preferred large houses like the ones back in London, with huge windows and lengthy front porches to sit on.

"It's… nice," she began, looking at the plants that grew up the right side of the house. Had that been an accident? Or was it some form of decoration?

"It's dainty," Florence said. Angie decided she'd use that word if anyone asked for her opinion on it, "I don't sleep here."

Florence put the cases down to knock on the door.

"Where do you sleep?" William asked.

"The guest house," Florence replied, pointing to the smaller building across the courtyard, "With the other Land Girls."

That made sense but Angie felt safe around Florence and part of her wanted to beg her to stay in the cottage with them. Her motherly presence alone would make Angie feel more secure, she imagined her brothers would feel the same.

As the woman opened the door, Angie smelt something cooking. Meat, she guessed, possibly some vegetables.

"Hello Mrs Miller," Florence called, gesturing for the Carter children to enter the cottage.

"Oh, Florence!" An older woman's voice replied, her accent unfamiliar to Angie's ears, "you've been gone for a while, I was getting worried!"

"Apologies, Ma'am," Florence said, "I got lost on the way there."

William, Michael and Peter had put their cases down by the front door and they were all kneeling to untie their laces. Just as Angie was about to wake Charles up so she could untie her own, Mrs Miller appeared in the hallway. She had an apron around her waist, greying hair tied back in a low bun.

"Please don't worry about taking off your shoes, boys," she said, shaking her head with a smile. It seemed unpractised - perhaps the woman didn't smile a lot, "Only when you go upstairs."

The woman came closer, to get a better look at the children. The three boys stood in a row like soldiers, just as they had at home that morning. Charles stirred, lifting his head up with a yawn.

"Bless you, boy," she smiled at little Charles in Angie's arms, "why don't you put the baby to bed, then we can have supper."

Baby? How many children did the woman encounter? Yes, he was a little small. But he didn't look like a *baby.*

"I'm four," Charles protested, hopping down, "and I'd like some supper as well, please."

Angie put a hand on his shoulder, proud of him for being so polite despite the fact he hated it when he was called little. Angie cleared her throat, deciding that, as the oldest of the five, she should introduce them.

"My name is Angeline. This is William, he's nine, Peter is seven, Michael is six," she explained, "and Charles."

"Who is four," Mrs Miller grinned, Charles smiling back.

The Carter's followed Mrs Miller into the dining room – Florence must have gone back to the guest house. Much to Angie's own surprise, she wasn't too nervous without her there. Mrs Miller seemed nice enough and her broth tasted wonderful. As the vegetables were soft and the meat was tender it was rather difficult not to gulp it down. Michael and Peter clearly did not care as they slurped away. Angie was about to open her mouth to tell them to eat more carefully, but Mrs Miller didn't seem to be bothered.

"So, how old are you Angeline? I must say, we were expecting five younger children," Mrs Miller said, looking up from her own bowl.

Angie looked down at her spoon which she had clanked clumsily.

"Sorry," she muttered, "I'm sixteen."

"Oh, don't you apologise," Mrs Miller tutted, "Luckily you're only small. If you were as tall as my daughter, I'd be afraid you wouldn't fit in any of the camp beds!"

William had finished his supper and was resting back on the chair, hands folded in his lap. Michael and Peter were on their last few mouthfuls and Charles was almost falling asleep, his head resting on the back of the chair.

"God bless him," Mrs Miller cooed, "We'll go and put him to bed soon. I made them all before you came."

"Thank you," William said politely. Michael and Peter followed, thanking her too.

Mrs Miller smiled, taking away the bowls and spoons. Just as she was about to take them out of the room a figure in the doorway caught Angeline's eye.

"Hello Dorothea," Mrs Miller spoke, disapproval clear in her voice.

The girl stepped into the light. She looked a little like Mrs Miller, her eyes the same piercing blue. The only difference really was that her pale skin did not have a single wrinkle and her hair was healthy and brown; soft waves, just brushing the tops of her shoulders. The first thing Angie noticed was that she would have been very beautiful without that hateful scowl on her face.

CHAPTER NINE

<u>Dorothea</u>

The first thing Thea noticed when she came in from a hard day working in the fields was the smell of food. Something nutritious and rich filled her home. That was when she knew something was different. Their evening meal normally consisted of some slightly stale bread and cheese, nothing that would fill the house with this delicious aroma. It suddenly fell into place– the evacuees.

Thea untied her muddied laces, throwing her shoes carelessly by the front door. She didn't bother changing out of her dirtied overalls, or to wash her dirty face, spotted with mud. Thea had vowed to herself not to follow their perfect, pristine ways. Instead, she planned to rebel against them. She wanted to prove a point; that life wasn't always ideal and spotless. To convey how she despised the way rich families brought up their children in a sugar coated world, where nothing bad ever happened.

She stood in the doorway, her eyes narrowed and calculating. There were four boys and a girl. The boy, who appeared to be the youngest, was half asleep, leant against his chair. They all had the same dirty blonde hair, other than the girl who had her back to Thea. Her hair had more of a golden hint to it. She also did not look much like a young child.

"Hello Dorothea," her mother greeted her disapprovingly.

Thea stepped into the dining room and the golden haired girl turned. Her hair framed her face, perfectly being dishevelled from her day of travel. A few freckles dusted her nose which, of course, was perfectly shaped as well; not too big or too small and with a slight turn up at the end that made her look positively innocent. Thea was pathetically taken aback by her beauty, specifically by those hazel eyes, which looked her up and down with a calculating gaze. This was undoubtedly the response a pristine city-girl like her expected; adoration and admiration for her looks. Thea had already declared her as a self-obsessed narcissist in her mind but the judgemental stare she gave Thea made it increasingly evident that they were never going to get on.

The boys, presumably the girl's brothers, mirrored the questioning look that their sister gave Thea. The boys also had the same hazel eyes, other than the tallest brother whose eyes were darker, like chocolate.

"Hello, Mother," Thea replied after taking in the guests.

She took a seat opposite the youngest boy who was now a little more awake than he had been a few moments before. Thea leaned over the boy sat beside her, grabbing a piece of bread from the bowl in the middle of the table. She took a huge bite, in what her mother would call an unladylike manner.

"Why don't you go and get changed? You could join us after," her mother asked her, tone laced with embarrassment.

"Well thank you for the offer, *Mother,*" Thea said, "but I'm comfortable as I am."

Thea looked over at the girl and the boy that sat beside her. She was hoping to be met with disgust but all she was saw was the pair trying to contain their laughter, as if Thea disobeying her mother was the most absurd and hilarious thing they'd ever witnessed. Thea wouldn't be surprised if it was.

"Please. You are filthy, Dorothea," her mother pressed.

"Alright," Thea said. Her mother let out a sigh of relief before Thea continued, "I may be filthy, but I am still rather comfortable, as I said."

"Leave this room, now," her mother snapped, the evacuees flinching slightly.

Thea decided to finally give it up, scraping the chair back as she stood. She slammed the door to her room, before leaning against it and looking down at her muddied attire. She smirked to herself.

After a long while and much procrastination, Thea changed into her sleepwear which was not the usual for a girl of her age, consisting of a large shirt that had previously belonged to her father and a pair of cotton pyjama pants that did not match. Anything was better than a nighty. Thea never understood them; dresses were uncomfortable so why would somebody willing where one to sleep in?

Her legs ached as they usually did after a long day's work, the mattress beneath her feeling almost too soft. She listened intently to the sound of her mother showing the evacuees to their rooms. Eventually the house's new occupants went silent and the only sounds were the old cottage settling; occasional cracks or creaks. It felt rather peaceful for a short while before the distinctive sound of Thea's mother's angry footsteps reached her. She didn't even bother knocking before turning the doorknob and stepping into her room angrily.

"You have humiliated me," the furious woman began, "thoroughly humiliated me!"

Thea sat up, crossing her legs.

"You wipe that grin off your face."

"Oh, Mother. Do calm down. You might give yourself a heart attack," she laughed.

"This is not a joke, Dorothea!"

"Mother, it was just a bit of fun."

"Fun," her mother lowered her voice, "what have I told you about first impressions?"

"They last," Thea shrugged, "so, they'll think I'm funny. That's an ideal first impression, if ever I heard one."

"I give up with you," her mother pointed out at the landing, "they have had a very difficult day."

"So, they're probably tired and you're being extremely loud and shouting at me," Thea smirked, "how inconsiderate of you."

"If my daughter hadn't been so persistent in her efforts to show off, I would not have had a reason to raise my voice in the first place."

"*Show off* is a new one," Thea remarked, "I'm used to stubborn, immature, childish…"

"Why do you behave as though you are so hard done by?" her mother asked, lowering her voice so she wouldn't wake her precious evacuees.

"I don't."

"You treat me like the enemy."

"Oh, Mother," Thea sighed, rolling onto her side to pick at her bed sheets, "Not everything is about you.

Do stop being so… what do you always say to me? *Self-centred*."

"That is hypocritical. I'm leaving this conversation here, it was bad enough in front of the Land Army girls. Continuing with our ridiculous disagreements will only put more stress on the children."

"Oh *boohoo*," Thea replied sarcastically.

She thought perhaps the stress would give the privileged children a glimpse at the real world. Open their eyes to the fact that things such as stress even existed.

"Goodnight, Dorothea," her mother responded with finality, "I do hope you wake in a better mood tomorrow. It would be nice if you could give Angeline a tour of the farm."

Angeline. She genuinely had the word *angel* in her name. Both of her parents must love her more than life itself. It was rather funny, in Thea's opinion, that her parents had set such high expectations with a name.

"Angeline," Thea scoffed, testing the name out as her mother left her room.

Thea rolled onto her back, glancing up at the ceiling as she attempted to get comfortable enough for rest again.

CHAPTER TEN

<u>Angeline</u>

As it happened, Dorothea's scowl at supper was just the beginning; she had ignored her mother's requests, argued with her and slammed her bedroom door when she'd stormed off. It was evident that Mrs Miller's daughter did not want the Carter children in the cottage.

Angie wasn't angry at Dorothea. She understood, possibly more than anyone, that personal space and privacy was essential for a teenage girl. When Angie was finally shown to her temporary room, she was thankful for the quiet after she'd tucked her younger brothers into bed.

Her new room was at the end of the landing, which was narrow with a low ceiling she wasn't used to.

The door to her room appeared isolated, with only one other bedroom beside it.

"If you get hot during the night," Mrs Miller explained as she entered the room and switched on the dim bedside lamp, pointing to the small set of drawers, "There are plenty of thinner sheets that you can use instead. They're all freshly washed, of course."

"Thank you," Angie replied, sitting on the mattress which was far stiffer than she was used to.

She couldn't imagine she would get hot during the night, the sheets she sat upon were thin and there was only one pillow on the bed. Angie was used to being surrounded by fluffy pillows, soft sheets and a mattress that practically moulded itself to fit her shape when she lay on it. This tiny camp bed would not be keeping her comfortable or warm.

"If you need anything during the night, my room is just at the top of the stairs."

Angie nodded politely, looking over at her case which was now at the end of her bed beside her satchel. She presumed Florence had put the cases in their rooms. Angie was used to things being done for her, but

Florence did it out of kindness, she wasn't a maid. So Angie appreciated it a lot more.

"Sleep well, Angeline," Mrs Miller said after a short while. "I apologise again for my daughter."

"It's perfectly fine Mrs Miller. I'm sure she'll come round. This will take a while for us all to adjust to."

Mrs Miller smiled at that, the wrinkles around her eyes crinkling, "You are such an understanding young lady."

Mrs Miller left her room, shutting the door behind her. Angie took a moment to look around; the small window above the headboard had been covered with cardboard due to the blackout regulations, the light from the lamp beside her was tinted orange, giving a warm tone to the bland white walls. Angie lay back on the poor excuse for a mattress, still wearing the blue dress her mother gave her that morning. She held on to the thought of her as she fiddled with the material. Her mother was only one day away but it felt like lightyears since she'd left London.

Her thoughts were suddenly interrupted by the sound of arguing, coming from the bedroom next door. Angie was never one to be nosey, knowing it was rude to stick her nose in another person's business. But Dorothea's voice was clear as day through the thin walls of the cottage. The farmer's daughter hadn't exactly made a pleasant first impression, so Angie thought if she listened into their conversation it wouldn't be such a bad thing. It was difficult to distinguish precisely what was being said. She could only make out a few phrases, but she got the general idea; Dorothea did not like the Carters, which had been obvious and didn't exactly upset Angie. She had enough friends at home and Dorothea wasn't someone she wanted to get to know anyway. It wasn't like this farm was ever going to become a home.

It seemed like choosing to befriend Dorothea or not wouldn't be a choice Angie got to make. Because Mrs Miller was suggesting Dorothea show her around the following day. Oh, joy, thought Angie. Finally, as Mrs Miller closed the door of the bedroom next door Angie clearly heard a word.

"*Angeline*" Dorothea said.

Angie found her cheeks heating at the mocking tone. She'd never been self-conscious of her name before. It was different, but not too uncommon. But when Dorothea said it, she felt like her own name was something to be ashamed of. Angie scowled at the thought, standing up stiffly to get changed into her nighty, praying the rude girl next door wouldn't cause her too much future trouble. Angie rolled onto her side and reached over, switching the lamp off and praying for sleep.

*

Angie awoke, unaware of the time or where she was. The room was as dark as it had been when she'd drifted into disturbed sleep. Her night of rest had hardly been that at all. She'd been woken up by noises from the room next door; drawers being slammed, creaky floorboards, *singing?!* Not even the good kind. It was as if Dorothea had wanted Angie to have a terrible night of sleep.

She sat up, pulling back the covers and tugging on her night robe after searching for a long while in her suitcase. Opening the door, she noticed how quiet the cottage was. If the window beside the bathroom had not been revealing sunlight, Angie wouldn't have been certain it was even day time yet. She tiptoed across the landing, hearing chatting coming from downstairs.

"You're up late, I was just coming to wake you up," William said from the bottom of the stairs as Angie walked down to him.

"I didn't know what time it was. There's no clock in my bedroom."

"Well, it's nearly eleven," William replied as he gestured to the dining room where all her brothers were sat with Dorothea.

The brunette had her hair pulled back in something resembling a bun and her feet up on the table. She was wearing pyjama bottoms and a baggy shirt, Angie wondered if she'd ever worn a dress in her life.

"Morning, *Princess.* Have a good sleep?"

It was clear from her expression that she knew that Angie most certainly *did not* have a good sleep. She didn't even bother replying.

"Dorothea made bacon," Charles held up a forkful before eating the entire rasher without bothering to cut it up.

Their mother would have been appalled.

"We only have bacon on Saturdays," Angie remarked, "It's Sunday."

"Dorothea said we can have bacon whenever we want!" Michael grinned.

How stupid was this girl? Was she not aware that there was a *war* going on? Had she even heard of rationing?

"Well, we can't," Angie said.

She scowled at Dorothea with her feet on the table. It wasn't that the dining table was a particularly nice one– if anything, it appeared old and scratched– but it went without saying that a person should never put their feet up somewhere food was eaten, even with socks on.

"Told you Angie's boring," Michael huffed, looking over at Dorothea as he dug into his breakfast. Angie assumed it was not his first plate.

"Aw, don't be mean Michael," Peter said.

Angie was thankful that somebody was defending her, even if he was continuing to shovel food into his mouth.

"I'm not boring. I'm just aware that we have to be careful with food."

Nobody looked up or even conveyed slight interest in what she was saying. Angie stormed out of the room with a scowl on her face, trying to ignore Dorothea's scoff from behind her.

Thankfully, Mrs Miller appeared at the top of the stairs just as she was about to climb them. She was sniffing the air suspiciously.

"Good morning," she walked down into the hall, "who is cooking?"

"Dorothea," Angie replied, head low to conceal her anger, "she cooked a ton of bacon."

"Bacon?" Mrs Miller gasped, storming into the dining room her blood boiling when she saw the mountain of food, "that was our very last batch!"

Angie stood in the doorway awkwardly, watching her brother's faces go pale.

"Oops?" Dorothea shrugged.

Mrs Miller snatched the plate from the centre of the table, looking at the boys with their terrified expressions.

"This isn't your fault boys, you couldn't have known," Mrs Miller looked down at her daughter, "it's eleven o'clock and I'm already furious with you. You are seventeen years old! Can't you act your age for once?!"

Dorothea took her feet off the table before grabbing one last piece of bacon from the plate her mother had taken away. The woman glared in disbelief at her daughter. Angie did too. She'd never met a girl so sure of herself, it was unnerving.

It made her heart pound.

"Get dressed," Dorothea said as she passed Angie in the doorway, "Not a stupid dress, something practical."

Angie looked at Mrs Miller pleadingly, praying she wouldn't have to suffer a day in Dorothea's company because there was *clearly* something very wrong with this girl. Mrs Miller didn't seem to get the message.

"Enjoy your look around the farm, Angeline," Mrs Miller said, "come on boys, let's go and wash your hands."

Charles looked up at Angie sadly.

"I won't be long," Angie forced a smile.

He stuck out his bottom lip and followed Mrs Miller and his brothers into the kitchen to wash his greasy hands. She didn't understand why her brothers couldn't come with her, perhaps Mrs Miller was clinging to the worthless hope that Angie and Dorothea would be friends.

Angie headed back upstairs to her room, feeling quite dizzy from the stressful atmosphere Dorothea had sprung upon her, first thing in the morning.

"Do you have any trousers?" Angie jumped in surprise, dropping the clothes she was holding as she searched for something 'practical'.

Dorothea was standing in her doorway her arms folded as she leant against it.

"You could have knocked!"

"It's my house," Dorothea said, taking a step into her room to look at the contents of her case.

She held up Angie's favourite dress. It was a bright red colour, her best friend Charity Smith back in London bought one too, so they matched. It reminded her of that life she'd left behind. Angie missed her friends terribly; she'd barely seen anybody other than her own family since the war began.

"Seriously? This is a farm, not a dance hall."

"Hey!" Angie snatched it back off her, "I could have been getting dressed."

Dorothea ignored her statement. It made Angie's blood boil, unused to being treated in such a way.

"It looks like you might have to borrow some of my clothes."

"You're far too tall," Angie said.

"You're far too small."

Angie looked in her case. She turned and looked the brunette up and down. She wore trousers and an old blouse; it was obvious it was old as it was slightly discoloured and certainly not to Angie's taste. Dorothea must have noticed her staring as she folded her arms uncomfortably, seeming visibly self-conscious. Angie was thankful a slightly vulnerable side of her had finally been revealed, because she'd been questioning whether Dorothea was an entirely different species, or just somebody who felt no emotions and was quite mad.

"Just pick me some clothes then," Angie sighed.

Dorothea returned a moment later with a pair of overalls. Dark green overalls.

"You can't be serious."

"What?" Dorothea explained, "They're my old ones, they're quite small. Should fit."

"But they're for boys!" Angie protested.

Dorothea scowled, "They're not. It's just people like you who say that."

Angie scoffed, snatching the overalls, "People like me?"

"Yeah," Dorothea mumbled as she left the room, "All stuck up and posh…"

Angie stripped the second she left, slipping on the uncomfortable material and the scratchy jumper Dorothea had handed her to go with it. She rolled up the excess material at her ankles.

"You think I'm stuck up now?" Angie said as she stepped onto the landing where Dorothea was waiting, "Get me a pitchfork or whatever farmers use."

Dorothea didn't say a word.

"And for the record," Angie finished fastening the straps on her shoulders. "I am not posh."

CHAPTER ELEVEN

<u>Dorothea</u>

Thea was proud that she'd managed to get Angeline's brothers to side with her during her bacon breakfast ordeal; it was a win. She'd made her mother furious and teased the hell out of perfect, pristine, stuck-up Angeline. Thea suspected she'd succeed in tormenting Angeline even further during the tour of the farm.

Thea was waiting on the landing for her to change into a pair of old overalls. Angeline would look ridiculous, never having worn a pair of trousers a day in her life.

"You still think I'm stuck up now?" Angeline stepped onto the landing, "get me a pitchfork or whatever farmers use."

"And for the record," Angeline continued, "I am not posh."

Thea turned around to look her up and down. She'd cuffed up the bottom of the legs; Thea let out a laugh.

"What?"

"You had to cuff them?"

"You have long legs!" Angeline protested.

Thea shook her head as she walked down the hall and stairs. Angeline followed, a little behind as she had knelt to un-cuff the overalls.

"So, where are we going first?" Angeline asked, Thea thought she sounded nervous.

"Probably the pigsty," Thea lied. She would be taking her to the cornfields.

"Pigs?" Angeline gulped.

"Or cows, I usually milk them at the weekend," Thea said. Another lie, Angeline's face was priceless.

"I didn't know you were so involved in the farm," Angeline said, walking beside her when she'd finally caught up on her shorter legs.

Thea pushed the rusty old wooden gate open.

"Let me guess; you thought jobs on the farm were all for men?"

"No," Angeline protested, but her face said otherwise.

"Well in case you hadn't noticed. I live on a farm and there are no men here."

Thea held the gate open for Angeline to pass through.

"And besides," Thea patted the wood of the gate, "I'm pretty strong."

Thea felt Angeline's gaze as she looked at her arms, inspecting them.

"Who taught you what to do?"

Thea looked down at her muddy boots as they trudged down the long path to the cornfields.

"My father," Thea murmured. "Not that that's your business."

Angeline was silent for a few moments, a thoughtful expression on her face as she walked carefully along the uneven ground.

"He must have trusted you," Angeline said.

Trusted? Why did everybody act as if he was dead? He *wasn't* dead, Thea thought angrily.

"He *does* trust me," Dorothea replied, her tone firm.

Angeline seemed to have taken the hint. Much to Thea's relief, she shut up for the rest of the walk to the first cornfield. When they arrived, Angeline looked around in puzzlement.

"Where are the pigs?" she asked.

Thea stifled a laugh.

"You aren't very bright, are you?"

"Hey!" Angeline argued.

"Well there are clearly no pigs!" Thea laughed, "it's a cornfield. I was teasing you before."

"Well, I may not know anything about farming, or when somebody is teasing me," Angeline said, "But you are a terrible tour guide."

Oh, she was arguing back now? Thea thought.

"How so?"

"Well to start with," Angeline pointed down the path they had just walked along, "You didn't explain what anything was."

"It was just a path and trees!" Thea argued, "Hasn't the city princess seen trees before?"

"Stop calling me that."

Thea rolled her eyes as she jumped over a fence into the field of golden corn.

"Aren't you coming, Princess? Shall I call for a handsome prince to carry you over the fence?"

Angeline stormed up to the fence, bracing her hands against the wood as she lifted her weight upwards, before suddenly yelping in pain and falling back to the ground. Thea jumped back over the fence, kneeling as Angeline held her hand close to her chest.

"Let me see."

"Go away." Angeline stammered in embarrassment.

Thea ignored her and took her wrist to look. It was a large cut and was bleeding quite a bit. She allowed Angeline to snatch her hand back as she stood to inspect the fence and found a nail sticking out of it, Thea groaned.

"We'll have to go back to the cottage and clean it. If it was just wood, I'd say we could carry on but not if it's a rusty nail," Thea explained.

"A nail?" Angeline yelped, "someone at my school got tetanus from that!"

Thea wasn't really listening; she was busy thinking of what she'd need to mend the fence.

"This is your fault!" Angeline continued, "if you hadn't annoyed me…"

"Give it a rest," Thea cut her off, "it isn't that deep, it'll be fine."

"You don't even care," Angeline didn't sound angry now, if anything, she sounded forlorn.

City princess was clearly used to everyone worrying about her, Thea thought.

"I do care," Thea grabbed Angeline roughly by the arm, "I care because I'm the one who's going to get told off for it."

Angeline pulled away and stormed down the path back to the cottage.

Thea was bordering on furious now, "I only call you a princess because you act like you're so bloody perfect."

"Jealous, are you?"

"No," Thea scoffed, "I feel sorry for you. You must be tired of faking it."

"Faking what?" Angeline asked.

"I see right through you, Angeline."

Angeline stopped walking and clenched both of her hands into fists, despite her cut.

"You know nothing about me. I've been here a day and you've done nothing but assume. I know it may surprise you, but I have feelings. I've left the person I love most in the world in London and I'm hurting." Angeline teared up.

"The person you love most… Oh, your prince charming!" Thea teased.

"No," Angeline spat, "my mother."

Thea felt like she'd been punched in the stomach with the way that Angeline's voice had broken as she tried not to cry. It mirrored Thea's own pain; the way Angeline missed her mother was just how she missed her father. Thea caught up with her just before they returned to the cottage. She cleared her throat as she prepared herself for something that would be extremely difficult. Perhaps the hardest thing she'd ever do.

"I'm sorry," Thea said in a rush.

"No, you aren't," Angeline said disbelievingly, "you just don't want me to tell your mother how horrible you've been."

"You don't have to believe me," Thea said, "I just wanted to say it."

She allowed Angeline to go through the gate first, locking it behind them.

"I won't tell your mother," Angeline said, "but I don't particularly want to be your friend."

"Well I don't want to be your friend either," Thea retorted.

Angeline stood by the front door as she waited for Thea to come and unlock it. The pair headed straight upstairs, Thea nodding to the bathroom. Angeline sat down on the wooden stool, glancing around the room as Thea searched in the cupboard for the first aid kit.

"Don't cry," Thea said, kneeling down with a cotton pad and antiseptic in her hand.

"I won't cry…" Angeline yelped in pain, "is it meant to sting that much?"

"I think it means it's working."

Thea kept her hand on Angeline's, pressing the cotton to her cut. She took it away after a short while to inspect it.

"It's not as deep as I thought," Thea hummed.

"Will it scar?" Angeline asked.

"Does that really matter?" Thea asked, gesturing to show off her the many bruises, scars, scratches and blemishes.

Angeline inspected them for a moment before pulling up the sleeves of her scratchy jumper, showing her entirely smooth and clear skin. Thea wasn't jealous of it.

A physical symbol of their differences, she thought.

"I haven't had a scar before," Angeline explained, "I suppose it'll make for an interesting story."

Thea nodded, cringing slightly at the fact scratching her hand on a nail classified as an 'interesting story' to Angeline. How boring was her life? Thea put away the first aid kit after passing a plaster to Angeline.

Thea cleared her throat.

"We can look around again," Thea suggested, mainly because her mother would be angry if she'd only spent an hour with Angeline, "If you feel up to it."

Angeline nodded and the pair headed downstairs and pulled on their shoes. Angeline was being overly careful putting on her shoes with her new injury. Thea couldn't help but roll her eyes.

She was certain she couldn't put up with this for much longer.

CHAPTER TWELVE

Angeline

Angie was conscious of her cut hand as she tied her laces. It took her far longer than usual as she tied them one handed. Surprisingly, Dorothea waited for her without comment.

"It's hard with one hand," Angie apologised as she stood up.

"It's just a cut," Dorothea countered.

"I know that."

Dorothea didn't say anything more, opening the door and heading out of the cottage in a different direction.

"Where are we going?" Angie asked.

Dorothea laughed, shaking her head as she unlocked a gate.

"What?"

"I prefer it when you're silent. And you talk to me an awful lot for someone who 'doesn't want to be my friend,'" Dorothea remarked.

"You said that too!" Angie protested as she waited for the farm girl to close the gate behind her.

"Yes, after you'd said it," she put the keys back in her pocket, "we're going to see the animals because apparently cornfields are far too dangerous for you."

Angie frowned but followed. She hadn't encountered many animals before; mainly just dogs and cats, pets that her friends or family members had owned. It was not that Angie was scared of animals; it was that she did not entirely trust the girl who was introducing her to them.

Angie glanced at Dorothea walking beside her. She had a bored expression on her face, as if she was counting down the seconds until she no longer had to be in her presence. Her hair was flowing behind her, Angie hadn't noticed when she'd taken it out of the bun but it was clear she had not even bothered to put a brush through it today. Surprisingly, it suited her. She struck Angie as the type of girl that would suit anything. Angie was jealous that she herself was not as naturally beautiful as Dorothea with her high cheekbones and clear complexion. Angeline wondered how she'd managed to keep her face unscratched, given that her arms were a catalogue of farming injuries.

"Do I have something on my face?" Dorothea asked, Angie brought back to the present to see blue eyes focused directly on her.

"No," Angie stuttered.

She'd have to remind herself to not stare for too long at her again. Because it was unsettling how Dorothea furrowed her brow and looked Angie up and down suspiciously. Angie was thankful when she eventually looked away.

It was clear they were approaching the livestock due to the smell, Angie scrunched up her nose in disgust.

"Does Florence help with the animals?" Angie asked hopefully.

"Florence?"

"Yes, the woman who picked us up from the station," Angie explained.

126

"No," Dorothea continued, "the only time I have the Land Girls assisting is when Mary helps milking the cows or when Peggy gives Edward a brush."

"Edward?" Angie asked as the pair approached a set of sheds.

"My horse."

"Ah."

Dorothea unlocked the door to what was soon revealed to be a pig sty. Angie scrunched up her nose in disgust once more at the obscene noises of the animals within.

"Hello piggies!" Dorothea shouted excitedly, making Angie jump. She assumed that was her intention.

The animals grunted as she tipped a bucket of some awful-smelling food into the pen.

"What is that?" Angie asked.

"Vegetable peelings, things like that," she explained, waving the empty bucket in Angie's face.

Angie squealed and pushed it away, Dorothea laughing loudly. She filled up a watering can with water, pouring it into the pigs' basins before turning back to Angie.

"These are pigs," she said, "anything else you want me to tell you so I can improve my tour guiding technique?"

Angie rolled her eyes, "No, this is fine. What now?"

Dorothea tutted, "Weren't you ever told to be patient, Princess?"

"I said stop calling me that," Angie demanded.

Dorothea grinned, locking up the door again.

"Let's go, I can show you some far more interesting places," she said.

*

Dorothea's idea of *more interesting places* consisted of a rich green wood and a path lit with the sunlight that filtered through the towering trees. It snuck its way through the forest, seeming endless. Angie had never seen so much greenery, in her entire sixteen years of living.

"This is on your property?" Angie asked, unable to stop her lips from parting in awe.

At home they had a couple of trees in their garden, but they could not be compared to this.

"Well, not exactly. But most of the farm is quite repetitive; fields, sheds, paths, fences."

"I see," Angie nodded, walking along the surprisingly smooth path of dirt.

"So, I thought I'd bring you here," Dorothea continued, leaning up against a large oak tree as Angie ran her fingers along the uneven bark.

"Because you're a show-off."

"I thought you were meant to be polite!" Dorothea said.

Angie smirked, mirroring the grin Dorothea so often wore.

"It's nice," Angie said, deliberately using a bland word to imply that she was not impressed.

"Nice?" Dorothea balked, "as if you've ever seen anything more beautiful."

The golden sun that had managed to sneak through the branches of the trees lit up Dorothea's face. Angie wasn't sure why she'd noticed.

"There are buildings in London just as beautiful," Angie said, Dorothea following her down the path.

"Buildings?" She scoffed, "alright, sure."

"Buckingham Palace? St Paul's Cathedral?"

It was best not to bring up the fact that buildings in London were mostly being turned to ash.

"Never heard of them," Dorothea said.

Angie tried to meet the taller girl's gaze but she looked away.

"Oh.. oh!" Angie laughed, "you've never been to the city, have you?"

Dorothea's cheeks flushed and she shrugged, looking at the trees to avoid eye contact.

"I'm happy here."

"But this isn't real life," Angeline remarked, "you're living a fantasy, really, and—"

"I'm happy here," Dorothea snapped, "I'll take over the farm."

"There's nothing for you here," Angie chuckled at Dorothea's obliviousness to the real world, "there are no theatres, no dance halls, and no gentlemen..."

"Maybe I like it that way!" Dorothea scoffed, coming to a halt, "God! Girls like you think that's all there is to life! Dancing and men and marriage and children!"

Angie stood still for a moment before turning to walk the way they'd just come.

"I don't think that."

Dorothea shook her head, storming in front of Angie. The walk home was silent; both girls alone with her thoughts.

Dorothea was wrong. Entirely wrong. Angie knew there was more to life and she knew the world was changing and that after the war it might be easier for women. They may have a choice to decide how they wanted to live. That freedom terrified Angie. With so many options, how could she choose what path to take? To marry and have children young, or to work and build a career? Would she marry the first man she fell for or wait? The whole concept was terrifying. And it made her wish that her childhood could last for an eternity.

The pair had not discussed where they were going, but they ended up back at the cottage. William and Michael were sat on the front step, with grazed knees, and sandwiches in their hands. Charles and Peter were running around excitedly with a ball on a patch of grass across the courtyard.

"We wondered when you'd be back," William said, "Mrs Miller made sandwiches for you."

Dorothea headed inside and Angie sat beside her two brothers, letting out a sigh.

"Are you two friends now?" Michael asked.

Angie laughed, "Definitely not."

"You should be," William remarked, "Dorothea doesn't have to be your best friend, like Charity, but you could still be nice to each other."

Angie wished she had her best friend's address to write to her, but Angie had been sent away before Charity had had the chance to write her a letter from wherever she'd moved to with her family.

"I'll try, perhaps" Angie said before stepping inside. It was easier to tell her brother that than the fact Dorothea had already refused to be her friend.

Angeline was not surprised to hear arguing from the kitchen, she looked around the room awkwardly. She'd only come to get her sandwiches.

"Hello Angeline," Mrs Miller smiled and turned away from her daughter who was sitting carelessly on the counter, "I made you sandwiches."

She passed her the plate.

"Thank you very much," Angie responded politely.

She left the kitchen as fast as she possibly could, cringing in discomfort.

"I don't like her, Mother!" she heard Dorothea say. "You can't force me to be friends with someone like that!"

"Keep your voice down!" Mrs Miller whispered.

Angie looked down at her sandwiches before swallowing and retreating outside to eat her lunch with her brothers.

If Dorothea wanted to be bitter, she was prepared to be bitter in return.

CHAPTER THIRTEEN

<u>**Dorothea**</u>

The thing Thea longed for most was her father or James to return home. They would have defended her rather than siding with some pathetic girl they'd barely known for a day.

"It sounds like everything Angeline said was perfectly fair," her mother said.

Thea scowled. It was just like her mother to play devil's advocate rather than agree with her own daughter.

"You're defending her?!"

Her mother whispered angrily, "I'm not defending her. I simply understand her point."

"You want me to leave the farm when this is over?" Thea laughed in disbelief, "go to the city and leave this all behind?"

"I only want that because it would be better for you," her mother explained, "you shouldn't set your heart on living on an isolated farm for the rest of your days."

"That's what you're doing!"

"Yes," her mother said, "but I lived first. I didn't meet your father on this farm. We travelled, had children."

Thea let out a sigh.

"You hardly know me at all," she looked down, swinging her legs as she remained sat on the kitchen counter. "I love the farm. I'm staying here even after the war is over. When Father and James come home."

Her mother turned back to the dishes, scrubbing at a cooking tray.

"And I'm not talking to Angeline," Thea continued.

Thea didn't care how childish she sounded. Angeline had clearly expressed that she wanted nothing to do with her and the feeling was very much mutual.

Thea jumped down from the counter and stormed down the hallway, praying Peggy would be around.

Thea had taken a liking to Peggy since she'd shown her the horses. She didn't mind Florence but they didn't speak much, Scary Mary didn't like her for some reason, and Heather talked too much. So, Peggy was her favourite of the Land Girls. Despite their different upbringings, they were similar in many ways; both had a closer relationship with their father than their mother, they enjoyed classic novels and of course, they both adored Edward and the other horses.

Thea found Peggy and Scary Mary outside the guesthouse, sitting on the bench. Mary had her eyes closed and was running her hand across a rosary that she held in her hand as she gripped the beads in concentration. Thea was religious and she believed in some kind of God. She thought there must be someone in control, but Thea had never understood praying the same prayers repetitively.

Peggy had her nose in a book. Thea would recognise the cover of *The Wonderful Wizard of Oz* anywhere.

"Hello Peggy," Thea said quietly, hoping not to disturb Mary.

Mary opened one eye and glared up at her. Thea gulped; she was not usually nervous around people but there was something about the way Mary looked at her. As though she knew something Thea didn't.

"Hi, Dorothea!" Peggy grinned, closing her book excitedly. She gasped, "Oh! I've lost my page!"

Thea picked up the book. It appeared new, unlike the copy she owned herself. The pages in her own copy were likely to begin falling out the next time she read it.

"Where were you up to in the story?" Thea asked.

"When Dorothy spotted the scarecrow, just after leaving *Munchkin Land.*"

Thea skipped to chapter three, knowing it was around there somewhere.

"There."

"How do you know the novel so well?" Peggy asked as Thea opened it on exactly the right page. "I don't know anyone who could guess where something was in a book."

"You clearly haven't seen Mary with a bible then," Heather giggled, swinging an empty watering can as she walked towards them.

Thea couldn't help but stifle a laugh as Scary Mary shot her usual threatening gaze her way.

"Hello, Heather," Thea smiled, watching Heather fill up the can and begin watering the flowers around the guesthouse. "My father used to read the book to me. I'm convinced he named me after her."

"I'd be flattered," Peggy said with a smile.

"Bet Mary is even more flattered!" Heather joked, placing the empty can on the ground. "Named after a saint."

Peggy shook her head with a laugh.

"That's a good one," Mary remarked, tilting her chin up stubbornly. "Now excuse me, I was busy."

Peggy waited a moment, until Mary had retreated inside.

"Ignore her," Peggy finally said, "she's been like that all week. I presume she's missing home."

That made sense. Perhaps Angeline was missing home too. Thea cringed internally; *you're defending her now?*

"Aren't we all?" Heather sighed, sitting beside Peggy in the empty space Mary had left on the bench.

Peggy looked sorrowful at the mention of home and Thea felt a pang of pity for her. Peggy's home would be so different when she'd return after the death of her brother, Thea's heart ached with sympathy for her.

"How was your day?" Thea asked her to divert the conversation, sitting on a patch of grass beside the bench.

"A little boring," Peggy admitted, "I'd rather spend the entire day with the horses."

Heather chuckled, "Be careful, Dorothea, she might steal them and ride them all the way back to the city."

Peggy smiled sadly, "I do love it here. I'd come back, under different circumstances."

"Only for the horses, of course?" Thea joked.

Thea didn't usually speak to people; it warmed her heart to think that these two people genuinely enjoyed her company, if they even did. She couldn't be certain. Anyway, Thea was grateful that Peggy, Heather and Florence were posted here.

At the thought of Florence, Thea looked around, realising she had not seen her yet.

"Is Florence inside?"

"The new girl came over, the blonde one," Heather said.

"She looked rather upset, I assumed she'd fallen out with one of her brothers," Peggy said.

Thea felt her heart race a little faster. Was Angeline upset? Had she heard Thea's conversation with her mother? She cursed herself again, why did she care? Why did it bother her? Thea had done nothing wrong.

"Are you alright?" Peggy asked, "you've gone a little pale."

Thea had no idea what was going on with these unfamiliar emotions.

"I'm always pale, I'm fine," she lied, standing swiftly.

"Weren't you giving her a tour of the farm today?" Heather asked.

"Yes, I was... I mean, I d-did," she stuttered.

Peggy fit the pieces together instantly.

"That's why she's upset," Peggy stated.

"I suppose," Thea rambled, "I wasn't unfair! I just– I kept calling her a princess, as a joke, and then she got annoyed and tried to prove she wasn't a wimp and then she cut her hand. After we'd patched it up she made me furious because she told me it was silly to never leave the farm and I– I may have got angry and I said I didn't like her."

"Well then," Peggy chuckled, "You two are a pair of opposites, hmm?"

"Never works in friendship, if you ask me," Heather said.

"Well, nobody did," Peggy scoffed, "Dorothea, you and Angeline are just taking your frustrations out on each other. It's an overwhelming time but I'm sure you two will eventually become friends."

"I don't want to be her friend."

"You came here to talk to us for a reason, I think you were upset," Peggy said.

Perhaps, deep down, Thea knew she was right but the prospect of making friends was unfamiliar and terrifying. She'd never had a best friend before, even when all the girls from her school had had a best pal, someone to play with when they were younger, a shoulder to cry on when they went through the struggle of teenage years. Thea had nobody.

"You should talk to her," Peggy smiled.

Thea sighed. Of course Peggy wouldn't understand. She was pretty and confident and people liked her, Thea imagined she would never have struggled making friends. Thea looked over at the cottage where Angeline was opening the door, perhaps to go to her room, or anywhere she would be unlikely to encounter Thea again.

"I'll see what I can do, I suppose," Thea said, defeated.

She headed in the direction of the cottage with her head down, wearing a frustrated expression.

"Dorothea!" Heather shouted.

Thea turned, "Yes?"

"Remember to be nice!" Heather called.

"I'm always nice," Dorothea muttered to herself.

It was getting darker. The familiar sound of her mother taping cardboard to the windows was the first thing she heard as she entered the cottage. Thea avoided her mother, apologising to two people in one day would be a step too far. Thea would rather say sorry to the city girl than her mother. Thea couldn't deny that she found Angeline's presence entertaining; she enjoyed teasing the other girl to see her reactions. That was all. It wasn't that she wanted to be her friend.

CHAPTER FOURTEEN

Angeline

A familiar smell reached Angie as she passed the kitchen. She stopped in the doorway, spotting the pot on the stove as it bubbled away. Peter was clutching a notebook, the familiar brown cover battered. It was a book of their family recipes, written in her mother's hand; food that could easily be made with rations. It was amazing how smells could make you feel at home which was, without a doubt, what Angie's mother was trying to achieve when she'd given them the book.

Peter spotted Angie in the doorway and waved at her.

"We're cooking Mother's food!" He called excitedly.

Michael was cutting up some carrots, his tongue stuck out in concentration. She felt a worried tug in her stomach at the sight of her little brother with a knife.

"Don't worry, Angeline," Mrs Miller said, reading her mind. She was holding some tape as she stuck cardboard on the kitchen window, "I'm keeping an eye on them."

"Thank you for letting them do this," Angie said, "It means a lot."

Mrs Miller climbed down carefully from the stool, setting the tape on the window ledge.

"I know how much a familiar meal can make you feel at home." Mrs Miller said as she pointed to the book, "I must say, there's a wonderful selection in there."

"They're mostly Maria's," Angie explained, "Our maid from home. Mother tended to help more in the kitchen once the war had started."

She also did more when the Carters had to let the cooks go when they couldn't afford to pay them, but Angie wouldn't say that.

Peter was pouting, clutching the book to his chest defensively.

145

"It's still Mother's writing," Angie said to Peter, "she still added all of our favourite meals."

Michael plonked the uneven chunks of carrots into the pot.

"Our mother isn't lazy," Peter mumbled to Mrs Miller.

"I don't think she is, Peter," Mrs Miller replied, "Maids are a godsend. We used to have a few when the children were younger."

Children. So, Dorothea wasn't the only one? Angie had assumed she was an only child, with the way she acted. Angie smiled her thanks to Mrs Miller, whose gaze had dropped to Angie's bandaged hand.

"Dear me Angeline!" Mrs Miller said, "How did you get that?"

Angie looked down, trying to think of anything to cover up what had happened during the tour of the farm.

She'd spoken to Florence about the whole Dorothea situation. Angeline could hardly believe she'd only known Florence for two days, her wonderful advice and motherly nature made it seem as if she'd always been around. She had advised Angie to attempt to be civil despite Dorothea's rudeness.

"I– fell," she said hesitantly.

"Fell? On what?" Mrs Miller came closer to get a better look.

Peter and Michael looked over curiously. Angie noticed their grazed knees and bruised elbows. It baffled her how nobody even looked the boys' way if they got hurt, but a slight cut on her hand was eliciting this response.

"I just fell. On a… rock," she lied.

Mrs Miller tutted, shaking her head.

Angie took the opportunity to leave the kitchen to avoid further discussion.

*

Angie found a comfortable place to sit beside the blacked out window in the living room. She took a book from a nearby shelf and inspected it. She wished there'd been room in her suitcase to bring more books from home but all she had was *The Wonderful Wizard of Oz* and she couldn't read that without her brothers.

She got a few chapters into the book she'd found before she'd come to the realisation that not a single word had sunk in; she had no idea what was happening in the plot or who the characters were. She knew it wasn't the book to blame; her guilt was spoiling her concentration.

It was an uncomfortable feeling in the pit of her stomach. Angie couldn't stop replaying what she'd said to Dorothea. How she'd dismissed her dreams, telling her the only option was to marry and move to the city. She didn't know why she had told her that. Perhaps because Angie was jealous of the freedom Dorothea had on the farm. She was conflicted with guilt from what she'd said and frustration at Dorothea for being so rude. Part of her felt like she should apologise but part of her thought she didn't have anything to apologise for.

"Angeline?" Florence called from the hallway of the cottage.

"In here," Angie replied, raising her voice so that Florence could hear her.

"I've been looking everywhere…" Florence stood in the doorway leaning on the door frame with her eyebrow raised and a knowing expression on her face, "What did I tell you about dwelling on your thoughts?"

Angie blushed and ducked her head, "I just feel guilty."

Florence sighed, "We've discussed this. She'll come round."

"What if she doesn't?" Angie asked, unable to disguise the way her voice wavered. She'd never really fallen out with anybody before.

"Then she doesn't!" Florence chuckled, "but trust me, I know girls like Dorothea. She may not have liked what you said but there's no excuse for her being so rude."

Florence came over to sit beside her.

"I ran a bath for the boys," she said, picking up the book Angie had been 'reading' to skim the back page.

"You didn't have to do that," Angeline said, "I would have."

"I know," Florence said as she put the book down, "but in case you hadn't noticed, I find your little brothers very sweet."

Angie stifled a laugh, "Yeah they are when they aren't in public. Honestly, they are so embarrassing."

Florence laughed and then pouted, "Oh, but Charles and his chubby cheeks!"

Angie smiled at her. Her love for the children was evident in the way her blue eyes sparkled and from the beaming grin on her face.

"You don't have children then?" Angie asked.

Florence tensed, staring at a spot in the distance for a while before she shook her head. The sudden melancholy atmosphere made it clear that Angie should not ask any more questions.

"I better go and set the table," Florence announced, clearing her throat as she stood, "The boys will be ready for dinner soon."

*

Angie took the time she had alone to look around the cottage. Not for anything in particular but simply to take her mind off things. She wandered into a room she hadn't seen before. It looked like a study apart from the beautiful piano, keys coated in a thin layer of dust. Angie felt drawn to it. She couldn't help but sit on the stool which creaked under her weight. She brushed away the dust, just over the keys she knew she would need. As she closed her eyes she allowed herself to remember the melody of *Clair de Lune.* She might have been playing for seconds, minutes or hours before she was interrupted.

Just as Angie allowed a moment of silence between verses she heard the distinct sound of another person's unsteady breathing behind her. Angie jumped, taking her hand off the keys as if they had stung her.

Dorothea was leaning against the door with her arms folded, as it seemed she always did. She smiled; a new smile that Angie hadn't seen before. Angie stood up and backed away from the stool.

"I'm sorry," she began, "I didn't know... it was yours...I just..."

"It isn't mine."

"Oh," Angie squeaked. *Had her voice always been that high pitched?*

"It's my father's," Dorothea said.

"Oh!" Angie's cheeks reddened. Her father. The absent man of the house that Dorothea could barely bring up in conversation without growing upset or defensive.

Dorothea shrugged and leant off the door frame to stand beside the piano, brushing away some of the dust that remained.

"I thought it would be out of tune," Dorothea said.

"It isn't," Angie replied.

"Well," Dorothea cleared her throat, "that's good then."

The pair made eye contact. For a moment it wasn't awkward.

"You play beautifully," Dorothea said, breaking the long silence.

Angie's mouth fell open, never expecting to hear something so generous from her, especially after the conversation she'd overheard between the girl and her mother.

"Thank you," Angie whispered back.

Dorothea looked at the floor, lips pressed together.

"Does that mean you forgive me?" Dorothea asked, finally looking up to meet Angie's eyes again.

"You don't have anything to apologise for," Angie blurted out.

Dorothea narrowed her eyes, looking at her closely.

"Did Florence tell you to say that?" Dorothea asked.

"What?" Angie furrowed her brow, "no."

"Oh. Peggy said you were telling Florence about me."

Angie glanced over at the piano to avoid the awkwardness of maintaining eye contact.

"Well I did," Angie remarked, "but you clearly spoke to Peggy about me too, so we're even."

Dorothea laughed and as she did, Angie's eyes wandered over the pale skin of her neck where she noticed a little birthmark, under her jawline. It was an imperfection in the midst of her beauty.

"Yeah. I guess we are," Dorothea grinned. "But you should at least owe me a favour."

"Oh and why is that?"

"For being so rude," Dorothea sighed dramatically. "For a city girl you have truly awful manners."

It was inevitable that even if they'd made up Dorothea couldn't resist some teasing. But for some reason, when Dorothea was smiling at her like that, she didn't mind. She didn't mind one bit.

CHAPTER FIFTEEN

<u>Dorothea</u>

Thea's father often played Debussy; more so when Thea had been younger. He'd gotten busier after a while when the farm expanded; he hardly had time for the instrument he'd abandoned in his study. Her father always teased Thea about her failed attempts at learning to play the instrument herself. She had what he'd called 'piano fingers' – meaning they were long enough to stretch to an octave, possibly more. But she'd never had the talent. Thea didn't have rhythm and was far too impatient to stick to learning one tune at a time.

It didn't bother Thea that she could not play melodies as her father could; hearing his beautiful music had always been enough. So when Angeline had sat herself on the stool and begun to play Arthur Miller's favourite song, Thea hadn't been able to take her eyes off her.

Thea adored music as much as she did her horses and books. Whether it be the music of nature; soft sounds from a stream, bird song, the wind whistling in the trees, or classical, (she'd always had a soft spot for piano and violin) Thea would listen intently to it. Thea enjoyed listening to songs on the radio from around the world, especially America. She'd taken a liking to their culture and how it seemed to mirror their own. She'd been happy about her introduction to the genre of Swing Music the year before– brilliant musicians like Louis Armstrong and Count Basie. It amazed her, the excitement of jazz and swing; the fact Black people in the USA were creating so much incredible art despite having being terrorised and tormented for years, provided a sense of comfort. Their music had reached the United Kingdom and beyond, across several oceans. It implied the world was maturing and beginning to accept people for who they were. Thea prayed that this would give her the opportunity to lead the life she desired on the farm without the prejudice that childless, working women had faced previously.

The sound of a bowl being placed on the table in front of her snapped her out of her daydream. She looked down at the unfamiliar meal.

"This is the Carter's mother's recipe," her mother explained, looking tense. She was probably praying that Thea would not say anything to offend the Carter children.

Thea nodded in thanks, Mrs Miller stepping away to sit in her own seat.

Angeline sat opposite Thea, tucking a serviette into the collar of her little brother's shirt. He swatted her away, his nose scrunched in frustration. Clearly the stubborn and independent nature ran in the Carter family.

"I did the stirring," one of the boys said proudly.

Thea looked over, trying to distinguish which of the four boys it had been. They all had similar blonde hair and dark eyes. The only way to tell them apart was their height, which was not very helpful when they were all sat down.

"Well done," Thea said to Michael? Charles?

"You did a wonderful job, Peter," Angeline replied.

Ah. Peter.

"Did you enjoy looking around the farm?" Thea's mother asked Angeline.

Thea prayed she wouldn't be thrown under the bus despite the fact they'd made up.

"Other than silly old me managing to fall on a rock, I had a lovely day, thank you," Angeline said politely.

For the first time, Thea didn't roll her eyes at her overly courteous words.

"Well," Thea's mother stuttered, eyes widened in surprise. "That's good."

"Can we look around tomorrow, please?" Michael asked.

Angeline cleared her throat.

"Well, we wouldn't want to take Dorothea away from her jobs again," Angeline mumbled shyly, "Maybe another day Michael."

Thea smiled across the table at the golden-haired girl, partly grinning because she had got one of the Carter boy's names correct but also because

Angeline was so... kind. *She was kind to everybody, it doesn't mean anything.* Thea's smile faded at the thought. It shouldn't have mattered anyway, Thea and Angeline weren't friends. They were just acting civil.

"Well, I could always take you to see the horses in the evening," Thea suggested with a shrug.

She didn't even have to look over at her mother to know that her jaw had dropped that Thea was genuinely suggesting something nice.

"I want to see the horses!" one of the boys blurted out.

"Of course you can," Thea said.

She could sense Angeline's searching gaze on her now, looking her up and down and making her stomach flip.

"I want to go too!" The youngest boy whined.

"You can," Angeline said to the boy, "can't he?"

Thea nodded, instantly regretting it. She could have sworn she'd seen Angeline smile to herself, from the corner of her eye. Perhaps, if she'd shrugged it would make her seem more aloof. After all, she was still stubborn, moody, rebellious Thea. She didn't want that reputation going down the drain. It was like a shield; it protected her.

*

The rest of the meal was eaten in silence; a surprisingly comfortable one. Thea looked over to check on Angeline several times because she couldn't stop thinking about how it felt when Angeline smiled at her. This, Thea thought, must be what it felt like to yearn for a friend. For the entirety of her childhood, she'd wished she'd had a friend, but she'd never specifically enjoyed the company of another person her age. Angeline wouldn't have been her first choice for a friend, and Thea would have to get used to her strange, posh accent and politeness, but she wasn't a terrible person. She'd be bearable after a while.

It was utterly absurd, Thea thought to herself, how swiftly her feelings towards Angeline had changed in the past twenty four hours.

Michael was the one to break the silence.

"I'm tired," the boy announced.

Thea respected his bluntness. He didn't beat around the bush like the other Carter children.

"It is getting late," her mother said.

"I'll put them to bed," Angeline said quickly, standing up.

Her expression seemed urgent, as if she was desperate to get away from the table. *Or away from you,* an unhelpful voice in Thea's mind added.

"Alright," Thea's mother smiled at Angeline as if she'd hung the moon, "will you help with the dishes, Dorothea?"

Thea stood up, glancing at Angeline. She was staring back with her light hazel eyes that appeared somehow green in the light of the dining room. Angeline looked away and Thea noted the way she slightly blushed. *Which didn't mean a thing,* Thea reminded herself, *she was an awkward person and blushed a lot anyway.*

"Yes of course, Mother," Thea finally replied.

Thea and her mother cleared the table swiftly. Angeline's brothers followed her upstairs like baby ducklings.

"So… are you and Angeline friends now?" Thea's mother asked.

She began drying dishes with an old tea towel as Thea scrubbed away.

"I suppose," Thea mumbled with a shrug, passing her mother a clean plate.

"You suppose?" her mother spoke clearly, as if she was hinting at her daughter to stop muttering.

"Well I don't know! I didn't exactly sign a contract."

Her mother let out a laugh as she placed the dried plate away, in the cupboard above her head.

"You don't sign a contract when you become friends with somebody, Dorothea," her mother said.

She knew that, she wasn't stupid. But rather than let it go, she voiced her thoughts.

"You sign a contract when you get married," Thea said.

"Yes, but that's different."

"How? Everybody says you're supposed to marry your best friend," Thea remarked.

"This is all besides the point," her mother said, "the relationship a woman has with a man is *very* different to the relationship a woman has with another woman."

Thea put down the bowl she was washing, staring at the soapy bubbles that stuck to the edge of the sink.

"But what if your best friend is a girl?" Thea said, her voice seemed to echo, circulating around her mind a few times.

Thea had dreamt of the possibility one too many times.

"What are you implying?" her mother asked frostily.

Thea looked up at her mother, into the same eyes she'd seen practically every day since she was born. They seemed cold now, like sharp icicles, piercing her hopes and dreams. Her mother cleared her throat,

"I'll finish the dishes on my own."

CHAPTER SIXTEEN

Angeline

Angie couldn't concentrate on her brothers; she was far too busy worrying if Dorothea was a mind reader. Putting her little brothers to sleep had been a disaster; she'd already called Michael Peter by accident, handed Charles the wrong toothbrush and nearly started humming a lullaby to William when it was in fact Charles that required one.

"Are you alright, Angie?" William asked after she'd dimmed down the gas lamp beside his bed.

Angie felt far from alright. Her mind was racing. There was something so captivating about Dorothea's smile and mannerisms. It had left her feeling dizzy.

Angie wanted to play her more music, just to see the way her blue eyes glistened in awe.

"I'm quite alright, William," Angie lied, leaving his room and quietly closing the door behind her.

She could feel his eyes on her as she'd exited the room, he could always sense when something was wrong. The truth was, Angie could not explain to her nine year old brother, or anyone for the matter, the burning desire in her chest to befriend Dorothea. A girl whom she'd known for a little over twenty four hours. Angie could barely understand the fixation herself and was certain that she hadn't felt this way about any of her friends back in London. There must have been something in the Welsh countryside air, she thought.

Angie marched to her bedroom and closed the door, pressing her back to the cold wood, forcing herself to release slow, steadying breaths as she reminded herself that she hadn't said or done anything to offend Dorothea. They'd made up. They were friends— of a sort.

Angie's head span until she fell asleep in a ball in the middle of her bed, unaware of the time.

*

Something was most definitely wrong. A week had passed. It had generally been uneventful, the Millers and Carters falling into a comfortable routine. But Dorothea had not spoken a word to Angie. *Not a word.*

The mysterious girl always left in the early hours of the morning, returning a little after lunch when everyone else had already eaten. She would make herself a sandwich and walk over to the guesthouse, past Angie and her brothers playing catch on a patch of grass in the courtyard. The girl would then sit beside one of the Land Girls and they would talk whilst Dorothea ate her sandwich with her still-muddied hands. The Land Girl beside her would talk enthusiastically and Dorothea always smiled in response.

Angie felt an ugly, painful jealousy in the pit of her stomach. What was so wonderful about that Land Girl? Why was her company better than Angie's? What was Dorothea so busy doing that she'd fallen back on her promise to show Angie and her brothers the horses? She always went to the stables with that stupid Land Girl. Angie had been so sure the reason Dorothea disliked her to start with had been because she was from the city, but the Land Girls were too. Now it felt personal.

After seven days, Angie had become so accustomed to these bitter, jealous thoughts that she'd barely realised she was thinking them. She'd grown angrier; being unfairly rude to everybody she'd crossed paths with.

"Fancy a walk?"

Angie glanced up from the book she was reading; if the definition of reading was 'occasionally skimming over a few words before looking up and glaring at Dorothea and the land girl.' Florence was looking down at her, her bouncing blonde curls framing her face.

"Uh…" Angie trailed off.

She did not fancy a walk. Not with Florence anyway. Florence would insist on drawing her out and she wasn't ready.

"In fact, that wasn't a request," Florence chuckled, grabbing her hand.

Angie was about to complain that she'd made her drop her book and lose her page but Florence knew she had barely been reading in the first place. They wandered down a pathway with Florence leading. After a few yards, Florence grabbed Angie's shoulders and shook her hard.

"Hey!" Angie protested, trying to escape her grasp.

"Did that shake some sense into you?" Florence asked, flicking her forehead.

"Ouch!" Angie glared, "What do you mean?"

She rubbed the sore spot on her forehead.

"Dorothea made up with you," Florence said, "why are you ignoring her?"

Ignoring her?!

"What?" Angie laughed, mouth falling open, "she is the one avoiding me!"

She felt like she could cry. A week of frustration and sleepless nights only to be told it was *she* who was ignoring Dorothea? Florence flicked her head again.

"Will you stop that?" Angie groaned, "I thought you were on my side!"

"There aren't any sides. You know how to make friends," Florence gestured to Angie, "she isn't as well practised."

Angie swallowed. Was that really what was happening, Dorothea was just… nervous? That just didn't seem correct. Dorothea was so stubborn, surely if she'd wanted Angie to be her friend she would have just made it happen.

"I thought she was ignoring me," Angie said, continuing to walk slightly ahead of Florence to avoid being flicked again.

"I don't think that's what's going on," Florence said, catching up and walking beside Angie, "if Dorothea wanted to avoid you; you wouldn't see her at all."

That seemed believable.

"But she didn't offer to take us to the stables," Angie said.

"She's even more stubborn than you," Florence admitted, "but do you want my take on her?"

Angie nodded.

"I think she's shy," Florence announced, "around you anyway."

That stopped her in her tracks.

"Why?"

"Because she isn't used to girls her age who don't tease her," Florence said.

Angie couldn't imagine anybody ever having the nerve to stand up to Dorothea, never mind tease her. Perhaps the bullies from Dorothea's childhood were the reason she had built an impenetrable wall about herself and she used to be more approachable.

"How do you know she didn't have any friends?" Angie frowned.

"Because Land Girls gossip and Peggy can't keep her damn mouth shut," Florence laughed.

"She did say she didn't want to be my friend," Angie protested weakly, rubbing her arm.

"It's hard for antisocial people to make friends," Florence explained as they reached a clearing of golden cornfields. Angie didn't think she'd ever get used to how spacious it was.

"I'm not that scary," Angie frowned.

"You have been this past week! Who knew you could be so moody?" Florence teased.

"I was never very good at making friends either," she admitted.

Florence smiled at her; a kind smile that felt so reassuring.

"Well, we're friends. You're a brilliant person Angeline," Florence smiled, "and Dorothea needs you."

Angie blushed, looking to the side and pushing away the elation that bubbled in her chest.

"I don't think she needs me," she said, "She doesn't need anyone. She also made it quite clear she doesn't want anyone."

"Have you been listening to anything I've told you? It's just stubbornness. She's shy."

Angie let out a long sigh.

"I'll talk to her," Angie finally said, "But I have to say; none of my friends back in London were this much hassle."

"With all due respect, Angeline, were any of your friends back in London as interesting?"

Angie shook her head, not even needing to contemplate the question.

"Sometimes, the things that are harder to fight for are worth it in the end," Florence said.

Angie looked up to meet Florence's baby-blue eyes as they turned to walk back, she appreciated how Florence didn't just roll her eyes at the petty teenage disagreement, she listened just like a mother and it was so familiar it was almost painful. But it was a good pain. A pain that ensured years of memories with her mother and her family back in London would never fade away.

"Like the war?" Angie asked after a while.

Generally, the topic was forbidden. Everyone had lost so much already and Angeline hadn't asked about Florence's family back at home. Or if she even had any left. All she knew about Florence was that she got touchy when they approached the subject of children.

"Do you think life will be better after the war?" Angie elaborated; her hazel eyes filled with hope.

"I think it will be different," Florence admitted, "who can tell whether it will be good or bad?"

Angie was thankful for her honesty, yet part of her had hoped for comforting lies. It baffled Angie how much of an impact the war would have. It was a game of dominoes.

"Good things will come out of it," Florence said, trying to cheer Angie up.

"Like what?" Angie asked with her head tilted.

"Like unexpected friendships."

CHAPTER SEVENTEEN

Dorothea

"See!" Peggy said, nudging Thea in the side with her elbow.

"See what?" Thea looked in the direction Peggy was pointing.

Angeline was across the courtyard, standing beside Florence.

"She's smiling at you!" Peggy said.

Angeline was smiling, that much was true but Thea couldn't be what she was smiling at. Thea looked to the ground for a moment before using every ounce of positivity within herself to smile back. From across the courtyard, she could see Angeline's lips part in surprise.

"Doesn't mean she likes me," Thea mumbled.

Girls at school had always smiled at Thea. It was their strategy to lure her in with a sense of safety, only to then turn on her. Thea rarely trusted a smile.

Peggy prodded her with her elbow again. Thea rubbed her arm as she watched Angeline return to the cottage.

"She likes you," Peggy sighed, "you know, you really underestimate yourself. It would be a privilege for anyone to be friends with you."

A *privilege*? Thea had mixed feelings about Peggy's praise. It was nice that the woman was so generous, but it was quite often unrealistic.

The rest of the late afternoon was spent mucking out the stables. The homely smell and hard work meant Thea could escape her own thoughts for a while. In late May, the sun set later in the evenings. Thea appreciated it when it finally rested lower in the sky; there was a cooler breeze that made it far easier to work. She thought of how days like these would be spent if her father were here. She'd have more time to herself. Thea remembered how she'd been so delighted the previous summer when it was finally warm enough to swim in the nearby lake. She remembered floating carelessly in

173

the clear water from the Welsh mountains, relaxed and free of dirt and sweat. Thea longed for the days of free time, less work and being in the company of those she loved. Her mother's company was unappealing at even the best of times so she'd have to wait for James and her father to return.

Thea didn't know how long she'd wandered around in the land of daydreams, but she was brought back to reality when Peggy poked her head through the stable door.

"Your mother has called you for dinner at least fifteen times!" Peggy complained, "I heard her from the bloody guesthouse!"

Thea had never heard Peggy curse before. It sounded so amusing with her posh accent.

"Sorry," Thea said.

"Go on then!" Peggy said, huffing and puffing as she returned to the house.

Peggy felt like the sister Thea had never had.

Thea wiped the sweat from her brow with the cuff of her sleeve. As she returned to the cottage, she realised she smelt like manure, pouting self-consciously as she knelt to untie the laces of her boot. It was surprising to her that she cared what she smelt like, that had never been a concern of hers before.

The table was set and everybody was sitting and looking rather impatient.

"Apologies," Thea cleared her throat, spotting Angeline look her up and down out of the corner of her eye. She felt increasingly worried about her appearance, which was perplexing. "I think I'll go and get changed quickly, please start without me."

Getting changed involved the quickest bath of her life and putting on freshly laundered clothes; a beige jumper and trousers.

Thea returned to the dining room where thankfully everyone was only halfway through their meal. She sat beside Angeline, the last empty seat. She looked down at her plate of cold food; and pushed it around absentmindedly with her fork as she pondered on the idea that Angeline had saved the seat especially for her.

"So..." Thea's mother spoke, her eyes downcast, "A letter arrived in the post today."

Thea's heart raced and she dropped her fork clumsily on her plate.

Her father and James had finally written back, she'd finally know if they were alright–

"It's addressed to Angeline," Mrs Miller halted Thea's train of thought in its tracks as she passed the letter over to Angeline.

Dorothea held back her frustration, the jealousy in her stomach bubbling viciously.

"It's from Mother. I can open it later," Angeline said, averting her gaze, "have you got any letters for Dorothea?"

The city girl sounded somewhat hopeful.

"Don't worry about that," Dorothea reassured her, "they'll write to us soon enough."

It had been the most words they'd exchanged in weeks and her mother looked at her daughter with eyebrows raised, not expecting the kindness.

"Can I read the letter?" Charles asked, "I want to hear from Mother."

"We can all read it later," Angeline announced.

"May we please see the horses tonight?" William asked eagerly.

He must have sensed the tension between Angie and Thea had subsided a little. Thea had been hesitant to take them to the stables because she was unsure of spending time with Angeline. Thea had no idea how to make friends but after a week of trying, she'd given up. It was thoroughly exhausting how they had been tiptoeing around each other.

"Of course, I'll take you after we've had pudding," Thea said.

Angeline, William, Peter, Michael and Charles all looked up hopefully with the same hazel eyes. Mrs Miller laughed.

"It's Sunday, we get pudding on Sunday," Thea's mother said, "you all look like you've never been fed!"

Angeline and William blushed shyly, but Michael, Peter and Charles fiddled excitedly, sitting up straight to make it clear that they had finished their main meal.

"I'll go and warm up the custard," Mrs Miller said as she stood up, "Dorothea, could you collect the dirty dishes?"

Thea followed her mother into the kitchen once she'd gathered them all.

"There were hardly any apples left," Mrs Miller sighed as she retrieved the apple pie from the oven, "I barely had enough."

Thea set a pan to boil for washing the dishes later.

"I've dried a lot of apples," Thea said, "they last longer."

"Ah."

The silence was awkward, but at least they weren't arguing.

"Make sure the boys are in bed before dark," her mother said as she got some bowls from the cupboard.

"Yes, Mother."

Her mother put the bowls down as Thea was drying her hands, and pulled her in for a very unexpected hug.

"I'm sorry your father hasn't written a letter yet," she said as she pulled away from their stiff embrace.

"It isn't your fault," Thea assured her as she helped carry the bowls into the dining room while her mother carried in the pie dish.

"I might cry," Angeline whispered beside her, eyes beaming at the dessert.

"Please don't, I bet you're an ugly crier," Thea whispered back.

She didn't actually believe that. Something told her Angeline would still look beautiful if she'd been stuck in bed for days with the flu. Angeline nudged her. It was gentle, friendly even.

*

To be fair to Angeline, the pie was truly delightful and if Thea had experienced a shortage of puddings, she imagined she'd be close to tears too. Feeling comfortably full and content, Thea helped with the remainder of the dishes before heading to the front door, calling to the Carters.

"Who's coming to the stables?" she asked.

Thea heard a harmony of 'me's' as she slipped her muddy boots on with practiced ease. Angeline spent a lot of time tying her brothers' laces. It took even longer since William, who insisted he could tie them by himself, had managed to get them tangled in a knot.

"I *can* tie them," William protested, looking up at Thea as Angeline knelt to do it for him, "I'm just out of practice."

"I believe you," Thea told him seriously as she opened the front door. She held it open as the boys rushed outside, Charles bouncing around with excitement.

"Thank you for this," Angeline said, as she waited for Thea to close the door behind them.

Thea looked at the girl and smiled softly, admiring the dress she wore, that suited Angeline's figure so perfectly.

"You don't have to thank me," Thea shrugged, "consider it an apology."

"An apology?"

"Yes," Thea was thankful for this moment alone as the boys ran ahead, "for lying."

"You lied?" Angeline asked. She looked positively heartbroken.

"I said I didn't want to be your friend," Thea met her eyes, "but I do."

CHAPTER EIGHTEEN

<u>Angeline</u>

Dorothea wanted to be her *friend*. That had genuinely passed her lips. Angie hadn't meant the silence that followed to drag on so long but she didn't know how to respond. The horses provided a successful distraction for the expectation that hung thick in the air.

"This is Edward," Dorothea said as she unlatched the top part of the stable door, a beautiful grey horse peered his head through the gap.

Angie's mouth fell open. Horses often appeared in the novels she'd read and there were many carriages drawn by horses in the city, despite the fact cars had become more common. Angie had never been this close to one. Charles stood on the tips of his toes and held out his little chubby hand.

"Wait Charles," Angie gasped, not knowing how Edward would react.

Dorothea laughed gently, picking up Charles and easily placing him on her hip. The action seemed far too affectionate for Dorothea, yet it looked so natural. It seemed that there was a hidden side to her. She allowed Charles a little closer to the opening of the stable door. He stuck his hand out again, stubby fingers stroking the horse's nose.

"He's huge!" Michael exclaimed.

Dorothea put Charles down.

"He's the youngest and smallest actually," Dorothea explained.

That horse was the *smallest*?

"He's bigger than any horse I've seen in London," Angie admitted.

"Yes well, they probably don't feed them the right stuff," Dorothea muttered as she fetched a stool.

Angie was growing used to Dorothea's disparaging attitude towards anything to do with the city.

The stool made it far easier for the boys to reach the horse. In the meantime, questions and answers were being exchanged between Dorothea and William, mainly technical things such as riding and feeding. Angie smiled; they were both so clever it was inevitable they'd get on like a house on fire. It wasn't long before Charles was practically sleeping standing up. Dorothea met Angie's eyes and nodded at the boys, then to the cottage.

"Alright boys," Angie finally said, "I think it's time for bed."

She picked Charles up and placed the boy on her hip; just as Dorothea had before.

William was reluctant to go to bed but did so with the promise that he could read the letter from their mother. Angie noticed the way Dorothea's eyes looked over at them wistfully. Dorothea hadn't received a letter from her father since the Carters had arrived, perhaps hadn't received one at all. Angie convinced herself not to dwell on it. It wasn't her fault, after all.

With their teeth brushed and the curtains drawn, the Carters settled in Angie's room to listen to their big sister read their mother's letter. Angie looked at the letter and the sight of her mother's handwriting making her heart race.

My darling children,

Angie took a moment to swallow the lump in her throat and take a deep breath.

I hope this letter finds you well; and that you are safe. To say I miss you, my loves, would truly be an understatement. Every day we spend apart is painful. I miss William's peculiar facts he'd read about in the library and then share at the breakfast table. I miss Peter helping Maria and I with the washing even when we insisted he did not need to. I miss Michael being stubborn and independent; I do hope you are listening to your sister. I miss reading to my dear Charles every night. And my darling Angeline, I miss your bravery, your positivity. They say you never realise how much you love something until it's gone; I've never understood that phrase more. However, do not worry my loves as I am sure we will be together again very soon.

I am safe here in London. Working with the post is increasingly more difficult, yet you know of the love I hold for my job. Writing to loved ones has never been more important and I'm truly honoured to be assisting.

Angeline, you'd be so proud of the women here. I know how you longed to stay and help with the war effort, but your brothers are so much more important. We may be miles apart, my dear children, but we are still working together.

Since your departure I have received a letter from your father.

William gasped.

"Keep reading!" Peter practically shouted, reaching over to grab the paper.

Angie felt guilty reading; she was glad she hadn't read this letter aloud at the dinner table in Dorothea's hearing.

He's safe, my dears. He's thinking of you and is in France. The troops have travelled across Europe, there's mention of American troops being brought over and he holds onto the hope that we will win. I pray this will be over very soon.

I love you, always,

Your Mother

Angie stared at the piece of paper, as if it would reveal more words. She longed for more words.

"Is that a picture?" Peter asked, pointing at a tiny square that had fallen onto Angie's lap.

She picked it up with trembling fingers, turning the paper over to reveal an image of their father. His thick brows were furrowed and he wasn't smiling. It had only captured his shoulders but it was evident that he was in his uniform.

Charles eyes brimmed with tears. Angie felt her heart drop.

"Let's take you to bed," Angie said as she picked up her youngest brother, his face buried in her shoulder.

Angie didn't miss the way Peter grabbed the picture and put it in his pocket before they all shuffled silently to their darkened bedrooms.

Charles was tense, even lying down. Angie stroked his hair softly, humming a melody.

"I want to go home," Charles sobbed.

Angie felt her throat tightening as she reached for his hand.

"It won't be long," she whispered.

Angie stayed with him until he eventually grew tired of crying and drifted off on his damp pillow. Eventually, Angie stood, closing the door behind her as quietly as possible. She crept across the landing until she reached her room. Her hand froze on the knob of her bedroom door and she looked at the door beside her own. Angie tried to resist, unsure why Dorothea's room suddenly felt like a magnet, pulling her in. She wanted to apologise that they'd heard from her mother and father, when Dorothea wasn't even sure whether her own father was alive.

Before Angie could stop herself, she knocked on the wood of the door. She heard the shuffling of feet, getting closer.

"Angeline?" Dorothea said her voice laced with confusion.

"Hi. Can I come in?"

Dorothea stared at her with an expression that was difficult to read.

"Why?"

The word seemed to echo for a moment.

"I don't know," Angie replied with an uncertain crack in her voice.

Dorothea watched her suspiciously for a moment longer before stepping aside to allow her to enter the room that had an uncomfortable chill to it. Angie rubbed her arms.

"Sorry," Dorothea said, "I was sat on the roof."

Angie looked shocked.

Dorothea shrugged dismissively, the hint of a smirk playing on the corner of her lips. It was as if she got a thrill every time she left Angie speechless.

"I'll show you," Dorothea suggested.

Angie nodded hesitantly as Dorothea pushed the window beside her bed wide open, ducking her head and climbing out.

"Dorothea!" Angie gasped; afraid she'd hurt herself.

"Shh!" The other girl laughed, sticking her head through the gap in the window, "you'll wake everyone up."

"Surely you're breaking blackout guidelines," she mumbled, shuffling hesitantly over to the window.

"Well, they recommend staying in your home after dark and blocking the windows," Dorothea said, "My windows are blocked and I'm not leaving my home. I'm just sat on top of it."

"You're a menace."

Dorothea opened the window a little more.

"Joining me, Princess?" Dorothea said, fluttering her lashes jokingly.

Angie didn't know how she'd never noticed how long they were before. Angie rolled her eyes and to prove a point, she climbed through the small gap in the window with surprising ease. Dorothea had her eyebrows raised as Angie perched herself beside her, looking up at the moon. The cornfields glowed a ghostly white under its light.

"How can people sleep?" Dorothea asked whilst letting out a long sigh after a few peaceful moments of silence had passed.

Angie looked at her; the slightly darkened bags under her eyes were noticeable.

"You struggle sleeping?" she guessed.

"No," Dorothea replied, keeping her eyes on the sky. "well, I do sometimes. I just don't understand how people can sleep, when the world is so magnificent at night."

Angie pondered on that thought for a moment, watching as Dorothea's blue eyes moved away from the sky, her gaze now fixed back on her. She felt lighter than air and that she was just floating away. Angie didn't deserve to feel this content.

"I'm sorry," she said, looking away.

"What for now?" Dorothea chuckled, shaking her head, "you apologise for everything."

"That you didn't get a letter from your father," Angie continued, "we've only been away for a few weeks and we've got a letter from our mother and heard from our father. It's not fair."

Dorothea stared at Angie just as she had the moon.

"Why do you always do that?" Dorothea asked. But her tone wasn't harsh.

"Do what?"

"Behave as though I deserve to be treated well," Dorothea shrugged, ducking her head, "Girls our age... they don't tend to like me. So, I- I'm not good with feelings and friendship stuff but... I think you're nice-good- great! I appreciate how kind you are."

Dorothea didn't look up once, but Angie knew she was blushing.

"You do deserve to be treated well," Angie replied with conviction.

The girl beside her didn't indicate in any way that she agreed.

"Dorothea?"

She finally looked up, her slightly chapped lips pressed together and her hair dark and messy around her face. Angie cracked a smile at her,

"I think you're nice-good-great too."

CHAPTER NINETEEN

<u>Dorothea</u>

Thea and Angeline sat in a comfortable silence. As time passed the air around them grew colder; that much was obvious from the way Angeline's teeth were chattering. Thea had grown used to the nightly chill, using it as a beacon to pull herself back to reality and to avoid getting lost in the dizzying maze of her own thoughts. But Thea didn't seem to feel any anxiety sat beside Angeline. She was thoroughly baffled that Angeline hadn't come up with an excuse to slip away to her bedroom. Thea let herself feel a slight thrill at the idea that Angeline wanted to stay awake in the light of the moonlight, beside her on the roof.

It was inevitable that Angeline would feel the cold; she was only wearing a thin floral dress. It was funny to Thea that her dress was detailed with flowers when she'd likely never seen the real thing beyond dying cut stems in florist windows, back in the city. Thea longed to show Angeline the beauty of the real thing, blossoming in the Welsh fields. Thea wasn't sure when her dislike for Angeline's industrial upbringing had been replaced with the desire to show off nature and the farmland.

When Angeline's teeth chattering cut through the silence of the night, Thea realised that it would be a good idea to head inside. She longed for the warmer nights summer would bring, wondered whether she'd spend any with Angeline or whether this thing— spending time together— would only occur once.

"You're cold."

"No, I'm Angeline. Nice to meet you."

Thea would never laugh at a joke that bad, unless it had come from her father.

"I think the chill may have gone to your head," she said without a hint of a laugh.

Angeline let out a long yawn before lying back on the roof, staring up at the night sky. She tilted her head to look at Thea, holding eye contact for a moment before cracking a smile.

"Maybe," Angeline finally replied.

Thea was hesitant in her movement but lay down beside her friend. *Friend.* That word felt so unfamiliar. Angeline yawned again.

"It's not even that late," Thea chuckled.

Angeline glared at her.

"It is!" she protested.

"It isn't even midnight."

"Oh."

"I normally go for a walk before bed," Thea said, averting her gaze away from Angeline and up to the sky again, "I'd invite you, but you seem too tired."

The way Dorothea said it was like she was challenging her. And as Thea had learnt previously; Angeline never turned down a challenge.

"I'm not *that* tired," Angeline announced, sitting up and widening her eyes as if to prove a point.

Thea raised a brow, chewing the inside of her cheek to hide a grin.

"I'm not!" Angeline said.

Thea sat up, their arms brushed as she did. Thea folded her arms.

"It's a long walk," she warned her.

"I can do it."

Thea stood up; hands on her hips as she waited with an expectant look on her face. Angeline stood up too, her arms folded. Their faces were close, closer than they had ever been. Thea looked down, starting to laugh.

"Are you standing on your tippy-toes?" Thea giggled.

Angeline's cheeks burned and she turned away.

"You're so small, honestly. How old even are you? Fourteen?" Thea said, knowing full well that fourteen year olds didn't have soft curves like Angeline's.

"I'm sixteen and you know it. You're so rude," Angeline said, "now, you've promised me a midnight walk."

"Sorry for leaving you waiting, Princess," Thea replied as she ducked under the window and headed back inside.

Angeline wandered over to the window, inspecting it to establish how to climb back in without embarrassing herself. The ledge was quite high up and difficult for somebody with such small legs to reach and she was wearing a dress. After a moment, a hand appeared through the gap in the window and Thea silently helped Angeline back inside.

*

The walk was more than pleasant despite the cold, they'd warmed up once they'd started moving and Angeline had fetched her cardigan. Thea decided that she'd save the meadows for another day, when all the colours would be visible. It seemed unfair to experience it in the dark.

"So, where exactly are we walking?" Angeline asked, her cheeks already flushed with exhaustion.

Her physique wasn't like Thea's, her jaw had more of a softness to it and where Thea was thin and pale, Angeline was healthy and flushed. Her cheeks weren't sharp like Thea's, instead had a tiny hint of childhood chubbiness. When Thea's days were spent walking miles, Angeline undoubtedly didn't do much more than gentle strolls and clearly wasn't used to Thea's fast-paced walking.

"Not sure," Thea replied.

"But you said it was a long walk!" Angeline argued, "you must know where we're going."

Thea grinned to herself.

"Are you like this with all of your friends?" Angeline asked. She had to walk at a jog just to keep up with her.

Thea studied the figure beside her even though she couldn't see her face in the darkness. Angeline surely knew she didn't have friends; Thea couldn't possibly strike her as a person other people genuinely liked.

"I don't get on with many people."

"Oh," Angeline said quietly.

Thea let out a long sigh. She'd been waiting for this conversation.

"I assume you have many friends back home."

It wasn't a question.

Angeline was pleasing to the eye and she was talented, her piano playing still echoed in Thea's mind.

She was interesting but didn't flaunt her intelligence and virtues, which only made her more desirable.

Desirable to men, of course.

"I have a few," Angeline said, shrugging dismissively, "but nobody like you."

Thea cleared her throat, "You mean, nobody that was mean to you?"

"No," Angeline replied, "you aren't mean to me, just took a while to crack. Like a tough egg. I meant nobody quite as interesting as you."

'Tough egg' didn't sound negative but Thea presumed 'interesting' wasn't a good thing.

"Interesting?" she asked.

"Well, I mean, you act like a boy," Angeline replied.

"Excuse me?" Thea scoffed, stopping in her tracks.

"In a good way!" Angeline protested.

"In what world is a girl being like a boy a good thing?" Thea said, her mouth remained open in offence.

"In my world," Angeline murmured, "I just mean you're fearless and… exciting. I suppose."

Exciting. Exciting. *Exciting.*

What did that mean?

"Girls can be fearless too," Thea said.

She wanted to educate Angeline; to get those ideas out of her head.

"I know…"

"Have you met our Land Girls?" Thea laughed, "I mean, they've chosen to leave everything they ever knew behind to help the country. They don't call it an army for nothing."

Angeline nodded in agreement as they continued walking.

"I wouldn't call Mary fearless," Angeline muttered, "She makes me rather fearful."

"Peggy thinks it's hilarious that I started to call her Scary Mary."

Angeline giggled, covering her mouth to stifle the sound. Thea wished she hadn't.

Thea continued, "She *is* terrifying."

It was true. Thea hadn't met anybody like Mary before, somebody that had such a creepy character. The way her dark eyes narrowed if you sat to close or asked her a question, the way she sat there in a trance, rosary held so tightly in her palm it must have left a red mark.

"I do agree," Angeline replied.

"She doesn't... like me," Thea said, with a hint of vulnerability evident in her tone. "I don't know why, or what I did but she watches me as if I've done something bad."

Angeline stood still, letting out a gasp. Thea span around, eyes wide with concern.

"Dorothea."

"What?" Thea asked, worried as to why she'd stopped.

"Have you not been saying your evening prayers?" Angeline giggled.

Thea rolled her eyes and carried on walking.

The pair spoke about anything and nothing, losing track of time in each other's company. They stayed away from the trees since Thea didn't enjoy walking through the woods in the dark. If she was a little scared, she imagined Angeline would definitely not enjoy it. For once; mocking, scaring and teasing were the furthest thing from her mind. The feeling in her chest was unlike anything she'd ever felt before. Thea hadn't felt this way about her brother. Her relationship with Angeline most certainly did not feel like a sibling bond.

It didn't mirror what Thea felt for her father, either. She thought that this much be what friendship felt like.

Thea could have walked on for hours, but the croakiness in Angeline's voice indicated that the city-girl was growing tired, unused to the amount of exercise or being awake at this time of night.

"We should go back now," Thea announced.

"I'm alright," Angeline sighed.

"Well, I'm tired," Thea said, knowing this was the only way Angeline would agree to return to the cottage.

"Oh," Angeline said breathlessly, she was obviously quite thankful for the promise of sleep.

*

Standing outside Angeline's door, Thea wondered if there was an instructional book entitled *'What To Say To Your New Friend After Being Unkind To Her At First But Now Really Quite Like'* that she could read. Doubtful.

"Goodnight," Thea whispered awkwardly.

That was a good start. *Right?*

"Night," Angeline replied.

There was something unspoken hanging in the air.

"Thank you," Thea added.

"For what?"

Being my friend? Being nice? Giving me a strange feeling in my chest?

"Being nice-good-great," Dorothea finally replied with a soft laugh.

Thea enjoyed the familiar way that Angeline's cheeks bloomed as she returned to her own bedroom. Thoughts of a beautiful golden haired girl circled her mind as she fell asleep.

CHAPTER TWENTY

Angeline

Angie hadn't slept so well since she'd been at home with her mother. It was a short but pleasant slumber, one that was filled with dreams of midnight walks. The figure beside her was not faceless, unlike most of her dreams. This person had dark brown hair and cool, blue eyes. In her dreams, Dorothea sat that little bit closer, their skin brushed more often and she smiled a little more brightly.

The morning air was filled with warmth; summer was coming. Angie had only experienced summer in the city in her sixteen years of life and that wasn't pleasant. There weren't any lakes to cool off in, no open areas where the fresh summer air could clear her lungs. Now she had a chance to experience summer in the countryside. And her mother wouldn't be there to experience it with her.

Angie rolled onto her side, kicking back the thin sheets. She saw her mother's letter discarded on the windowsill, knowing that if it had been any closer she would not be able to refrain from reading the words over and over again. When she finally allowed herself to read it again, she analysed every word like she'd studied English Literature at University. Which in truth, she would love to do. She adored words, poetry, classic novels and analysed new meanings within simple phrases and sentences. Angie didn't think she would never be able to follow a path like that, because she was a girl, and that wasn't what her family expected of her.

She put the piece of paper down carefully, folding it along the creases set by her mother. Strangely, seeing her mother's writing in front of her and holding something that her hands had once touched made her feel even more distanced. *At least you've heard from someone you love. Think about how Dorothea feels*, she thought. It was peculiar how Angie instantly felt an attachment to Dorothea, this burning need for her to smile properly. Not that half smile she did, that always made her look like she was hiding something. Angie had convinced herself it was because, like Florence had said, none of her friends back in London were as interesting as Dorothea.

The sound of someone shuffling across the landing alerted her. Angie stood, slipping on her gown before looking in the mirror. Her hair was a mess, coming up in wild ringlets. Curly hair as fashionable nowadays, yet when her friends at home said they were jealous of hers, Angie couldn't help but laugh. They clearly had not seen her hair in the mornings, when it closely resembled a bird's nest. She wished she'd pinned it up but she hadn't done so for the past few weeks; there hadn't been a reason to. She tended to braid it or tie it back. But now she felt the need to look nice and braided the top half, getting carried away until she'd pinned two neatly plaited braids around her head, resembling a crown. This was how a princess would wear her hair, or perhaps Dorothy from *The Wonderful Wizard of Oz,* she thought.

Once she'd finished dressing, she looked in the mirror one last time to see her cheeks flushed and her own eyes bright with happiness.

*

"Is there a fancy dress party somebody didn't tell me about?" Michael asked, staring at Angie as she entered the dining room.

She whacked his arm.

"Shu'dup," she said, humiliated.

If this was how her brothers responded, she dreaded Dorothea's reaction. Angie didn't know why her friend's reaction mattered so much. It wasn't like she'd dressed nicely *for* Dorothea. Or for anyone. It was for herself.

"I think you look pretty!" Charles beamed.

Angeline smiled at his sweetness.

"Thank you, Charles. Guess I know whose team I'll be on for dodgeball later," Angie smirked at Michael.

Catch and other ball games were the newest pastime for the Carters, there was little else to keep them entertained and now they had the space to play. However, now that Dorothea and she were a little closer, Angie hoped there would be more jobs around the farm that would keep her and her brothers busy.

"Where is Mrs Miller?" Angie asked.

"Making breakfast," William said, licking his lips. The boys were always hungry.

Angie wanted to know where Dorothea was, but she rarely joined them for breakfast. Part of Angeline hoped that after last night she'd want to spend more time with her. And the boys, of course.

"Good morning, Angeline," Mrs Miller said, "you look nice."

Why did everybody seem so surprised? This was how she always dressed back in London. Had she really looked that terrible during the past few weeks?

"Thank you, Mrs Miller," Angie began to explain, "wearing nice clothes tends to boost my mood."

Mrs Miller nodded, "I feel the same way."

Mrs Miller placed a plate of toast on the table. Angeline noted that there was a smaller stack than usual. She prayed the shortages weren't getting too bad.

"Sorry there are no eggs this morning," Mrs Miller sighed.

"You're wrong there, Mother," a voice announced from the hallway.

Angie looked up, seeing Dorothea walk in clutching a basket.

"The chickens were apparently feeling generous this…" Dorothea met Angie's eyes as a slight gasp escaped from her mouth, "morning."

"Oh, fantastic!" Mrs Miller said, taking the basket from her daughter, "I'll be in with them in a short while."

Dorothea hadn't said anything but sat on the spare seat beside Angie.

"Angie looks pretty!" Charles announced.

That did not help lessen her embarrassment.

"She does," Dorothea croaked.

Angie was pretty sure she was about to pass out.

"Thanks," Angie managed in a shy voice.

It wasn't long before Mrs Miller returned with the cooked eggs. Dorothea ate three and a piece of toast.

"Have you got lots of work to do today?" Angie asked her.

"Yes," Dorothea said, "the weather's warming up, so I need to check all the water pumps."

"We lost some crops last year because we couldn't get water to them," Mrs Miller explained as she buttered her toast.

"Can I help?" William asked shyly.

Dorothea looked at the boy sympathetically.

"Well…" she sighed, "I'm actually doing it with Florence and Mary. We wouldn't want it to get too overcrowded."

Angie felt her stomach drop at the thought of Mary. They'd teased her the night before, nothing too cruel but perhaps the strange feeling Angie had was guilt. But then, Dorothea had looked so vulnerable talking about how Mary didn't like her for no apparent reason. Dorothea didn't seem scared of anything so Angie disliked the idea Dorothea would have to spend the day with Mary, the only person who Dorothea seemed unsettled by. Hopefully Dorothea's fear was just irrational overthinking, because Angie did not like the idea of Mary being cruel to her.

"I'm sure you can find other jobs for them," Mrs Miller suggested, although it sounded more like an order than a request.

"Mother, this job is really important. I have to get it sorted before…" Dorothea began.

"It will take a few moments," Mrs Miller said firmly, brow raised expectantly.

After breakfast, Dorothea told William and the boys to put their wellington boots on. Angie put a hand on her arm.

"I can take them somewhere else," Angie whispered, "you've got work to do. Besides, they aren't your brothers. You shouldn't have to deal with them."

Dorothea was staring at Angeline, frozen to her spot with her lips parted. Angie pulled her hand away, touch still lingering on her fingertips.

"You wouldn't mind?" Dorothea replied, the hope in her voice evident.

"Of course not," Angie shrugged, "Maybe I could take them into the village?"

"Perhaps, if Peggy went with you," Dorothea said, "I wouldn't want you to get lost."

"Not Florence?"

She'd barely spoken to Peggy since their arrival and would have preferred to spend time with Florence, who adored the children and reminded her of home.

"Peggy knows the village better," Dorothea replied, looking to the boys who were waiting patiently with their wellies on.

Angie remembered how Florence had struggled to navigate her way back to the cottage from the station; perhaps somebody with a better sense of direction would be better.

"She also needs a few groceries from Henry's," Dorothea added, "the girls cook their own food at the guesthouse, see."

Angie nodded in understanding, clearing her throat.

"Change of plan, boys," she told her brothers, "we're going for a walk around the village."

Only William had managed to conceal his disappointment.

"But walks are boring," Peter complained.

Angie decided that she'd never disagreed with Peter more. Walks, specifically with Dorothea, were marvellous in Wales. London had streets that all looked the same but places here were so varied.

"Well we can make it fun!" she said, pulling on her coat.

Angie could feel Dorothea's gaze on her as she skipped onto the porch and down the steps, twirling around in her dress. Charles giggled excitedly and started twirling around with her. When the world stopped spinning, her eyes met Dorothea's where she watched appreciatively.

CHAPTER TWENTY-ONE

<u>Dorothea</u>

Peggy was known to dilly dally. She always took twice as long to do any chores around the farm and ten times as long to answer the front door. Thea let out an audible groan of impatience. She could sense Angeline's gaze on her, which seemed to have become a common occurrence lately.

"Does she always take this long to answer the door?" Michael asked, letting out a long sigh.

Dorothea liked him. He was straightforward, not caring what anyone else thought. He often just said what was on everybody else's mind.

"Yep," Thea sighed, popping the 'p.'

"I hate late people," Michael mumbled. Angeline whacked him across the back of the head.

It wasn't very hard; Thea used to hit her own brother much harder.

Seeing how Angeline acted with her brothers; arguing constantly, telling them off, surprisingly made her miss her own brother terribly, even though they'd drifted apart in recent years. As James had grown up, he had discovered the magic of late night pubs and women. When it came down to living without him, it made her realise that arguing with him was far more entertaining than arguing with her mother.

"I hate late people too," Thea agreed. Michael stuck his tongue out at his sister.

After five minutes, four knocks and enough whining from Michael that even Thea was beginning to get annoyed at him, Peggy finally opened the door. Her hair was pinned in waves; she was dressed in a silk night gown and had mascara stains under her eyes.

"About time!" Thea proclaimed. "Get dressed; you're taking the Carters into the village."

Peggy rubbed her tired eyes and Thea caught a glimpse of Angeline's uncomfortable stare.

"We can go a little later," Angeline insisted.

"No, you should have been up anyway, Peg!" Thea chuckled, leaning on the wall. "It's past ten and it isn't even a Saturday!"

Peggy groaned, turning away before mumbling, "Give me fifteen minutes."

"Ten!" Thea called after her.

She stood up straight and gestured towards the bench where Peggy and she often sat to enjoy sandwiches and read in the light of the late afternoon sun. Michael, Peter and Charles sat on the bench instantly. William and Angeline both pointed at the empty space as if to say "Would you like to sit?" to Thea.

"No, you sit."

Angeline silently allowed William to take the space, seizing the opportunity to stand beside Thea as they waited for Peggy. They were already side by side but Thea moved a little closer to Angeline. Close enough for their arms to touch.

The door of the guest house opened and Florence appeared a moment later. Thea knew it wouldn't have been Peggy as she was most certainly not capable of getting dressed that swiftly. Florence was wearing the Land Army uniform of brown boots and baggy dungarees that all the women wore, quite a contrast to when the women had all arrived in dresses.

"Good morning all," Florence said with a smile.

Thea noticed the way Angeline's face lit up and how she took a step away from her, their arms no longer touching. It felt like a painful loss to Thea, even though Angeline probably hadn't even registered that they were touching in the first place.

"Morning Flo," Angeline said with a smile.

Flo? She'd given Florence a *nickname.* How was that fair? Angeline was *her* friend.

"Don't you look lovely," Florence gasped, taking Angeline's hands and inspecting the dress she wore.

Lovely didn't cover it, Thea thought to herself. Her hair was golden and her eyes bright, the apples of her cheeks flushed with a pink glow. The dress she wore was flowing at the skirt, but hugging her curves subtly in a way that made Thea's breath catch in her throat with jealousy... but it didn't feel quite like that. Thea didn't want to be Angeline she just... wanted— needed— something.

So, *lovely*, was not the word Thea would use.

"Thank you," Angeline muttered shyly, looking up at her briefly.

Thea was getting frustrated.

"Well, Florence, we should get started," Thea blurted out.

"Now?"

"Yes, I need to sort the horses out before we clear the water pumps," Thea confirmed, looking at Angeline for less than a second. "Have fun with Peggy."

Angeline opened her mouth, but Thea walked away before she could say a word.

"You're rushing. What's your problem?" Florence asked as they reached the stables.

"Problem?" Thea cleared her throat, opening the latch on the stable door, "I don't have one."

"Yes, you have," Florence pressed, "Please don't tell me you two have fallen out, I can't cope with Angeline being upset again."

Angeline was upset when they'd fallen out? That made Thea equally satisfied and devastated.

"No," Thea picked up a watering can and filled it up, taking a mental note that the pump she had just used worked fine.

Florence watched her suspiciously. She clearly wouldn't be giving in until she got a satisfactory response.

"I just think *lovely* wasn't the right word," Thea admitted, instantly regretting it. She despised how speaking her mind came so naturally to her.

"Ah, jealousy," Florence nodded in dawning comprehension.

Thea nearly dropped the can into the stables as she poured the fresh water into the horse's basins.

"I am not jealous!" Thea shouted.

"Hm," Florence raised a brow, "if you want me to lend you some dresses…"

Thea burst out laughing. Florence thought she was jealous because Angie looked beautiful. That was funny.

"It's not that."

Florence took a moment, considering Thea with a thoughtful gaze.

"What word would you have used?" Florence carefully asked.

Thea put the watering can down, on edge and uncomfortable.

"I don't know," *Beautiful, magnificent, alluring, wonderful.*

Thea coughed to fill the awkward silence.

Florence continued watching her, but thankfully said no more on the matter.

Once the pair had tended to the horses they returned to the guest house to wait for Mary. How Thea dreaded spending the day with Mary's hateful gaze focused on her.

*

Checking water pumps was about as exciting as one would imagine. Thea ended up doing most of the work, mainly because she'd insisted, and the difficult task had proved to be an effective distraction from Angeline and all the peculiar feelings she caused. After a while, Scary Mary seemed to get bored and feel it necessary to spew her usual negativity over proceedings.

"What's the point of us being here if we're not doing anything?"

Thea turned around, noting Florence was equally shocked by Mary's rudeness.

"W-well, you'll have something to do as soon as we find the blockage," Thea replied hesitantly.

Scary Mary continued glaring at her as if Thea had dropped a house on her sister.

"Just because you're in a mood doesn't mean you have to make us suffer," Mary said, still scowling.

"I'm fine," Thea replied haughtily, standing up to wipe the sweat from her brow with the back of her hand.

"Fine?" Mary spat, "you're pouting like a child and are far too stubborn for your own good."

"Excuse me?" Thea stood still in shock.

"You have far too many opinions for a young woman," Mary continued.

Thea felt her face burning red as she opened her mouth to respond.

"Alright you two," Florence stood between them, "calm down."

"I'm just saying what we were both thinking," Mary shrugged innocently.

Florence continued, "I disagree, Mary."

Thea looked down as she switched on a water pump, water spraying everywhere.

"Here!" Thea said, turning the water off, "A hole. You can fix that whilst I go and check another one."

She stormed away. She despised Scary Mary. Who did she think she was? Times were changing and she clearly didn't understand that, it was like she lived in the 1800s. After digging to get to a pipe and sweating from exertion and anger, she heard footsteps behind her. Thea jumped in surprise, holding up her spade to use as a weapon.

"Woah there! It's only me!"

Thea ducked her head as she lowered the spade, "Sorry."

"That's alright," Florence said.

"Do you need another job to do?" Thea asked to dispel her embarrassment.

Florence shook her head, perching herself on a fence and patting the spot beside her for Thea to sit.

"I know you and I haven't really talked," Florence began, "in comparison to you and Peggy."

Dorothea met her eyes cautiously.

"I know an awful lot about you but I fear you know nothing about me," Florence said.

Thea kept eye contact to show she was paying attention.

Florence cleared her throat before she spoke, "I know you don't like how I've taken such a liking to Angeline. It's the same with the boys. Peggy told me you don't have many friends, I understand that you feel possessive over them... over her."

Thea went to deny it but Florence cut her off,

"I'm not here to take your friend away. It's just, for somebody who can't have children, looking after them just makes me feel... whole."

Dorothea's eyes flew wide, mouth falling open. *Well that was unexpected*, Thea thought

"I..." Thea began.

"I'm not looking for sympathy, Dorothea," Florence managed a weak smile, "It doesn't upset me too much anymore. I found out years ago, when I was a bit older than you, a stupid medical complication that obliterated my dreams of the life I wanted. Processing it wasn't easy but time heals even the worst wounds."

It took a while for Thea to understand what she'd been told, especially when it had been so out of the blue. It did make sense; Angeline and Florence were so similar, they both came from similar backgrounds and they'd instantly connected with one another. Thea had nothing to be jealous of, Angeline was still her friend and she didn't prefer Florence over her, Florence was effectively her temporary family. She felt so ridiculous for being petty. It wasn't like Angeline was hers.

"You'd think being with other children would make me feel worse, but in truth the worst thing about it was falling in love with my fiancée back home," Florence admitted, "knowing that no matter what happened; we'd never get to hold a baby of our own."

"I'm so sorry, Flo," Thea said. She didn't know why she had used the nickname, but her full name had felt too formal for a situation like this.

"I'm lucky enough to have my fiancée, somebody who loves me no matter what," Florence smiled, a dreamy look on her face. "Like Angeline, she stuck with you even after your little disagreements."

Thea froze on the spot, her heart pounding out of her chest.

"I-I don't know what you're implying..." Thea began.

"I'm not implying anything," Florence said, putting a hand on her arm.

Thea released a shaky breath as she realised she'd forgotten to breathe in the last few moments, she gripped the fence so hard it hurt.

"And I want to tell you about my cousin at home," Florence declared, "He trusted me, which went both ways. On New Year, late 30s, he and I were watching the fireworks and he told me something I swore to never repeat, and I haven't until now but I know he'd want me to tell you. See, my cousin had fallen in love. He talked about this person with beautiful eyes, these gorgeous long lashes, dark skin, which never bothered me of course," Florence smiled.

Thea smiled back, still unsure of where the story was going but was glad Florence was so accepting of something that really should have been normalised anyway. That wasn't going to happen anytime soon with a British government of old, fat, white male capitalists. Thea wasn't used to seeing people with dark skin around Wales, she didn't think she'd seen a single immigrant in years, but she got furious whenever she heard a bad word about them.

"And I asked him, 'John, if you love her so much why don't you take her dancing?' We knew of bars where both skin colours could dance together. He said, 'Flo, I wish I could. But he doesn't like me back.' I sat there in shock for a bit but then I really thought about it; He and She. It's a difference of one letter, isn't it? We're all humans, we're all built the same inside and yet poor John had spent his life burying that down. He deserved better than that. He wasn't sick, he wasn't wrong or crazy. He was just in love, and not even the law should be able to stop that."

Thea's eyes welled up with tears; she really did not want to cry in front of Florence, who had just shared something so personal to alleviate her own insecurities. But it was so freeing, uplifting, to know that people like her existed. John loved a man so maybe it was alright, that Angeline made Thea feel like she was floating. Maybe it was alright that seeing her in a dress made her heart race and palms sweat. Maybe it was okay that Thea wanted to know what Angeline's' lips felt like against her own. But then... if it was normal why had she never heard a word about it before?

What if she was the only girl in the entire world who felt this way?

"Oh, sweetheart," Florence put her arms around her, pulling her into her chest. Her embrace was so soothing. She would have made an amazing mother.

"I'm sorry," Thea croaked out, "I don't know what's wrong with me."

Florence leant back and held her face, "Don't you dare say that. There's nothing wrong with you."

"Nobody's ever wanted me to be their friend," Thea said, "I think my mind's just... muddled everything up. What I'm feeling it's not– it can't be real..."

"And if it is real?" Florence interrupted.

Thea didn't even want to think about that. How would she live her life if she was attracted to *girls* instead of boys?

"She's my friend above anything else."

She was also Florence's friend. What would she do if Florence told Angeline?

"Please don't tell her." Thea begged.

Florence hugged her tightly again, tucking a piece of hair behind her ear. Her father used to do that. Thea couldn't think of him right now. Not when he'd be so disappointed in her.

"I wouldn't do that. I didn't tell on John and I won't tell on you," Florence replied comfortingly.

They sat together on the fence for a while; Mary was no longer at the pump when they returned. Walking back together, Thea felt as if a weight had been lifted from her shoulders but it had been replaced with a newer, heavier one. The weight of fear as she'd finally accepted the truth. What she felt for Angeline could not be entirely explained by friendship at all.

This notion terrified Thea; more than Scary Mary, more than the uncertainty of war, more than losing her father and brother. She would forever be a disappointment; if not to everyone else, then to herself.

CHAPTER TWENTY-TWO

<u>Angeline</u>

It was a relief to finally walk on the smooth pavement into the village, as opposed to the rocky pathways that snaked their way through the farm. Angie was still getting used to walking on them and she'd frequently trip over, Dorothea teased her for that and many other things. The smooth pavement reminded her of the paved streets of London, though she was a world away from home and her mother.

The route that Peggy led Angeline and her brothers down into the village was far shorter than the one Florence had used the way back from the train station, which felt like a lifetime ago now. Dorothea was right that Peggy knew her way around the area far better than Florence.

Michael and Peter climbed up on an old sandstone wall and began walking along it, which was far too dangerous for Angie's liking. She tried to take Peter's hand.

"Be careful," she said worriedly.

Peggy smiled, shaking her head as she lifted Charles up to the wall as well.

"It's fine, Angeline," she tutted, "they're little boys. What's life without a little danger?"

"Safer," William replied, still standing beside Angie.

Angie gasped when Michael wobbled a little, holding his arms out to balance himself.

Peggy chuckled, "No wonder Dorothea teases you for being a city girl."

Angie scowled before climbing up onto the wall behind her brothers, cautious not to ruin her dress. Angie much preferred Florence to Peggy. Florence was kinder; gentler with her words. Peggy was much rougher around the edges.

When the wall ended the boys jumped down, Angie copying their actions with less grace. The boys ran ahead, William following.

It left Angie standing uncomfortably beside Peggy.

"She likes you really," Peggy announced, "I know you try and prove yourself to her."

She gestured to the scab on Angie's hand from the fence incident back on the first day. Angie frowned, clenching her hand. *Did Dorothea really have to tell Peggy everything?* She wondered.

"You don't have to though," Peggy continued, "like I said, she likes you as you are."

There were another few moments of silence as they both watched the boys run around giggling and playing. Peggy had a melancholy smile on her face.

"Are you alright?" Angie asked softly.

"Yes," Peggy responded instantly, "they just remind me of my brother."

Angie didn't want to ask any more questions, the pain in Peggy's eyes said it all.

"Bombing, back in London," she said, "he was only ten."

Angie's heart nearly broke. He was almost William's age. She couldn't bear to imagine life without him.

"Why didn't he come here with you?"

"It happened when the Blitz first started," Peggy explained, "he was playing in the street. We heard him calling for us and I tried to get out of the shelter to get to him, but I heard sirens and my mother pulled me back in. He was buried under the rubble, his football beside him. I could see his shoes sticking out from under the…"

Angie had to swallow, trying desperately to think of something – anything –she could say to make Peggy feel better. There were no words that could ease her pain.

"I'm not sure why I told you that," Peggy admitted with a sad laugh, "I suppose we should learn from it, and remember to tell people what you want to tell them. I wish I'd told him I loved him, just one last time."

Angie nodded in understanding, looking at her brothers. She vowed to herself she would tell them every day, if not for her own sake then for Peggy's.

"I don't think Thea hears it enough," the woman said after a while.

Angie contemplated the thought, which sort of made her want to give Dorothea a hug and tell her that she cared, she really did.

*

William insisted on carrying all the paper bags from Henry's, like the gentleman he would one day be. Henry had been unlike any shopkeeper that Angie had encountered back in London. He'd willingly made conversation with them and even asked how their day was going. It made her like the place a little bit more, the sense of community was a real comfort.

"He was nice," Michael noted, putting her thoughts into words, as usual.

"It's a family business I think. Henry loves his job," Peggy said, "not like the shops in London, is it?"

"Definitely not," William said, peering into the brown paper bags, "the vegetables at home never look this green."

Angie smiled, putting Charles on her back as he'd been complaining that his legs ached after the long stroll into the village. *This boy is getting heavy*, Angie thought to herself. She'd never tell him that, he was the youngest and Angie didn't want him to grow up just yet. She wanted him to be small enough for a piggy-back for as long as he possibly could be. She didn't like how fast they were all growing up and she still refused to believe William was almost ten years old.

"Are you sure you don't want me to take a bag or two, William?" Peggy chuckled, since the boy could hardly see through the multitude of groceries he had gathered in his arms.

"Maybe," William mumbled.

Peggy took a few bags from him, leading the way back to the farm.

"Do you want to take an apple to Dorothea. I always buy her one when I go to the greengrocers," Peggy said once they got back, holding out the fruit to Angie.

"Don't you want to take it to her?"

"No, I'll see her later. She always brings me a sandwich," Peggy explained.

Angie lowered Charles from her back and took the apple. William was right. Everything from Henry's was fresher than could be found in London.

Angie looked up across the courtyard, heading to the gate that Dorothea had led her to on the very first day she'd taken her to the fields. Angie looked around hesitantly, chewing her bottom lip as she decided she'd try to jump over the fence. She put one hand on the wooden beam, apple in the other, swinging both legs over. She stood up straight, laughing in surprise that she'd managed to do it, brushing down her dress and beginning to walk down the path.

She stopped when she saw Florence and Dorothea stood nearby.

"Uh- I thought I'd try to… jump over," Angie lowered her voice "like you do."

Dorothea nodded as she took a step closer to Angie. She stood so close that Angie could smell the earthy scent of dirt and hay and something sweet like lavender. She took the apple from Angie's hand, their fingers briefly touching.

"Is this for me?" she asked.

"Peggy told me to bring it for you."

Dorothea hummed appreciatively, taking a bite as she walked up to the gate and vaulted it.

"It was an easy job," Florence said cheerfully, "we're done already."

"That's good," Angie said as she watched Dorothea walk away briskly and disappear into the stables without saying another word.

Angie looked at Florence nervously. "Did you say something to her?"

"What? No!" Florence laughed, putting a comforting hand on Angie's shoulder. "She's fine."

Angie wasn't convinced.

"Where did Mary go?" she asked.

"She buggered off," Flo laughed. "You know what she's like with Dorothea."

"She mentioned it."

"Mary just doesn't like her," Florence shrugged, "always says, 'there's something wrong with that girl.'"

Angie thought that was absurd.

"Must be the bible talking," she joked.

Florence suppressed a laugh then smiled down at her with that affectionate gaze that so closely resembled how Angie's mother looked at her.

"I missed you, kiddo," Flo admitted.

"I was barely gone half a day," Angie laughed, "is Dorothea really that bad?"

She asked in jest but in truth, she desperately wanted to know.

"No," Flo shook her head, "she's a sweet girl. She really adores you, you know."

"You aren't the first person to say that today," Angie claimed, unable to stop smiling as they reached the guest house.

"Who else said that?" Flo asked as she knelt to pull off her wellington boots.

"Peggy," Angie replied.

"Well, Peggy is very close to Dorothea," Flo said as she stood up, wellies in hand, "I think you should believe her."

Her cheeks were tinted pink at the idea of Dorothea genuinely appreciating her as a friend.

"See you later." Florence looked at her with a peculiarly knowing smile as she went inside.

CHAPTER TWENTY-THREE

Dorothea

Thea was sure she could never face Angeline again.

Her mind was clouded with images of her; of Angeline's soft fingers touching her own. Their hands had barely brushed for a second when she had given her the apple. Anyone who wasn't longing for touch wouldn't have noticed it. But that was the issue; Thea was longing for touch. She'd never felt so vulnerable.

Thea had run off, certain that if she stayed around her any longer, she'd slip up and say too much. Then Angeline would know. *But know what exactly?* Thea asked herself. All Thea knew was that her feelings for Angeline were like an eternal flame in the very pit of her stomach; it seemed to warm her in a way that nothing had before. At the same time it exuded smoke that made her chest tighten, resembling the physical effects of the emotion Thea knew all too well– guilt. She wasn't quite sure whether the flame came straight from heaven or straight from hell.

Sitting on her roof, Thea closed her eyes and felt the summer air brushing her cheeks, the sensation of her hands on the rooftop tiles, the whisper of the wind– she could imagine for a moment that it was last summer. Before war was declared... she could pretend that her father was sat beside her.

The thought of her father made her chest grow tighter. *How could you be so selfish?* Her father was fighting in a war. He was alone, undoubtedly forced to fight apart from her brother James. Thea had barely thought about him, instead she was troubled with the petty issues of a pathetic teenage friendship. Thea was confused about many of her feelings. There was one thing she was sure of, though: she hated herself.

She was selfish.

Selfish.

Selfish.

"Dorothea?" a voice as soft as silk reached her.

Thea had never been happier to hear her voice but her eyes widened in surprise, Angeline must have let herself into her bedroom.

"Angeline," she said breathlessly, standing up to help her out of the window and onto the rooftop.

"You worried me," Angeline climbed out of the window to join her. "You didn't come down for dinner."

"I..." Thea began.

"Why were you sat so close to the edge of the roof?" Angeline demanded to know.

"I sit there sometimes," she shrugged.

Angeline was standing close, looking up at her. Her neat brows were furrowed and her pink lips pulled into a pout. Thea banished away the thought that she looked *adorable.*

"You worried me."

"I'm sorry."

Thea would never normally apologise to anyone; this was getting out of hand.

Angeline moved away from her, looking out at the farm cast into darkness under the night sky. She began shuffling closer to the edge of the roof, Thea watched her with a concerned gaze.

239

"What are you doing?" she murmured, beginning to raise her voice, "Angeline."

Angeline turned to face her, settling herself where Thea had been sat just a moment ago. She swung her legs over the side of the cottage and let out a loud gasp, threw her arms up and pretended to fall. Thea feared she'd truly fallen and bent down instantly to grab her upper arm.

"Aw," Angeline giggled, looking at Thea's hand on her arm. "You do care."

Thea snatched her hand back and folded her arms. *So, Angeline played pranks now?*

"That wasn't funny," she spat.

Angeline stood up, stepping away from the edge. She came closer.

"Well now you know how I felt," she smirked.

"I wasn't sat *that* close to the edge," Thea mumbled.

Angeline laughed, her smile lighting up like rays of sunshine.

Stop.

"Aren't you hungry?" Angeline asked as she lowered herself back down to sit beside Thea. She hadn't wanted to attend dinner, not after her discussion with Florence.

"I'll take a sandwich when I walk," Thea shrugged.

The pair sat in silence. Thea had to constantly remind herself to stop staring at Angeline. The braid in her luxurious golden hair and the way dress suited her so perfectly.

"Can I come?" Angeline asked when an invitation didn't seem to be forthcoming.

"For a walk?" Thea asked.

She wanted to spend more time with...

Stop.

"Yes," Angeline blushed, "If that's alright."

Thea nodded and then met her hazel eyes for a moment, noting how they seemed greener in this light which looked so...

For the love of God, stop.

"What were you thinking about?"

"Sorry?"

"Before I came out here," she said, "you seemed deep in thought. We're friends. You can tell me."

Thea felt the flame in the pit of her stomach grow hotter. Angeline had just said they were *friends.*

"My father," she admitted after a while.

There was a moment of silence.

"He's your best friend, isn't he?" Angeline guessed. Her tone wasn't condescending like the girls Thea had encountered at school.

"Yes," Thea said shortly. She despised being vulnerable, yet Angeline's responses were always so soothing that she hardly minded opening up to her.

"My mother is one of my best friends," Angeline said, "there's nothing wrong with that."

That wasn't the issue, Thea thought. She wished Angeline could know the truth.

"I feel guilty," Thea replied. "He's out there and I'm here."

"Women can't fight. How is that your fault?"

"No, I mean..." *Why can't you just see, Angeline,* Thea thought, "I've barely thought of him. I've been too busy thinking about..."

She trailed off.

"The farm?" Angeline guessed.

Thea was going to explode.

"*You!*" Thea blurted out.

The world stopped spinning on its axis. She had to look away, bile rising in her throat.

"Me?" Angeline repeated.

"I'm hungry," Thea blurted out, climbing back up to the window ledge.

She heard Angeline following her inside. Thea sprinted out of her bedroom, closing the door to buy her more time to get away.

"Hey!" Angeline called behind the door.

Thea took the stairs, preparing to make the quickest sandwich of her life to make good her escape. *Which was proving to be rather difficult when her hands were shaking*, Thea thought. She could hear feet striding quickly across the kitchen tiles; she squeezed her eyes tightly shut. This was not happening. Angeline didn't move any closer.

She probably didn't want to.

Shoving the sandwich carelessly into a brown paper bag, she tried to get past Angeline, who was standing in the doorway.

"Let me through," Thea demanded.

"Only if I can still come with you," she bargained.

Thea groaned in frustration, as she walked past to pull her boots on.

Angeline followed her out of the house, closing the door quietly so she did not wake the sleeping household. Thea didn't care right now. She paced ahead; taking a route that lead to the cornfields as she swiftly ate her sandwich. Angeline managed to stay close enough to not get lost.

"Dorothea," she said after a long while, panting a little. "Can we talk?"

"We're talking now."

"Stop being immature," Angeline scoffed.

Dorothea faced her with a scowl.

"You sound like my mother," she said as she threw her sandwich crusts into a bush.

"That's because you're acting like a child," Angie remarked.

Thea did not respond, stopping when they finally reached the first field where Angeline had scratched her hand on the rusted old fence. The two girls stood in silence, both recalling that moment how much everything had changed since then.

"Tell me what you meant," Angeline whispered, "please."

Thea had never heard the girl sound so desperate.

"My father is my best friend," Thea said finally, "you were right about that. But there's something I haven't told you... I haven't had friends, real friends before. Of course, I have Peggy but... this is different."

Thea gestured between them.

"I had a few friends in London," Angeline admitted. "Charity was my closest friend."

Thea felt a pang of jealousy at the way Angeline smiled at the memory.

"And this boy called Albert," Angeline cleared her throat uncomfortably.

"Oh," Thea said coldly, "was he nice?"

"He was fine," Angeline replied half-heartedly, "I don't care much for boys."

Thea's heart raced faster, "you don't?"

Angeline shook her head.

"I've never even kissed a boy," Thea whispered.

"Neither have I."

Thea sighed heavily, "I've never had a friend before you. I've struggled with the concept."

"Friends are meant to help you when you struggle," Angeline put a gentle hand on her arm.

Thea looked down at her hand; she wanted to hold it...

Stop.

"I feel guilty, for spending all my time being concerned about you instead of my father," she blabbed, "I mean *of course* I still care about him... and you! I just... don't know how to reconcile these feelings."

Angeline removed her hand from Thea's arm slowly.

"Feelings?" she asked.

"Yes."

Stop. *Stop.* Say no. Take it back.

"What kind of feelings?" Angeline asked nervously.

Thea didn't even think before she started talking, she wished that she had.

"I think you're magnificent, Angeline. I haven't felt this way for anybody before."

Angie was silent for what felt like hours before she finally relaxed and looked straight at Dorothea.

She opened her mouth to speak.

CHAPTER TWENTY-FOUR

Angeline

"I think you're magnificent, Angeline. I haven't felt this way for anybody before."

How could Angie respond to that? What did that even mean? Her friends back in London had never said anything like that. Not even Albert had. Everything about her friendship with Dorothea had been so unclear until now; nothing made sense. She'd been certain the other girl hated her more than anything at first. It seemed as though Dorothea said one thing but meant something completely different, completely at odds with her forthright nature.

When the shock had subsided, her brain processed the information enough to form words.

Dorothea looked at her with hope in her clear blue eyes. As if Angie's next words would be the most amazing thing she was to ever hear.

"You don't," Angie replied shortly.

Dorothea looked like she wanted nothing more than for the ground to swallow her up. The look of disappointment on her face was the most painful sight Angie had ever seen. Until her expression morphed into something bitter. Her thick brows drew together, lips in a thin line, much like how she had looked at Angie in the beginning. When she believed that there was nothing more to her than being a snobbish city girl. It appeared to Angie that all the walls she'd finally broken down to reach Dorothea's vulnerable side had been built back up in an instant, with reinforcements.

"I don't?" Dorothea spat, "so, you think you can tell people how they feel now?"

Her harsh tone tightened a painful knot in the pit of Angie's stomach.

"I…" she began.

"You know what," Dorothea interrupted, "you're absolutely right. I don't feel that way."

She jumped down from the fence, scowling at Angie.

"You're just like everybody else."

Angie felt every ounce of bravery she'd gained over the past few months begin to disappear. This was worse than being crammed in a bombing shelter in the dark.

"I'm n-not," Angie croaked.

"You are," Dorothea laughed mockingly, not even bothering to face her. "You're self-obsessed, like any other city girl. You think you can put on a pretty frock and be treated like a princess? You think that you're special and different. And do you know the worst thing about you, Angeline?"

"Stop," Angie had tears streaming down her face. Dorothea wouldn't allow herself to care.

"You're a liar," Thea said.

A *liar?* Of all things? Angie had never lied to Dorothea. She rarely lied to anybody without good reason.

"You can't accept the truth, so you run away from it. You pretend nothing is going on. You're lying to yourself."

"I don't know what you're talking about,"

"Yes, you do."

Angie prepared to deny the statement, mouth falling open.

But before anything more was said, Dorothea surged forward and cupped her face. Angie felt a warm pressure on her lips. Her eyes closed on instinct.

Dorothea was *kissing* her.

Her hands rested on Angie's freckled cheeks, the gesture unpractised.

Angie couldn't move.

After a short while, Dorothea leant away. Angie's cheeks burned like they'd been branded by Dorothea's fingertips. Angie was the first to open her eyes, the other girl stood close with her eyes still closed, lips parted. Her breaths were coming fast.

Angie's tears had stopped, her sadness and confusion replaced with one thing. Rage.

"What in *God's name* was that?" Angie demanded.

Dorothea's eyes snapped wide open. Angie was quite shocked at her language herself and took a step back.

"Why did you do that?!" Angie demanded again, louder this time.

Dorothea flinched again.

Angie was sure her face had never been so red. Her eyes stung and her heart was beating out of her chest.

"I thought," Dorothea whispered, "you wanted to…"

"Well you thought wrong!" Angie cried. "What planet are you on, Dorothea?"

Dorothea looked like she was being led to the gallows. The worst part was that she seemed resigned to it; as if she believed she deserved to be punished for what she'd done. Angie's fiery fury dulled a little.

"That isn't right," Angeline said. "That's not… normal."

Dorothea was biting her lip so hard, Angie thought she'd draw blood.

"I know," she murmured in shame.

There was a beat of silence.

"I had to do it, just once," Dorothea whispered.

Angie looked up; Dorothea's eyes were glassy as she met Angie's.

"I don't understand you," Angie admitted, "you said you hated me. You were mean. You called me a liar. You said all that and then you..."

"I'm sorry," she interrupted, not wanting to be reminded of her hateful words.

Or perhaps Dorothea didn't want to hear the word kiss again. *Because then it would feel real,* Angie thought, *Dorothea kissed me.*

"Is that all you have to say?" Angie laughed.

"No," Dorothea continued, "I was scared. I *am* scared. I wasn't misleading you; I didn't have friends before. I tried to be cruel to you at first to make you hate me. At first, I swear I thought it was only friendship, my feelings for you."

"What is it, if not friendship?" Angie pressed.

"Something else, I suppose," she said, looking away, "Florence was just... she made me feel safe, accepted. I suppose I got carried away and expected you to... I know you don't like me back but I–"

"Flo knows about you? About this?" Angie gasped in horror.

What if Florence thought it was reciprocated? What if she told her brothers? Or far worse, Mrs Miller?

If that happened, the Carters would be sent away from the farm. Would they have to go back to London? Would they have to listen to the planes, sirens, bombs, screams, cries...?

"Don't worry," Dorothea spat, practically reading her mind, "Flo knows I'm the only unnatural one."

The words were laced with hatred, not for Angie, but for herself.

"Just because I'm not... like you doesn't mean I hate you."

Dorothea smiled sadly.

"It doesn't make a difference if you do or don't, you'll never behave the same way around me."

Angie considered the idea for a moment.

"I suppose... you're right," Angie admitted.

The silence between the pair had never felt awkward, even before they'd settled their differences. Now, stood in the middle of a cornfield after midnight, standing several feet apart, Dorothea looking out beyond the towering trees of the ancient wood, Angie keeping her gaze down; now, it felt uncomfortable.

Part of Angie wanted to turn back time to before Dorothea had kissed her. Anything would be better than watching the girl whom she'd taken so long to befriend, try so hard to stifle her sobs as tears trickled slowly down her cheeks, glistening in the light of the ghostly moon.

*

When her tears cleared up, Dorothea didn't say another word. She simply turned away and stalked back to the cottage. Angie managed to keep up but maintained a distance.

Before Dorothea jumped over the gate to exit the cornfield, she froze, suddenly alert.

"Did you hear something?" she asked, lowering her voice.

"No…" Angie replied hesitantly, listening intently to her surroundings.

She hopped down from the fence, picking up a spade that had been discarded on the ground. Dorothea stood in front of Angie protectively. Angie wasn't sure whether it was a subconscious movement, but she appreciated it anyway, unprepared as she was for any kind of altercations.

Angie listened very closely before she heard it, the distinctive sound of the rustling of leaves. On such a calm night, it couldn't have been the wind. Dorothea pointed to a bush, looking back at Angie before creeping towards it slowly...

"Girls?"

Angie yelped in surprise; Dorothea's hand ghosted around Angie's waist for a moment, only lowering when she recognised the approaching figure.

"Mary!" Dorothea said breathlessly. "You scared the life out of us."

"I believe it is the other way around," she nodded to the spade Dorothea held defensively right under Mary's nose. She lowered it.

"What are you doing out here?" Angie asked, avoiding the question she and Dorothea were both dying to ask: how *long* have you been here?

"My window was open," she explained. "I heard you pass the guesthouse."

Angie couldn't put a finger on exactly what it was, but something about her tone didn't sit right.

She was trying to hide her panic stricken expression. If Mary had been here since they'd passed the guesthouse, it would mean she'd witnessed what Dorothea confessed and the kiss.

"I think you should go back to your own bedrooms. Don't you think, girls?"

Dorothea cleared her throat, lifting her chin up like she did when she was trying to seem confident.

"Well, it's a good job that that is where we are heading now," Angie cut in.

"Oh," Mary grinned, a crooked smile that was nothing short of terrifying, "that's good. I think some time apart would be healthy."

"What do you mean by that?" Dorothea demanded harshly, as the three of them began to walk towards the cottage.

"I just mean time apart is necessary for a healthy friendship," Mary said, her tone cold as ever.

"I couldn't agree more" Angie cut in again.

Judging by the way Dorothea's cheeks were burning red, she was getting more and more furious. Angie prayed they got back before she said something stupid.

"Well I disagree, Mary," Dorothea said.

Oh God.

"Do you now?" Mary asked.

Mary looked exactly how Angie imagined witches looked from her books; hair prematurely greying, unruly brows and dark eyes that were almost black, and an air of malice. If she was green, she would have looked like *The Wicked Witch of the West.*

"Yes," Dorothea stuck her chin up again, "we don't need interference from a woman like you."

Angie nearly tripped over her own feet, her mouth hanging open.

"A woman like *me*?" Mary laughed darkly, "Oh, Miss Miller, you only have to take a look at yourself to know what kind of *people* cause real problems."

The way she said 'people' in reference to Dorothea was in a way that implied she was not even worthy of being called human. Angie could tell Dorothea was speechless that a guest had the audacity to say anything of the sort.

"A word of advice, Angeline," Mary continued, "don't lose sight of who you are. You have a good life ahead of you. It would be a shame if somebody was to stand in your way of that."

With that, Mary detoured to the guest house.

Angie faced Dorothea, prepared for her to be furious, to lash out.

"She's right, you know," Dorothea said.

Angie's stomach flipped.

No. No. *No.*

She was not about to let Scary Mary take her away.

"No, she isn't," Angie protested.

Dorothea met her eyes.

"You said it yourself, Angie," her heart jumped at the nickname, "it isn't normal. It isn't right."

Angie's eyes were burning. It had taken so long to get here; to become close to Dorothea.

"Goodnight, Princess," Dorothea mumbled.

Angie knew that she didn't mean 'goodnight'. She meant something entirely different.

She meant goodbye.

CHAPTER TWENTY-FIVE

<u>Dorothea</u>

Her bottom lip trembled and her eyes pricked with tears she tried to keep them at bay. It was pointless. She stormed up the stairs, taking two at a time and praying Angeline would not follow. Why would she after what Thea had done?

It wasn't that Thea didn't want to be in her company; she cherished every hour they spent together, every minute, every second. Maybe it was best that she had finally acknowledged what she believed to be the truth. She wasn't good enough for Angeline and she'd known that from the very first time she'd laid eyes on her. Even more so when she learnt of her gentleness, her kind smile, her graciousness and compassion.

Thea unbuttoned her overalls, letting the tears spill at last as she tugged her pyjamas on with no care for herself, catching her skin with the buttons. She didn't bother getting under the sheets; Dorothea didn't deserve any comfort at all.

Not after what she'd done.

Any hope of remaining close to Angeline had been entirely obliterated. It was nobody else's fault but her own. How could she sleep when she'd lost the most important thing in her life since her father and James had left? And, really, that was what Angeline had become. It was more than just the fact she was the first girl her own age to acknowledge her. Angeline had made her realise something that, despite how challenging it was to accept, made Thea who she was.

Distracted by the slightest sound from the room next door, she struggled to relax enough to close her eyes. Her heart was heavy and filled with regret. Mary had been right; Thea had to stay away from her. She was a bad influence. That was an understatement. Thea knew that it would never be okay for someone like her to love freely. A young woman who loved other girls, it was wrong and would never be accepted. And yet, her mind was fixated on the kiss. She memorised exactly how Angeline's breath had hitched in her throat. Thea didn't doubt that it had been out of disgust though she preferred to think it was longing and relief that Thea had finally kissed her— it was a pathetic fantasy but Thea couldn't stop— her lips had felt so soft. Everything about it had been perfect. Other than the fact that she hadn't kissed her back; she'd shoved her away in revulsion.

Thea felt she would drown in her panic.

*

"Dorothea, let me help," Peggy ordered.

"I'm fine!"

Snapping at people had Thea's go to response over the past few weeks. The only person she'd speak to when she was in a mood like this was her father and that wasn't happening any time soon.

Thea continued shovelling the aggressively. The soil was going everywhere, her trousers covered in the brown muck.

"This is getting absurd," Peggy said as she snatched the spade from her hands.

"Peggy!" Thea screeched.

With her hands finally empty there was nothing to distract her, emotions threatened to overwhelm her completely when she wasn't distracted by work.

"Talk to me! I can't help you if you won't tell me what's wrong! Friends tell each other when they feel down," Peggy shouted back, throwing the tool aside.

Angeline had said something like that all those weeks ago, on the best and worst night of Thea's life. It was a pathetic statement. From the few experiences with friends that Thea had had, they'd all let her down, even if she was the one at fault.

"Stop pestering me," Thea glowered as she stormed over to retrieve her spade.

"Pestering?" Peggy laughed, "Dorothea, I know you haven't had many friends before but that is not how you talk to someone trying to help."

"Oh, save it Peg," she uttered.

"No," Peggy said, as she pulled the spade from her grasp once again, "I'm fed up with this. Stop pushing everybody away."

Thea laughed bitterly, folding her arms, "It isn't deliberate. People *want* to get away from me."

"Nobody wants to get away from you," Peggy lowered her voice, sensing the depth of Thea's distress.

"Angeline did! And you know what? I bet James and my father were thankful to get away from me too!"

Silence.

Peggy's face softened. She appeared to be searching for an appropriate response, but she hadn't met Thea's father. She'd only known how much he meant to her

"You don't truly believe that."

Yes, Dorothea did now she understood her true nature. Her father wouldn't want a daughter who thought and acted as she did, she was a disgrace.

"You don't know anything about me, Peggy," she hissed. Perhaps if she pushed everybody away, nobody would be disappointed in her, "And neither does my father. If he did, he'd hate me."

With that Thea snatched the spade back and began digging once again.

She saw Peggy in the corner of her eye, leaning against a fence.

"I'm not going to fight you for more information. It's your business," she cleared her throat, "but from everything I've heard, your father adores you."

If Thea wasn't as well practised at suppressing tears, she imagined she'd cry right there and then. It had been true. Arthur Miller loved his daughter more than anything.

The night before the dreaded train had pulled up to the station to take him away, he hadn't left Thea's side. They'd sat in his study on the creaky piano stool. He'd been grinning, dancing around with a small whisky in his hand, as if it weren't the last night in his home before leaving to fight for his country.

"Would the beautiful lady at the back like to request a song?" he'd joked in a posh accent.

Thea had giggled, hiding her face in her hands. She remembered the way he'd come over to her, pulling her hands away from her face. He'd smiled down at her, eyes glossy.

"Won't you have one last dance with your old man?"

Thea wished she'd told him that it wouldn't be his last dance, but she'd been overcome with tears. She only managed a jerky nod.

It hadn't really been much of a dance; Thea had started crying and was sure he had too. She buried her face in her father's shoulder, taking in the smell of whisky and tobacco. He stroked her hair, swaying side to side. Thea wished she could go back to when she was little and needed to stand on his toes to dance.

"I'll come back for you, Thea," he'd said, pulling away to look into her eyes. *"The next time we dance will be your wedding day. I'll come back. I want to see my little girl show everyone how magnificent she is. I want to watch you grow into a woman, see you have children and fall in love..."*

He'd choked up, unable to continue so Thea put her hands on top of his, nodding hard.

She felt a pang of guilt now as she looked up at Peggy, her eyes filling with tears.

"I'd like to be alone, please."

"Doroth—"

"Alone," Thea repeated.

With that Peggy, pushed away from the fence and walked back to the guesthouse.

Thea thought she'd feel better alone, but now she felt far worse. She wiped her eyes with the cuff of her sleeve and tossed the shovel aside in rage. Over the previous weeks there'd been two people she'd tried to avoid; Angeline and Mary. Now she'd have to add Peggy to that list.

"Hello, Dorothea,"

This had to be a joke.

She opened her eyes to be faced with Mary's dark blue ones. Thea had managed to stay away from her for weeks; *why now?*

Thea tried desperately to get past, "I'm sorry Mary, I'm not in the mood…"

Mary stood in her way with a glare plastered across her prematurely wrinkled face.

"Well, I've been trying to speak to you for days," the woman said, "it's almost like you've been avoiding me."

Thea shot her a cold stare.

Sensing her impatience, Mary continued, "I'll be quick then, hmm?"

Thea folded her arms, trying to appear nonchalant.

"I just wanted to say you're doing the right thing," Mary said, her glare softening slightly.

"Great," Thea tried to shove past.

"I mean it," Mary affirmed, "if you continue to stay away from Miss Carter, I'll have no reason to inform your mother of the incident from the other night."

Thea froze.

"You'd tell my mother about what happened if I spoke to Angeline again?"

That couldn't happen. She wouldn't drag Angeline down with her.

"Well, yes," Mary said piously, "it would simply be for your own sake, Dorothea."

"You're threatening me," Thea nervously laughed, in shock.

"I am not threatening. I'm warning you."

Thea was sure life could not get any worse.

"Well don't worry," she said, "Angeline won't ever want to speak to me again."

"Excellent," Mary smiled, "I'll be on my way then."

Thea returned to the cottage just as a few fat drops of rain fell from the sky; she lifted her head and let them trail down her cheeks. She entered through the back door of the cottage, so she could avoid bumping into anybody else.

She'd been threatened. Her one chance of friendship had been destroyed but now she couldn't even talk to Angeline, not that she'd been talking to her anyway. She had been the only person who truly understood how she felt without her father.

Thea had never felt so lonely.

CHAPTER TWENTY-SIX

<u>Arthur Miller</u>

Since leaving home, sleep had been infrequent. He was constantly aching from carrying his rifle and marching across uneven terrain in the uncomfortable boots provided by the British Army. His chest often felt tight and he persistently coughed into his arm. The blood he spat into his handkerchief was something he neglected to tell anybody else. Arthur had been equally lucky and unlucky due to his age; it was difficult to march as his wheeze grew worse but he was still considered young enough to be called upon to fight when the allies had required more troops. It came as a surprise to everyone when workers of reserved occupations were sent to war. However, there were some benefits that came with being the eldest in his squadron. He was offered the only cot, spared a position on the front line and was generally treated with respect not afforded the younger lads.

He'd been thankful for the opportunity to join the army. The stories his mother told him of his father's heroic bravery in the First World War had been with him his entire life. Her eyes would twinkle with pride as she told the tales. He hadn't known his father too well as he'd passed in 1918, just before the war had ended. All he'd known about him was that he'd been devoted to the Miller farm. How could Arthur stay idle when his father had fought, despite the importance of his work at home? He'd intended to follow his legacy; to prove himself as honourable a man.

James had insisted he follow his father and Arthur couldn't deny him that. Being separated from his son would remain the most painful experience of army life. It should have been expected. James was young and healthy; he'd be perfect on the front line. Arthur was older, so he'd not been able to fight alongside him.

A violent cough rising up his throat distracted him from falling down a hole of despair, jolting him back

271

to reality. He tried to remind himself to be grateful he was participating in a war that would provide a better life for his dear family. Thea and his darling wife Maggie were the most important people in his life, as well as James who was now beyond his protection. He knew most men would put their country before anything but Arthur could never do that. If he were to die, his last thought would not be that he'd die a hero. The last images swirling around in his mind would be of Maggie walking down the aisle to meet him in a white dress, eyes glistening with tears. Holding James in his arms for the first time, his hand so tiny as it wrapped around one of his fingers. Or Thea, his beautiful girl smiling up at him, the apples of her cheeks rosy red as she giggled at a joke he had told.

He was so proud of Thea. Despite how destructive war was, it came with advantages for her. She would be able to prove herself as the hard-working girl he knew she was. She'd look after the farm with the care that was always present in the way she dealt with things she loved. Thea was ahead of her time and she deserved a life where she could show everyone how strong women could be. He missed her bravery, which had always filled him with hope.

Arthur had to take a breath to compose himself, not that he was embarrassed to be displaying his emotions. Men cried in war; that was something his mother had never mentioned. Men cried, a lot. He wasn't ashamed to cry for the life he'd left behind, it was a life to be proud of.

He allowed himself a moment like this whenever he had a chance. So long as he could see the sky, even in unfamiliar territory, he felt closer to his loved ones. It would be the same sky Maggie looked at when she went out to view the stars on a warm summer evening. The same sky James would see from the trenches, looking up, so vast and free. The same sky Thea watched as she sat on her roof, looking out at the cornfields and trees covered in a blanket of darkness at night.

Thinking of his loved ones brought more tears. He opened his eyes to look out across the deserted ground, its emptiness mirroring the images of death he had already witnessed. He preferred to look at the sky.

After he hacked out another cough he closed his eyes.

Maggie is wearing a beautiful sky blue dress; her lips are red and her hair is styled in elegant waves. Thea is sat beside her on their familiar bench at home. When they are sat beside each other it's evident how similar they are. Thea was smiling widely at her father. She's wearing her favourite overalls and she's a little muddy but that's alright, she's happiest when she's outside and a little scruffy. His son is stood beside the bench, his mop of brown curls lopsided as he smiles, holding his hand out to his father.

There's blood on James' shirt. It looks like a bullet wound but Arthur doesn't want to ask. Maggie and Thea look bright but not quite like James does; he appears almost as if he has a halo, its golden glow brightening his features. He looks at radiantly and peace.

"Come with me, Dad." James says.

Arthur hears himself asking, "Where?"

"It's time for us to go."

Arthur knows. He knows where he's going because this doesn't feel like life; he doesn't feel like he's alive anymore.

But he's not scared.

"What about them?" Arthur gestures to Maggie and Dorothea.

"They'll look after each other," James replies firmly.

Arthur takes James' hand. He is suddenly overwhelmed with a feeling of loss.

"I love you, Arthur," Maggie calls, voice like honey.

Arthur manages a smile, and begins to walk into the familiar woods holding James' hand.

"Save me a dance," he calls back to Thea.

James squeezes Arthur's hand and he squeezes it right back.

He wasn't scared.

CHAPTER TWENTY-SEVEN

Angeline

William was the most mature of Angie's brothers but that didn't mean he wasn't competitive.

"Angeline you're meant to be on *my* side!" he shouted.

Michael blew a raspberry at William, holding the ball up in triumph. Angie had wanted to take a shot but Michael had managed to grab it first.

"Just because we're on the same team doesn't mean you get to take *all* the shots!" Angie argued, watching Charles run after Michael.

She'd begun spending every waking hour with her brothers. It served as a distraction from *the incident* and how much it ached to see Dorothea every single day only to be entirely ignored.

William huffed and ran after Michael who threw the ball to Peter, who hadn't managed to catch it, much to William's satisfaction. He skidded across the grass to pick it up and throw it to Angie who blew a raspberry right back at Michael. She jogged over to Charles.

"Don't give it to Charles!" William groaned.

"William!" Angie tutted, "he can play too."

William didn't seem to undertake ball activities as a game but rather as a matter of life or death.

"But he always drops it!" William argued.

Charles threw the ball down angrily.

"Charles!" William shouted as Peter grabbed the ball.

The youngest boy started sobbing and ran off along the path back to the cottage, until he tripped over his own two feet and hit his chin on the ground. He let out a wail. Peter dropped the ball and they all ran over to their little brother. William's face had paled significantly.

"I'm sorry!" William teared up, "I didn't mean to upset you, I just wanted to win."

Angie sat Charles up. He buried his face into her side as she inspected the bump on his chin, his cries beginning to subside.

"I'll take him inside and patch him up and get him a glass of water and..." William babbled.

"It's fine, William," Angie interrupted, "I'll take him in now."

She lifted him up and rested him on her hip, carrying him across the courtyard and into the cottage.

"I'm not that bad," Charles was mumbling as Angie struggled to open the door with one hand, "I don't always drop the ball."

"I know," Angie kissed the top of his head, "you know what they're like when they start playing games."

Charles nodded as she finally managed to get inside. She sat him on the bottom of the stairs and untied his laces, pulling his shoes off before kicking her own pumps aside. She picked him back up and headed to the kitchen to find Mrs Miller.

She'd considered for a moment whether she could use Charles' injury as an excuse to see Dorothea; she'd claim she couldn't find Mrs Miller and didn't know where the first aid kit was. This was a lie, Dorothea had used the first aid kit to patch her hand up when she'd scratched it on the fence, but she doubted Dorothea would remember that. After a few moments of contemplation, she'd decided that that would be rude; to use Charles' accident to her own advantage. If Dorothea wanted to speak to her, she wouldn't have been avoiding her for weeks on end.

When Dorothea ignored Angie, it made seconds feel like minutes, minutes feel like hours and hours feel like days. It made Angie feel it was all her fault.

But she hadn't instigated the kiss.

"Are we going to find Mrs Miller then?" Charles asked, bringing Angie back to reality.

"Yeah, sorry," Angie opened the kitchen door.

Mrs Miller was sat at the table with her head in her hands. Her breaths were coming rapidly and she had telegrams placed on the table in front of her.

She clearly hadn't noticed the children's presence as she released a loud sob, muttering to herself,

"No, no, no."

Angie froze. She didn't know if Mrs Miller needed medical assistance, from her frantic breathing.

After a moment the woman stood, picking up a glass of milk she had next to her. She launched it at the ground, the sound of the glass shattering making Charles gasp.

Mrs Miller snapped her head up, looking at the pair with red rimmed eyes.

"Oh, goodness," she croaked, "I'm so sorry."

She picked up the telegrams and clutched them to her chest, as if guarding them with her life.

"Mrs Miller, should I call for Dorothea?" Angie asked timidly, not sure what else she could do.

Selfish, Angie thought to herself. Even when seeing Mrs Miller in a state, she still longed to see Dorothea.

"No!" Mrs Miller snapped, bracing herself with one hand on the kitchen counter, "You have to promise me. You can't tell Dorothea about this."

This? What was this exactly? Clearly Mrs Miller had received some upsetting news. Angie looked more closely at the telegrams and saw: **'Royal Armed Forces'**.

From the army.

Oh.

Oh.

"Oh…" Angie's breath caught in her throat, "I'm sorry. I'm sorry for your loss…"

Mrs Miller interrupted, "Don't."

She held her hand up, eyes becoming glossier.

Mrs Miller let out a wail. Angie put Charles down and made her way towards Mrs Miller. She didn't even have to bring her arms up before the woman hugged her.

Charles lingered in the doorway as Angie hugged her tightly. Mrs Miller was crying into her shoulder and she could feel the material of her dress becoming damp.

"You can't tell Dorothea," Mrs Miller pleaded.

"Oh, of course I won't," Angie nodded, "it's not my place."

"No, I mean we cannot tell her they're gone," she explained.

Angie tensed. She didn't want to tell her own daughter that her father and brother were dead. How could Angie deny Dorothea that knowledge? She'd need to know as soon as possible, she'd find out eventually and she didn't deserve to be lied to.

"Sorry?" Angie wanted to ensure she'd heard her correctly.

"She won't be able to live without him, Angeline," Mrs Miller sobbed, "you don't understand. I can't lose her too."

Mrs Miller never showed any affection towards her daughter yet now there was nothing but love in her eyes.

"She has to know," Angie blurted out.

Mrs Miller held Angie's face, a little too tightly.

"You have to promise me you won't tell her," Mrs Miller warned, "if you do, I can't promise that you and your brothers will be able to stay here anymore."

That was a threat, if ever Angie had heard one.

Mrs Miller took her hands away, taking a deep breath to compose herself as she hid the telegrams at the back of the cutlery drawer.

"Now, how can I help you Charles?" she said, with a forced smile. As if the previous conversation had not happened, her denial washed over the room.

Angie stared at the woman in disbelief. She was insane. Angie couldn't understand her motive; Dorothea would have to find out her brother and father were dead at some point, so why put it off? Lying only caused more heartbreak.

"I bumped my chin," Charles mumbled, lifting his chin up for her to see.

Mrs Miller tutted and knelt to him. She was talking but Angie couldn't hear the words; she could only see her lips were moving. Angie turned, her eyes filling with frustrated tears. The worst news of Dorothea's life awaited her soon and Angie knew about it before she did. She'd never forgive her if she ever found out she'd withheld the truth from her.

*

Angie had to tell Dorothea. It was no longer about what had happened. Part of her was thankful she now had an excuse, a real reason to talk to her. She'd suffered countless sleepless nights, trying to think of what she could say to Dorothea about the incident. She could just tell her the news and comfort her. How she longed to comfort her.

Judging from the sounds Angie could hear from the room next door, Dorothea was struggling to sleep as well. Angie frequently heard her window opening and closing as she ventured outside to sit on the roof. Sometimes, when she hadn't heard anything for a while, she'd stand outside Dorothea's door, her hand barely brushing the doorknob as she considered going in to check on her. She would always turn around and go back to her own room, too scared to enter.

Angie wasn't scared of Dorothea. The kiss had not frightened her at all. It had opened a door of endless possibilities, frightening possibilities of what might have happened if she'd kissed her back.

But tonight Angie had a motive, a duty to her friend. She slipped out of her bed and opened the bedroom door hesitantly, closing her eyes and taking a deep breath. She prayed it wouldn't be difficult to tell her about her father and brother. Perhaps Dorothea would be grateful she'd told her the truth. Maybe Angie would get to see the vulnerable side of her again and she'd seek comfort in form of a hug or a...

She knocked on the door.

A beat.

Two beats.

Three beats.

The door creaked open.

"Dorothea," Angie whispered. It felt so good to say her name out loud.

Dorothea didn't even meet her eyes.

"You have to go."

"No, I don't," Angie felt a sudden wave of confidence as she pushed Dorothea's door further open.

"Angeline," she pleaded, her voice cracking.

"Dorothea," Angie said.

The door was now open wide enough that Angie could see Dorothea's entire body. She was slouched, dressed in an oversized shirt and bottoms that did not match. She looked paler than usual, her eyes and cheeks hollowed.

"You don't understand," she whispered, "you can't see me anymore."

Angie laughed.

"What is this, *Romeo and Juliet*?" she asked.

"We aren't lovers."

The phrase seemed to echo in the air for a moment.

"I know that."

"Good," Dorothea moved to close the door.

"But you want us to be," Angie said.

"No, I don't," Dorothea blushed.

"But you kissed me."

"Stop!" Dorothea snapped.

Angie shook her head, putting a foot between the doorframe and door so Dorothea couldn't close it.

"I'll stop," Angie met her eyes, "I'll do whatever you want; if you just let me talk to you."

"Why?" she asked.

"Let me in, and I'll tell you."

The phrase 'let me in' had two connotations in this instance. Angie wanted to be let into the room, but also to be let back into Dorothea's life, for her to trust her again. Dorothea watched her with narrowed eyes.

Angie stepped inside.

CHAPTER TWENTY-EIGHT

Dorothea

Angeline was uncomfortable; Thea could tell by the way she dragged her feet across the bedroom floor. She couldn't blame her for that considering they hadn't spoken for almost a month.

"Uh," Angeline began, "should we sit on the roof?"

Thea tensed. They couldn't sit anywhere in plain view. Not after Mary's threat. Thea wouldn't risk Angeline being sent away from the farm just because she had given in and spoken to her the second she'd seen those hazel eyes.

"No. We should stay inside," Thea said.

She was slightly offended by the way Angeline stiffened.

"Why?" Angeline asked.

Thea rolled her eyes as she sat back on her bed.

"I'm not going to kiss you again, Angeline," Thea replied, her voice betraying her as it cracked.

The thought of Angeline seeing her as someone blinded by her own wants and desires pained her. However, much to Thea's surprise, Angeline looked down almost sadly. *Did she want Dorothea to?* She quickly banished that thought from her mind. *That would be absurd, Angeline wasn't like her.*

"I know you won't do anything, Dorothea," Angeline whispered.

Her voice was soothing as she sat on the end of Thea's bed just beside her socked feet.

"But I did," Thea admitted.

Angeline met her eyes, seeming to contemplate that for a moment. Before the kiss, Thea had appreciated every second Angeline spent watching her but now she felt vulnerable, exposed.

"I need to talk to you," Angeline finally said as she folded her arms around herself.

"Yes, that's why you're in my bedroom," Thea laughed.

Angeline let out a little giggle as she nudged Thea's leg.

The sensation seemed to spread up her leg, like the colourful sparks of fireworks filling every part of her being. Even meaningless touches felt like the most important thing in the world if it was Angeline touching her.

"Talk to me then," Thea said, sitting cross legged.

Angeline swung her legs onto the bed and sat cross legged too. Thea suddenly realised how close they were, their knees practically bumping and their faces were inches apart, their hands in their laps as they mirrored each other's body language.

"I found something out and I can't keep it from you," Angeline began.

"Something?" Thea asked.

"Yes."

"Alright," Thea replied hesitantly.

Angeline didn't say anything for a moment, simply keeping her eyes on Thea.

"Are you going to say anything?" Thea asked.

"Why didn't Mary tell Mrs Miller about what she saw?" Angeline blurted out.

Something told Thea that that was not what she'd intended to say. Yet, she didn't know how to explain that Mary *would* tell Thea's mother, if she saw them together again.

"I don't know," Thea rubbed the back of her neck.

"You're lying," Angeline stated.

"Sorry?"

"You rub the back of your neck when you lie," Angeline shrugged.

"I do not!" Thea laughed.

"Yes, you do!" Angeline pointed at her accusingly, speaking far too loudly for Thea's liking.

Her eyes flew wide and she put a finger to her own lips. Angeline furrowed her brow.

"We have to be quiet," Thea murmured.

"Why?" Angeline asked.

"You ask a lot of questions," Thea groaned as she leant back on the headboard of her bed.

"And you are avoiding my questions," Angeline pressed.

Dorothea closed her eyes for a moment and felt the bed dip beside her. She didn't want to open her eyes in case the warmth next to her was only a figment of her imagination.

"I don't care what Mary says, Thea," Angeline whispered after a while.

Her stomach flipped.

"Thea?" Thea chuckled a little at the nickname, unheard of from Angeline's lips.

"Sorry," she stammered as her freckled cheeks reddened.

"No," Thea whispered, "I like it."

"Guess you have to think of a nickname for me now, huh?" Angeline smiled.

Thea furrowed her brow.

"I already have one."

"You do?" Angeline asked, eyes wide.

"Princess," Thea teased.

Angeline whacked her arm lightly, shaking her head.

"You know, I'm not even rich," she said, "I grew up rich but my father's business went bankrupt a few years ago."

"You still act like a princess." *And look like one,* Thea didn't say.

She was surprised at Angeline's mention of her life at home when she'd been so private for months. It filled Thea with hope. *Angeline trusted her.*

"I do not!" Angeline gasped.

"You wore that fancy pink dress, remember?" Thea said. "You had your hair in that crown… braid thing."

Angeline's eyes seemed to sparkle.

"You remember that?" Angeline tilted her head to the side.

"Of course, I do," Thea shrugged, as if she hadn't pictured how beautiful Angeline had looked that day many times since.

There was a moment of silence before Angeline spoke again.

"I wore that the day you kissed me."

Thea averted her gaze away from Angeline, afraid that all she'd see on her beautiful face would be a look of disgust.

"I'm sorry," she uttered.

Angeline's gaze didn't move from Thea.

"I can't pretend it didn't happen," Angeline said.

"Neither can I," Thea replied, voice hitching in her throat. "That is exactly why we can't be friends—"

"Stop it," Angeline shook her head slowly. "Thea, stop it."

"—so, I think it would be best if you say whatever you have to say and leave."

It ached to say that.

"I liked it!" Angeline blurted out, sitting up straight.

She tucked her knees up to her chest, arms tightened around her legs as she squeezed her eyes shut.

"You didn't," Thea laughed sadly, "You pushed me away."

"Because I was scared!" Angeline snapped. "This isn't supposed to happen."

Thea let out a low scoff, sitting up slowly.

"You think I don't *know* that?"

Angeline loosened her grip on her legs, opening her eyes. She seemed entirely overwhelmed, as if suffering with a terrible internal conflict. Thea was convinced it had been a lie, yet she looked so troubled it was hard to not believe her.

"I'm still scared," she whispered.

Thea sat right beside her, their knees bumping.

"That's alright."

"It's not."

"Fine, it's not."

Angeline let out a laugh through her sobs. Thea hated to see those eyes glossy with tears. Thea wasn't very good at comforting people. She put a shaking hand on top of Angeline's. Her skin was just as soft as her lips had been. Angeline bit her bottom lip as she smiled.

Thea did something she wished she'd done first, before the kiss. She linked their fingers.

"You have tiny hands," Thea said.

Angeline wiped her eyes with her free hand and stuck her tongue out.

"No, really," Thea put their palms together, inspecting the size difference, "you're tiny!"

"Thea," she whined, nudging her head on Thea's shoulder.

Thea smiled, closing her eyes and intertwining their fingers once again, resting her chin on top of

Angie's hair. It smelt like the soap everyone else used but mixed with Angeline's natural scent it smelt far nicer. Despite the unfamiliarity of touching Angeline this way, it felt so wonderful that she momentarily forgot she'd never see Angeline again if Mary caught them together.

"Stop thinking," Angeline mumbled into her shoulder.

"That's quite hard to do."

"Please. For me?" Angeline leant away, looking up at Thea with long lashes and twinkling eyes.

God, Thea wanted to kiss her again.

She put her hand on Angeline's right cheek hesitantly, thankful when she tilted her head into the touch, letting out a sigh through her nose. Thea was so lost in this dream like world she had forgotten that Angeline had originally entered her room to talk to her about something.

"You were going to tell me something."

Angeline's breathing changed and she sat up, moving away from Thea's touch.

"Does that matter now?" Angeline asked, "I mean... we can be friends again now. I can tell you later.

Thea swallowed, looking away.

"You can't be serious?" Angeline scoffed.

"What?"

"You… you comforted me… you held my hand!" Angeline cried, "now you're just going to disappear again?"

"Angeline," she reached for her hand again, "come on."

She stood up, folding her arms around herself once more.

"We can't be friends," Thea began to explain, "you have to understand I'm doing this for your benefit."

"No, you aren't!"

"What if Mary told my mother what she saw and you were sent away from the farm?" Thea spat, "God knows where you'd go. My mother wouldn't care. Heck, she'd probably send you on a train back to London!"

"I don't care!" Angeline sobbed.

"What about your brothers?" Thea asked. "You want them to get buried under rubble like Peggy's brother?"

Angeline went silent, shaking her head as the tears in her eyes finally fell.

"That was *mean*."

Thea shook her head, standing up and looking down at the beautiful golden-haired girl. She cupped her cheek again, too nervous to do anything else.

"You'd never listen to me, if I wasn't mean."

Angeline met her eyes, stiff in her touch.

"I hate this," she mumbled.

Thea brushed her thumb over Angeline's cheekbone, wiping away the dampness of her tears.

"Believe me," Thea smiled, "if Mary hadn't threatened me, I'd be spending every waking hour with you."

"She threatened you?" Angeline hissed, "I hate her."

Thea smiled at the way Angeline scowled.

"That's why I stayed away from you," Thea admitted.

"That's why you wouldn't sit on the roof," Angeline realised, "in case Mary saw us."

Thea nodded, lowering her hand. Angeline quickly took it, linking their fingers together and squeezing gently. Whatever Angeline had originally come in to say was forgotten, but it didn't seem to matter anymore.

"Thank you," Angeline whispered, "you were only trying to protect me."

"That's all I ever wanted to do, Angie," Thea said.

"There's the nickname," Angeline chuckled.

CHAPTER TWENTY-NINE

Angeline

What on earth had she been thinking? Angie hadn't been able to do it. Dorothea stood there, already wrought with nerves. Angie wouldn't have even known how to word the news. *Hello Dorothea. Sorry, it slipped my mind for a moment. Your father and brother are dead; your mother knows and is refusing to tell you.* Angie cringed.

She'd settled on telling Dorothea something else. Something she didn't even think she'd ever be able to say out loud.

"I liked it!"

Angie could still picture Dorothea's exact expression. Her brows pulled together and her lips had parted. In that moment, time had slowed for Angie and she believed Thea felt the same. Angie had liked the kiss; she'd just been overwhelmed with fear to accept exactly what that meant. In truth, Angie had pushed down that dreaded feeling but she'd rather admit that she'd enjoyed the kiss to Dorothea and see her face light up with relief than tell her the news she'd come to share and see her shoulders drop and tears stain her cheeks. It was quite possibly the most selfish thing Angie had ever done in her life.

The worst part wasn't the guilt eating away at her but the fact that Dorothea had comforted her. They had lain beside each other and Angie could smell the faint scent of lavender and fresh grass on her bed sheets, along with a hint of hay and stables. Dorothea had held her hand, linked their fingers and stroked her cheek, close enough for Angie to feel her warm breath caressing the surface of her skin. It should have been Angie soothing Dorothea that night as she mourned the loss of the two people she loved most in the world but Angie hadn't even told her.

She knew she'd never get to sleep after what had happened, even with the calming ghost of Dorothea's touch on her cheek. Her eyelids felt as heavy as her heart as she closed her eyes. She was certain sleep would be far from reach, but thankfully she fell into a slumber; dreaming that Dorothea was lying beside her, their arms brushing.

It seemed in Angie's dreams, she'd always find her way back to her.

*

"Angie!"

Angie sat up in her bed with a gasp, immediately imagining the worst. *What if Dorothea had found the telegram? What if she knew Angie was keeping her father and brother's death a secret? What if...*

"Get up sleeping beauty!" Dorothea interrupted her thoughts, banging on the wood of her bedroom door.

She swung her legs over the side of her bed and walked over to turn the doorknob. Stood in the doorway was a fully-dressed Thea, William and Michael. Peter was running down the hallway noisily with Charles giggling as he hugged Peter's neck, enjoying the piggyback ride.

"I told you she wouldn't be dressed," Michael huffed.

301

"What's going on?" Angie managed to ask through a yawn, rubbing her eyes and wrapping her arms around herself at the morning chill.

She felt mildly intimidated being confronted by five dressed people when she'd just woken and was in her pyjamas, looking a mess. Yet, Dorothea's gaze lingered on her, eyes twinkling.

"Hide and seek!" Charles called with a toothy grin.

"Dorothea's taking us to the cornfields" William explained.

"And we're having a massive game of hide and seek!" Peter interrupted.

"Hey!" William pouted, and then continued, "it has to be in pairs so we don't get lost."

Dorothea's head was tilted as she looked Angie up and down.

Her voice was soft, "if you're too tired, you can stay here."

Angie wanted to spend every moment she could with Dorothea, she wouldn't be staying in bed.

"No, I'll come," Angie insisted.

"Angie, look at my scab!" Charles tilted his chin up, gesturing to where he'd fallen yesterday, "Dorothea said it makes me look like a brave soldier."

Dorothea chuckled at Charles as Angie's heart clenched. Dorothea's father and brother were brave soldiers. *Brave, dead soldiers,* Angie's mind unhelpfully supplied.

"We'll leave you to get dressed," Peter said, spinning around with Charles still enjoying a piggyback.

"Be careful! Please don't drop him," Angie squealed, reaching out to place a hand on Charles' back.

Dorothea met Angie's eyes, the corners of her lips turning up in a smile. It wasn't mocking in the slightest but rather reassuring.

"I'll keep an eye on them," she said.

"Alright."

With that, Angie closed her bedroom door and rushed to her wardrobe, heart in her throat. She inspected her items of clothing, settling on a cream, floral dress. It wasn't ideal for running around in a field but impressing Dorothea felt more important, which was absurd. It wasn't like anything could ever come of their relationship. They'd undoubtedly remain friends, or whatever this was for as long as they could. Perhaps it would only be until war was over and Angie returned home. That thought provoked a pang of pain in Angie's heart. This was a friendship unlike any other she had experienced. A friendship with lingering glances, loving stares and brief touches that felt like touches from an angel, or something otherworldly.

She was ready in a few minutes and on her way out of the room she stopped to look at herself in the mirror for a moment. All she saw was a liar. Dorothea trusted her and was taking time out of her day of essential work to spend it with her and her brothers. She didn't even need to do it, she'd *wanted* to. Angie was certain Dorothea wouldn't want to look at her again if she knew what she was hiding.

"Are you done yet?!" she heard Michael shout.

She opened the door as she heard Dorothea speak.

"Give her a second," Dorothea nudged him.

"Finally!" Peter sighed, Charles now on Dorothea's back instead.

"I wasn't that long," Angie argued.

"You weren't," Dorothea cut in, "if I were to look even half as nice as you, it would take me ten times as long."

Angie ducked her head, rubbing her arm.

"You're only being nice because you want Angie to be on your side when we play," Peter remarked.

Dorothea threw her head back in a laugh, Angie subtly admiring the contours of her exposed neck.

"And why would I want that?" Dorothea asked, putting Charles down so they could make their way down the stairs.

"Because I'm tiny and can hide in small places," Angie said, raising a brow.

"Hmm," Dorothea shrugged, tying her shoes before helping Charles get his wellies on, "that's true, but the other boys are also small."

"Yes but Charles is clumsy, Michael's loud and William and Peter are extremely competitive so it gets rather annoying."

"Hey!" William and Peter complained in unison.

Angie grinned as she reached for the pumps she'd thrown aside carelessly the day before.

"You're also clumsy and loud," Dorothea teased, helping Charles onto her back, "And I hate to tell you, but competitiveness runs in your family."

Angie stuck her tongue out at her, unlocking the front door.

Dorothea stayed a few yards behind Angie as they passed the guesthouse, undoubtedly concerned that Scary Mary would spot them together. Angie truly despised that woman.

It didn't take Angie long to regret wearing pumps on the uneven terrain. Dorothea was watching her knowingly as she caught up to her, when the guesthouse was out of sight. William, Michael and Peter ran ahead.

"Maybe I should be giving you the piggyback," Dorothea remarked.

"I'm fine," Angie muttered, she didn't mind the teasing anymore. It seemed to give her a rush of adrenaline. Maybe it always had.

Charles was humming absentmindedly as they snaked their way along the paths of the Miller Farm, his head lolled on Dorothea shoulder. Angie spoke to

Dorothea, since Charles was paying little attention to anything.

"So… if I'm clumsy, loud and competitive," Angie recalled with a smirk, "why do you want to be on my team?"

"Because…" Dorothea shrugged, "we're friends."

"So, you aren't friends with any of the boys?" Angie asked teasingly.

"No of course I am," Dorothea's cheeks heated up. "We just have… a different friendship."

"A different friendship?" Angie pressed.

"Yes."

Teasing was fun. Part of her understood why Dorothea did it. Dorothea looked at her, nose scrunched and sticking her tongue out as she mouthed "I hate you."

Angie giggled behind her hand, before taking it away to mouth back "No, you don't."

Once they'd reached the vast planes of the golden fields, they split into teams. William and Peter; who were bound to win due to their competitive nature, Charles and Michael and Angie and Dorothea.

"I can count to ten!" Charles shouted, "I want to count first!"

"We need longer than ten seconds to hide," Peter groaned, "Michael should count."

"No," Dorothea shook her head, kneeling to Charles.

She took his hand and held up five fingers.

"Every time you count to ten, put a finger down," Thea explained, "and when you have no fingers left, you can come and find us."

Angie's heart pounded, both at the heart warming sight of how wonderful Dorothea was with him and at the anticipation of hiding with her.

"Five ten seconds is fifty seconds," Michael said after a while with a nod.

"That's enough time to hide," William agreed.

"Let's hide then!" Angie blurted out.

Charles jumped excitedly, holding his five fingers up proudly. He used his spare hand to cover his eyes.

"ONE!"

Angie looked at Dorothea, who nodded in a direction before sprinting. Angie ran as fast as she could, struggling to keep up on her smaller legs.

"Are you there?" Dorothea called behind her.

"Yes!" Angie shouted back. The only sounds she could hear were the numbers in the distance and the blood pounding in her ears.

"I don't think we should make it too difficult for him," Dorothea said as she changed her sprint into a gentle jog.

Angie couldn't help but grin.

"You have a soft spot for Charles, hmm?" she teased.

"I suppose," Thea smiled, "he's just a smaller version of you. Well, not *that* much smaller."

Angie shook her head with a smile, closing her eyes briefly, plants brushing across her legs as she jogged through the field, feeling the warmth of Dorothea running beside her. In that moment, she forgot everything she was hiding from her. She felt at peace, but doubted it would last.

CHAPTER THIRTY

<u>Dorothea</u>

The sun was warming her cheeks. It wasn't too hot or too cold; it was perfect. Angeline was right there beside her, lying with her hands rested above her head and her eyes closed, long lashes brushing the tops of her freckled cheeks. She appeared so at ease in Thea's presence, it was impossible for her not to smile. Thea rolled onto her side, using her hands as a pillow and letting out a sigh through her nose.

Angie opened her twinkling eyes and Thea felt guilty for disturbing her. She'd looked so beautiful. Not that she didn't look beautiful awake, Angeline would look stunning no matter what.

"What?" Angeline whispered, her warm breath tickling Thea's nose.

"Nothing," Thea whispered back too shy to tell her how dazzling she looked in the golden sunlight.

"You're staring."

Thea put a finger to Angeline's lips.

"Shh. We're hiding."

"I'm quite sure that lying in a field is one of the worst hiding spots ever," Angeline raised a brow.

Thea didn't care about the game of hide and seek. She reveled in every moment she could spend beside Angeline. *Her friend*, Thea had to remind herself. She was risking so much by being friends with her and knew that Mary would tell if she saw Angeline and Thea in each other's company. Thea was seriously pushing her luck.

"Thea," Angeline's voice, soothing as bird song, distanced Thea from her stressful thoughts.

"Sorry," Thea muttered, "I got distracted."

"Yes, I could tell," Angeline said, slanting her mouth suspiciously.

"I'm fine," Thea said, forcing a smile. "Honestly."

"It's a Saturday," Angeline said with confidence, as if she had already thought it through entirely. "Mary has a lie-in on Saturdays. She won't see us."

Thea's heart swelled. Angeline had thought strategically about it to protect her. She could almost read her thoughts.

"I don't care," Thea lied, rubbing the back of her neck.

In truth, she cared far too much. Not about the social shame if the truth were revealed but the possibility that she may never see Angeline again. She longed for her to stay close. She longed to protect her for eternity.

"Would your mother make you leave?" Angeline asked.

Angeline didn't need to elaborate.

"Wouldn't any good, Christian mother?" Thea said with a sad laugh.

"I don't think mine would," Angeline admitted.

"Well of course she wouldn't. Because you aren't…" Thea halted. How could she word this? *A freak? An abomination?* "Like me."

Angeline frowned, leaning away from Thea with a furrowed brow.

"I am," Angeline said.

"No, you aren't," Thea sighed heavily.

She didn't want Angeline to be like her and endure this. She didn't want Angeline to leave the farm when war was over, knowing she was attracted to women and that she'd be at risk if she ever had a relationship with one. That she'd have to go through years of burying her feelings, ignoring her true self just as Thea would have to do. She didn't want that life for Angeline.

"I told you that I liked the kiss last night," Angeline whispered.

"But you've kissed boys before," Thea protested, "Albert, or whatever his name was."

"He didn't kiss me!" Angeline laughed, "we barely knew each other! He just had a well-off family!"

"Yes, he didn't even kiss you," Thea said, "you might have enjoyed it if he did."

"But he didn't!" Angeline shout-whispered in frustration, "why won't you listen to me?!"

"I am listening," Thea said, "I think perhaps you only believe you like me because I'm the only one around."

Angeline's jaw dropped and she sat up haughtily. It seemed she no longer cared about being found.

"That isn't true," Angeline muttered. "I like you."

Thea had dreamed of Angeline returning her feelings, but now it frightened her and she struggled to believe it. Angeline lay back down beside her, closing her eyes.

"I like you a lot," she repeated.

"We need to talk about this," Thea shook her head, "later. When we aren't playing hide and seek."

"It feels like all we talk about is the bad," Angeline groaned, "I wish I could travel back and enjoy my first weeks here, all over again."

"What? With me teasing you?" Thea laughed.

"No," Angie chuckled, whacking her arm gently, "like when you made me wear dungarees for the first time."

"That was disturbing."

"Disturbing?" Angeline said, "I thought I looked spectacular. Hardworking and attractive."

"No. You definitely look far better in dresses," Thea sighed, "but that was an excellent description of me."

Angeline laughed.

"What about when you tried to jump over that fence?" Thea teased.

"I would have made it if I hadn't scratched my hand."

"Whatever makes you feel better. At least I patched it up for you."

"That you did," Angeline smiled, eyes closing as she recalled the memory.

That was the day Thea had first imagined what it would be like to kiss her.

"Left a scar, though," Angeline showed Thea her hand.

"Hmm," Thea shrugged, "I'm covered in scars."

"At least you aren't covered in freckles," Angeline remarked.

"Freckles are pretty," Thea said, outraged.

"My mother used to tell me they were kisses from angels," Angeline's eyes seemed to twinkle in delight as she remembered her mother.

"I think I'd very much like to meet your mother. She sounds nicer than mine," Thea admitted.

There was a beat of silence.

"Angie?" Thea furrowed her brow.

"Sorry," Angeline replied, "I- I need to tell you something. Something I found out."

Thea leant up on her elbows.

"Is this the thing you were planning to tell me last night?" she asked.

"Yes," Angeline continued. "It's really bad. That's why I put it off. Also, because I feel it isn't my place to say."

"Well you have to tell me now," Thea chuckled.

There was another moment of uncomfortable silence.

"It's about your…"

"FOUND YOU!" Charles shouted from across the field.

Angeline and Thea both shot upright, Thea looking at Angeline with expectation.

"About my what?" Thea asked.

"I'll have to tell you later," Angeline replied. She'd paled noticeably.

"Just tell me now," Thea insisted under her breath, watching Charles and Michael come closer as they trudged through the thick grass.

"This is not a 'just tell me now' kind of situation," Angeline snapped back.

Taken aback by her tone, Thea frowned. Whatever it was, it seemed to be serious enough that Angeline was digging her nails into her own palm in frustration.

"That was a rubbish hiding spot, we found you two first," Michael said.

"Why did it take you so long then, huh?" Angeline teased.

It seemed Angeline used her brother's company to break the tension, something she'd done a lot since Thea had been avoiding her.

"Because the farm is huge!" Charles giggled, holding his arms far apart for emphasis.

"Ah, well that is true," Angeline nodded. "At least you have Thea and I to help you find Peter and William."

"Actually," Thea interrupted, standing up to stretch her legs, "I think I'm calling it a day."

"What?" all three Carters said at once.

"It's getting late," Thea continued with a shrug, "I'd better get to work."

"But it's a Saturday!" Charles complained, "Saturdays are for fun."

"Well, you know what they say. Farming never stops," Thea sighed.

Angeline was watching Thea cautiously, clearly believing that she was trying to get away from her. Which wasn't entirely true, Thea was frustrated that she'd have to wait to find out what Angeline was keeping from her. And, judging by the position of the sun in the sky, it was almost midday. Mary would most definitely be awake and on the lookout for them.

"I hope you find them," Thea smiled weakly.

She met Angeline's eyes for a brief moment. They seemed clouded with sadness.

The walk back to the cottage was lonely. After spending most of the night and morning with Angeline, she'd grown used to her company. She dreaded how boring life would be when Angeline returned to London. *But at least she would see her father and brother again,* Thea thought. Part of her was angry that she hadn't received a single letter from either of them, but she had put that down to the fact that mail was bound to be slow during a war. She refused to consider the other possible explanations. At that moment, it felt that the return of James and her father was all she had to look forward to.

Seeing them again was the light at the end of tunnel.

CHAPTER THIRTY-ONE

<u>Angeline</u>

It felt like she was back to square one with Dorothea, for the second time. The way she'd swiftly found an excuse to head home had made it blatantly clear that she wanted to be out of Angie's sight as soon as she possibly could. But of course she would be annoyed Angie was hiding things from her.

Perhaps it was also partly because Dorothea was so fearful of Scary Mary spotting them together; she seemed to always put people she cared for above herself. It frustrated Angie that Dorothea couldn't see how she deserved to be treated with the upmost respect as well, that she didn't even let people care for her every once in a while. She'd made it evident the night before that she was concerned about Mary telling Mrs Miller about what she'd seen because she didn't want to lose Angie, not because of the consequences to herself. Dorothea truly did put everyone else before her own wants and desires. That was what Angie admired about her, among many other things.

Venturing slowly back to the cottage, Charles on Angie's back as she delved deep into the twisted maze of her thoughts. At first, she had rejected the idea of telling Dorothea that she knew of her father and brother's death, she'd planned to keep it hidden from her so the walls she'd worked so hard to break down wouldn't be slammed back into place. But Angie didn't want to hide it anymore. It was selfish of her to even consider denying Dorothea the truth, the course of their lives would be difficult enough without this lie between them.

Angie didn't want to be the cause of Dorothea's grief, but she knew that she would never forgive her if she didn't share the information.

"What were you and Dorothea whispering about? Is it a secret?" Charles asked.

Michael agreed, "I want to know too."

"I think it's rude to ask what a person was discussing in private if you weren't involved in the conversation," Angie snapped, which didn't happen often when dealing with her brothers.

"Somebody's angry," Michael laughed.

Angie was very tempted to whack him in the back of the head.

"She's probably jealous she didn't win," Michael continued.

She was very *very* tempted.

"You make it sound as if hide and seek is actually important," Angie huffed angrily, "it's a baby's game."

Angie was instantly filled with remorse when she felt Charles stiffen before wiggling to get down from her back.

"That isn't true," Charles mumbled, "we're not babies."

Angie's lips parted as she racked her brain for something to say.

"Don't listen to her, Charles," Peter said, stepping forward to swing an arm around his little brother, he looked back at Angie reproachfully, "We'll play without you next time. You're clearly too grown up for games now."

Angie gulped as Michael, Peter, Charles and even William trailed ahead, leaving Angie to walk back alone.

When she finally returned to the cottage, she could already hear the boys squabbling inside. She smiled to herself at the familiarity, for a moment she could close her eyes and imagine she was back in London.

She saw Dorothea out of the corner of her eye, shifting bales of hay and only occasionally stopping to wipe the sweat from her brow with the back of her hand. Angie had been at the farm for long enough to know that Dorothea did the more physically demanding jobs when she was angry or upset. When Dorothea eventually paused to take a breather, she met Angie's eyes for a moment. Angie realised she'd been rooted to the spot watching her work, she lifted her arm to wave, attempting to cover up her distraction. Dorothea's eyes flew wide and she raised her brows as if she was trying to tell Angie something. She was bewildered until Dorothea nodded towards the guesthouse, where Mary stood watching them; her eyes narrowed and face calculating.

Angie grabbed the door handle, running inside the cottage and slamming the door behind her. She rested against the back of the door, letting out a few shaky breaths.

*

Dinner was another meal from the Carter cookbook that their mother had given them. It was a homely taste, a family favourite when money from their father's business grew scarce.

"This is our father's favourite," Peter said as he glared at the Woolton pie as if it had murdered his family.

Peter rarely held grudges and seemed to have forgotten that he'd even had a disagreement with Angie earlier in the day so she felt comfortable enough to place a hand on his back in comfort.

"Well, we should enjoy it in his honour," Mrs Miller announced, raising her glass of water.

The woman never drank alcohol around the younger children but Angie wasn't oblivious to the generous drinks she poured herself in the kitchen once the boys had gone to bed. Since her husband's death, the volume of alcohol she consumed had understandably increased. Angie wondered if Dorothea would drink her sadness away when she found out.

Speak of the Devil, Dorothea entered the room with a spring in her step and slumped in a chair, still wearing her filthy overalls. She seemed to raise her brows, as if challenging her mother to say something about her muddy clothes. She did not.

"This tastes swell, Mrs Miller," Michael said with his mouth full.

Angie couldn't help but grin, looking at Dorothea to see if she'd smiled too but she seemed to be in a world of her own.

"Have you heard the news?" Dorothea asked, directing the question to nobody in particular.

"You're going to have to elaborate," her mother remarked.

Dorothea didn't even roll her eyes; she sat up straight with a smile on her lips.

"The German Army in North Africa has surrendered to the allies," she said.

Her voice was laced with hope.

"What does that mean?" Charles asked.

Dorothea's smile grew, showing off all her teeth.

"That's a major defeat!" Thea continued, "not to mention the surrender at Stalingrad..."

"Dorothea," her mother warned.

"I know it, I know it's going to be over soon," Dorothea's smile made Angie's eyes prick with tears, "my father is—"

"Dorothea!" Mrs Miller shouted, the chatter in the room coming to a grinding halt.

Angie was too close to crying, she needed to excuse herself before she said something.

"He's coming back, mother," Dorothea lifted her chin up in defence, "I didn't sense it before but now I do. It's like he's here, in the room with me. It's like he's telling me it'll be alright. That he and James will..."

"That's enough," her mother hissed.

"But..."

"Enough!" she snapped.

Dorothea froze in her seat.

"So... can we go home?" Peter asked, he still hadn't touched his food.

"Now look what you've done," Mrs Miller spat, glaring at Thea accusingly.

Angie felt the rage bubbling up, yet her own response still surprised her. She stood upright, her chair scraping across the wood of the dining room floor.

"Dorothea hasn't done anything wrong. She's still hopeful because you haven't told her the truth," Angie pointed at Dorothea, "she deserves nothing but honesty—"

"Say any more," Mrs Miller interrupted, standing up too, "and you will no longer be welcome here, Miss Carter."

Dorothea was looking frantically between the two and for a moment Angie feared she'd side with her mother. But she joined them in standing, moving protectively in front of Angeline.

"If you send her away, I'm bloody going too," Dorothea snapped.

Angie's heart pounded.

"To London? With what money? And you should watch your language, young lady."

"Oh, do save it, Mother."

Peter tugged on Angie's sleeve, nodding toward the door.

"Boys, go and sit in the living room. I'll be there in just a moment," Angie instructed firmly.

"So," Dorothea began, "how is this going to end? Are you going to tell me this secret, Mother?"

Mrs Miller shook her head slowly, ignoring her daughter as she scoffed at Angeline.

"You know, it's amusing that you believe Dorothea will choose you over the farm," Mrs Miller glared at her.

"You know nothing," Dorothea snapped.

"Oh Dorothea, don't be absurd. She'll go back to London and forget you ever existed," Mrs Miller raised her chin, "I will not let a spoilt city girl take the only family I have left away from me."

Angie's tears finally spilled.

Dorothea went silent for a moment, allowing the words to hang in the air.

"Only… only family?" she asked, her voice wavering.

Angie felt the air leave the room.

"Yes, Dorothea," her mother said with a shaky voice, "your father and James are dead."

CHAPTER THIRTY-TWO

<u>Dorothea</u>

The silence became deafening.

If anybody spoke, Thea couldn't tell through the high pitched buzzing in her head. She felt somewhere between consciousness and unconsciousness. Was this real or some kind of sick joke?

Thea wanted to be told it was a lie. It *had* to be a lie.

Bile rose in her throat and she was certain she was going to throw up. Stumbling backwards, Thea grasped the back of the chair, her legs felt like they no longer belonged to her. The soundless atmosphere was now filled with the noise of her heart beating. Thumping. Pounding right out of her chest. She felt a hand on her upper arm, a gentle hand that would normally ground her.

"It's alright," Angeline whispered in reassurance.

It had never been further from alright and it would never be alright again. Her brother and father were *dead*.

She looked at Angeline's round, sympathetic eyes. She was biting hard on her bottom lip, so hard she thought it'd split. Her expression was strange... almost... guilty.

"You knew," Thea croaked out, jolting away from her touch as if it had burned her.

"I..." Angie began.

"You– you sat with me last night! We played hide and seek with your brothers!" Thea interrupted, "and the entire time, you knew! You acted like everything was fine, like you didn't know half my family were bloody dead!"

"People like her are always good liars, Dorothea," Thea's mother cut in.

Angie let out an uncontrollable sob.

Thea looked up at her, mouth wide in disbelief. Angeline had stepped back, beating a hasty retreat to check on her brothers. Or perhaps she was fearful that Thea would hurt her in a fit of rage.

"Angie isn't the liar here, Mother," Thea said, Angeline halted in the doorway.

"Oh, for goodness sake. Don't paint her as such a saint," Thea's mother spat.

Angeline watched Thea storm towards her mother, their noses practically touching.

"She could have told you," her mother continued, "but she didn't. You really think she cares that much?"

"You could have told me!" Thea shouted.

"I know," her mother admitted after a few moments of silence, "but I couldn't bear to watch you fall apart."

"That's exactly why I couldn't say anything," Angeline said quietly, "I didn't want to see you fall apart either."

"And yet you decided to force my hand," Thea's mother spat at Angie, "so I look like the villain."

Thea finally looked back at her mother, meeting the blue eyes that matched her own.

"You are the villain." Thea said before turning to Angie, "Where did she put the telegrams?"

"Dorothea..." her mother began.

"Don't," Thea snapped as she held her hand up in her mother's face.

Angeline didn't reply for a moment. Her hazel eyes were filled with remorse, fearful of the future. After all, it was unlikely Thea's mother would let her stay at the farm now. In fact, it seemed inevitable that she would be forced to leave. Thea was already lost to her grief and pain; she didn't want to contribute to her suffering by being forced to leave.

"In the cutlery drawer," Angeline managed, defeated, knowing that the truth was all that mattered now.

Thea shot like a bullet to the kitchen, she needed to see the proof. As she pulled the telegrams out of the drawer, she thought it was no wonder they were nicknamed the *Angels of Death*.

Post Office Telegraphs

Was embossed at the head of the paper. Thea spent time reading the three words over and over, praying that something would indicate that the message was a counterfeit. She skimmed over the regiment information, trying to focus:

The Secretary of War desires me to express his deepest regret that your Son Sergeant James H. Miller was killed in action on 26th April in France.

Thea couldn't hold back the tears, unfolding the second telegram with clumsy hands.

The Secretary of War desires me to express his deepest regret that your Husband Corporal Arthur R. Miller died of sickness on 1st May in Italy.

They weren't even together. Thea felt a tug on her heart strings, reading the impersonal words repeatedly. *Died of sickness.* That meant he could have been saved. Somebody could have attended to his illness, he could have been honourably discharged and sent home to heal, he could have been sent home, and he could have been safe. He could have— he—

Thea lowered the telegrams to the counter top and glared at them as tears trickled down her cheeks. Before anybody could speak, she shoved past her mother and Angeline who were hovering in the kitchen doorway. Thea couldn't be in the cottage any longer. Not with her father and brother's belongings there. Her father's coffee mug that would never be drunk from again, James' comic books he'd collected since he was a child, never to see their owner again. Because they were gone, they were dead.

The light at the end of the tunnel had gone out.

*

Thea had always avoided the woods once the sun had fallen behind the hills. It was far too dark and unchartered for her liking. But in that moment, the woods felt far more comforting than the cottage. The cottage. That was all it was, not her home anymore.

As she ran through the maze of towering trees, she was careless in her movement. Her feet hurt from running in shoes with no socks, but the pain felt good.

Eventually, Thea reached a clearing; a grassy blanket as far as the eye could see. It had a small lake in the centre, surrounded by rocks and moss. The trees around her felt like a wall to block out the world. In the comfort of her own solitude, she removed her shoes and took a step onto the grass. Thankful that there was enough light coming from the moon; Thea knelt down. If she looked close enough, she could admire the flowers, growing freely amongst the thick grass. A part of her wondered how beautiful the place would look in daylight and how marvellous it would be to share the sight with Angeline.

Thea had already lost so much; her heart ached at the idea of losing her too. She considered that far more frequently than she cared to admit. She had been afraid when her admiration for Angeline grew beyond friendship, when she'd kissed her and now, as her mother claimed Angeline would no longer be allowed to stay at the farm.

Angeline was sunlight. She brightened any day with her presence and no matter what she did, Thea could never hold it against her for long. Even if what she felt for Angeline could not be fully reciprocated, Thea still felt loved and needed her like the flowers need the sun.

"Thea," she heard a voice, soft as an angel's.

Thea turned around and let out a breath; blinking a few times to make sure she was not dreaming.

Angeline stood, out of breath. Her hair was tangled, her dress ruffled and knees scuffed. The blood was evident even in the dull glow of the moon.

"You're hurt," Thea noted, taking a step closer to see her injury.

Angeline let out a wet laugh, her breath hitching in her throat.

"It's nothing," Angeline sobbed, "I– I'm so sorry. I know you won't ever want to see me again. I know I'm a liar and a bad– terrible! *Terrible* person."

Thea took in her appearance. She still looked breath taking even with her tearstained cheeks, fumbling for an apology.

"I understand," Thea said, calm as she'd ever been.

Angeline's brow furrowed, her nose crinkling the way it always did when she was confused.

"Thea, this isn't the time for jokes," Angeline said, defeated.

"I understand why you didn't tell me."

"Why forgive me and not your mother?" Angeline asked.

"Because you, Angie," Thea laugh-whispered, stepping closer, "you came running straight after me."

Angeline nodded jerkily, tears that shone in the moonlight falling down her cheeks.

"I'll always come running a-after you," Angeline stuttered. "I didn't know what you'd do– I had to check you weren't hurt– in case you did something reckless."

Thea didn't understand.

"You always said you loved your father so much," Angeline explained, "that you couldn't live without him. I thought you'd—"

Oh. *Oh.*

Thea knew that there was a possibility Angeline didn't want to be touched by her but she couldn't help it. She cupped her cheek.

"Angie. I'd never do that," Thea promised.

A tear that had slipped from Angeline's eye settled on her cheekbone, where Thea wiped it away with the gentle brush of her calloused thumb.

"I can't live without you," Angeline sobbed, "I know that's... dramatic. But when I was running here it just– well I couldn't even bear the thought– I..."

Thea understood. How she understood.

"Sit down," Thea said, "let me look at that cut on your knee."

Angeline obliged, sitting on the grass with her legs out in front of her.

"You would have giggled if you'd seen me fall," Angeline remarked as she sat beside her.

"No, I wouldn't have."

"Thea, I didn't even trip over a branch or anything," she chuckled softly. Thea had missed that sound. "I tripped over my own feet."

Thea bit her lip to hold in her laughter, wiping Angeline's abrasion with a clean handkerchief she'd retrieved from her front dungaree pocket.

"I'm just glad you're alright," Thea said.

"You always put other people before yourself," Angie sighed, "I want to take care of you for once."

Thea prayed any mention of her father would be avoided. For one more night she wanted to pretend that he wasn't gone. That James and he were not lying dead and alone, far from home.

"I'm fine…"

"No, you aren't," Angeline raised a brow, "nobody's expecting you to be fine. You're allowed to be sad."

The pair didn't speak for a few moments.

"Angie, can… can you do something for me?"

"Of course, Thea," Angeline shuffled closer, her hazel eyes sparkling with care, prepared to do anything asked of her.

"I want to stay here with you," Thea admitted, "until the sun comes up."

Angeline's expression was unreadable until her lips pulled into a smile and Thea felt her hand in hers.

"Until the sun comes up," she promised.

CHAPTER THIRTY-THREE

Angeline

Dorothea's hand in hers was hesitant; as if she wasn't too sure of its welcome. Angie looked at their joined hands; they seemed to complement each other perfectly. Dorothea's hands were far larger than Angie's and the skin was rough, her nails short. Angie's hands were tanned, her nails long and the back of her hands dotted with freckles.

"What is it?"

"Nothing," Angie replied, trying to meet Dorothea's restless eyes.

"You don't like holding my hand," she guessed.

Dorothea had never been further from the truth.

"No," Angie assured her.

Dorothea swallowed audibly.

"This is the part where you say 'as a friend'," she mumbled as she picked at the grass they sat upon with her free hand.

There it was; the elephant in the room.

"I thought I'd told you already," Angie said, "it's more than that."

Dorothea's hand stilled.

"Are you doing this to make me feel better because of what happened to my father and—"

"No," Angie interrupted quickly.

Dorothea nodded, pulling her hand away and glancing to the side.

"You don't believe me," Angie groaned in frustration.

Dorothea seemed to put herself down all the time; whether it was consciously or subconsciously, she didn't believe she was good enough for love. As tempting as it was to lecture Dorothea on how wrong she was, now wasn't the time to deal with that. Dorothea had requested they spend the night in each other's company, being at odds all night long was not part of the plan.

Angie noticed the flowers surrounding them, colours muted by the moonlight, but still beautiful.

"Violets," Dorothea smiled as she noticed Angie looking. Her voice was so quiet it was barely a whisper in the breeze.

"Are they rare?" Angie asked, kneeling to gain a closer look.

"I can't see what species they are in the dark. Some types are rarer than others."

"They're my favourite flowers," Angie smiled softly, "I've never seen them growing in the wild before."

"Well," Dorothea knelt beside Angie, picking a flower and putting on a posh accent, "One wild violet for the beautiful lady."

"I think I prefer your normal accent," Angie grinned contagiously as she took it, running her fingertips across the velvet-soft purple petals.

"Here," Dorothea said as she took the violet back, tucking it behind Angie's ear.

Angie smiled, thankful that Dorothea finally met her eyes.

"What now, Romeo?" Angie joked.

"Hey," Dorothea laughed, "Why am I the man?"

"Men are always the hopeless romantics," Angie explained, "in novels."

"Well, I know it may surprise you, but neither of us are men," Dorothea teased with a smile that didn't reach her eyes.

"Juliet and Juliet," Angie whispered. "The new and improved star-crossed lovers."

The pair basked in the tranquillity of the moment; wind rustling in the trees around them, the splash of water from the lake that glistened in the light of the moon piercing the silence. For a moment, they could pretend Dorothea hadn't lost her family and that these feelings they had for each other weren't forbidden. Angie wasn't concerned for the future. Even if she was sent away from the farm, something told her it wouldn't be the end of their story.

"Do you think my father would still love me, if he knew what I am?" Dorothea's question hung in the air, circulating around them.

"Dorothea…"

"Please just answer me honestly," she begged.

"I didn't know him," Angie squeezed her hand.

"But just…" Dorothea choked, "pretend you knew him."

"Thea—" Angie began.

"Please," she interrupted.

"It's… it isn't the norm," Angie said, "I don't think he'd understand. But I don't think he'd love you any less. After all, he'd want you to be happy."

"He always told me he would dance with me when he came home," Dorothea croaked out, "he always talked about how proud he'd be to see me get married."

Angeline's heart sank right down into the very pit of her stomach. A wedding was not in Dorothea's future.

"He'd still be proud of you," Angie promised.

Angie wanted to hold her face, stroke her cheeks and bring her close and–

"Even when you go back home you have to write me letters. Promise me you won't leave me," Dorothea whispered.

"I won't leave you," Angie vowed.

"If my mother sends you away, I'll come with you," Thea promised, "you're the only person that matters to me now."

Angie didn't want to think about that now.

"Can you just– can you please kiss me?" Angie asked breathlessly.

Angie didn't know where it had come from, but her heart had ached with longing as Dorothea's lips pulled into a smile. Suddenly, gentle hands were placed on Angie's cheeks, a thumb brushing across her cheekbone as she always did; a gesture that seemed to make all her worries fade away. Her lips were soft, hesitant and gentle. As if Dorothea feared if the kiss wasn't perfect, Angie would push her away again.

The soft pressure only lasted for a blissful moment, before Dorothea pulled away and pressed their foreheads together, her eyes remaining closed. This time it was Angie who initiated the kiss. Dorothea let out a short gasp in surprise before returning the kiss.

Dorothea's hand cupped Angie's jaw, tilting her head. It was like electricity travelling up her spine, reaching every nerve end and filling her entirely with sparks of satisfaction. Her whole body sang in triumph and Angie's arms now seemed to know exactly what to do as she wrapped them around Thea's neck. Both of Dorothea's hands went to her waist, keeping Angie steady as she kissed her deeply. Angie had never felt so safe; she didn't want to move away, she hadn't ever felt so close to another person in her entire life. Her stomach erupted with butterflies, a sensation she'd never experience when she was kissed on the hand by Albert, or when she noticed boys at home looking at her longingly. This was something so perfect that it felt sacred.

"I should never have pushed you away in the first place," Angie muttered once Dorothea had pulled away to catch her breath.

"None of that matters now," Dorothea promised as she pressed their foreheads together again, bumping their noses.

"It matters to me," Angie pouted, "you must have been so worried I'd tell."

Dorothea seemed to think for a moment, pursing her lips.

"You know, strangely, I wasn't."

"Weren't you?"

"No," Dorothea shrugged, "I knew you wouldn't tell. I think I knew you were like me."

Angie wasn't offended as she knew exactly what she meant. It was an unspoken acceptance between the two, filled with lingering glances and subtle touches.

"I'm so sorry Mary threatened you," Angie said, "I should have said something to her or…"

"If you keep feeling sorry for me, I'll throw you in the lake," Dorothea's face was stern.

"You wouldn't dare."

"Oh, wouldn't I?" Dorothea said before standing and hooking her hands under Angie's arms, swinging her around.

"THEA, STOP!" Angie laughed contagiously.

"I'm going to do it!" Dorothea teased, swinging her right over the edge of the lake, "Let's hope there aren't any crocodiles!"

"There aren't any crocodiles in England!" she squeaked.

"Well this is Wales!" Dorothea giggled, stumbling back onto the grass, Angie landing right on top of her.

Angie burst into a fit of laughter as she rolled off her.

"I'll tell you the tales of the monstrous Welsh crocodiles one day," Thea said.

"Shut up," Angie chuckled.

She glanced up at the sky; it was the same sky her mother would see if she looked up. Angie felt a pang of guilt in her chest, she'd barely thought of her since she'd been overwhelmed with Dorothea and how much she had lost.

"What's your favourite thing about the night?"

"The stars," Angie whispered.

"How original," Dorothea teased, Angie whacked her arm.

"Well what's yours?" she asked.

"The quiet," Dorothea replied, closing her eyes.

"Well that's boring," she giggled, Dorothea whacked her arm back.

"Everything is so busy when it's loud. When the sun's up it's like you're blinded by the colour, light and sound, so much so that you don't think deeply enough about things," Dorothea explained, "We think so much more when it's night because there are no distractions."

"Well, that doesn't sound like a good thing," Angie said.

"That depends on how you look at it," Dorothea looked at Angie, "If we think about negative things, it's bad. But thinking about good things? It makes you appreciate everything more."

Angie stared at her, taking in the sight of her dark hair spread across the grass and the flush to her cheeks while she absorbed her words.

"You're so beautiful," Angie whispered instinctively.

She vowed to never forget the way Dorothea's face lit up, blue eyes wide.

"Nobody's ever called me that before," she admitted.

"Then I'll have to tell you a thousand times," Angie said, "to make up for it."

Dorothea smirked in her familiar way, putting her arm out in Angie's direction. Her lips curled into a smile and she shuffled across the grass, lying beside Dorothea as she wrapped a protective arm around her.

CHAPTER THIRTY-FOUR

<u>Dorothea</u>

There weren't many things Thea was certain of anymore. Her father and brother were gone. Her relationship with her mother was strained; Thea imagined they would never be able to repair what little relationship they'd had. Thea was partly relived by this. She'd have no expectations to live up to, no responsibilities as a daughter. The crushing truth was that, without her mother, Thea was not a daughter anymore.

Angeline was the only bright spot that remained. Time slowed down when they were in each other's company and her problems simply melted away, which is what made her grief all the more soul-destroying when she was faced with a dark, empty room that provided no distractions from her depressing thoughts. Thea didn't even bother changing into her sleepwear; she climbed onto the bed and didn't get under the covers. No number of blankets could warm the chill inside her.

It was unlikely Thea's mother would change her mind about sending Angeline and her brothers away. She'd made a promise to care for the children, and it hadn't been the boy's fault, they'd had nothing to do with it. It wasn't Angeline's fault either; she'd simply wanted to tell the truth for Thea's sake. Her mother wouldn't see it that way.

Her mother had claimed she didn't want to see Thea grieve and would rather lie to her. Thea was convinced it was the most ridiculous and self-serving thing she'd ever known a person do. It seemed entirely irrational until, in that moment, it dawned on Thea; it *had* been totally rational.

Her mother had lost the love of her life.

The love her mother had for her father was unlike any other she'd ever seen. Thea was only now having her first taste of love and wasn't she suffering the same, knowing that Angeline might leave her forever?

Thea could still remember how often her father would hold her mother; he'd spin her around and kiss her cheek, telling her how beautiful she looked. She'd giggle and whack his chest playfully, but she would smile for the rest of the evening. Thea's mother would sit on the fence and watch him work even in the winter, discussing trivial things but it hardly seemed to matter, as long as they were together. He'd still been trying to teach her how to play the piano. Thea could remember one evening when she'd glanced in her father's office to see them both squeezed onto the piano stool, her father chuckling when she'd play the wrong chords.

That was why it stung when her mother became so lifeless and grey. Thea had never had the greatest relationship with her mother; it had always been James who'd looked up to her. But the loss of her smile following their departure had been painful, Thea too tangled up in her own mind to appreciate that her mother was suffering too.

She had to swallow a lump in her throat. Thea was good at holding grudges but it was impossible to hate her now she understood the extent of her suffering. She hadn't wanted her daughter to feel the same pain. Yet ironically, this is what sending Angeline away would do.

After hours of tossing and turning, she finally drifted off.

She dreamt of her father.

*

"Dorothea…"

"Dorothea!" she heard again, more panicked this time.

Her mind was clouded with images of her father, suffering from an illness with nobody there to comfort him, no one to hold his hand as he died–

"Dorothea, please wake up," she heard a broken sob.

"Let me try, Mrs Miller," Angeline. Her voice was clear as day, it seemed she could always reach her, even in her sleep.

"How can you help?" she heard her mother ask between cries.

Suddenly Thea became aware. This was a nightmare, just a nightmare. Thea realised all she had to do was breathe.

"Come on, little one," Thea would recognise that voice anywhere, it was her father.

It felt like all those times he'd got her through her nightmares by stroking her hair and holding her close.

Thea let out a sob.

"That's it, Thea," her father whispered, she could feel his hand stroking her hair.

"That's it, Thea," it was Angeline talking now; it was Angeline's worried hazel eyes that greeted her when Thea finally opened her own.

She sat up on her elbows after wiping the sweat and tears from her eyes. She wasn't even under the sheets, yet they were soaked with her sweat.

"Father…" Thea mumbled, "he was here."

Her mother was kneeling beside her bed, her hand in Thea's hair. Angeline was sitting right beside her too.

"I hallucinate sometimes too," Angeline smiled sadly.

"No," Thea said, "h-he was here."

"Dorothea," her mother shook her head, "you'll only upset yourself more."

Thea nodded weakly, there was no in point dwelling on it. She was here, in her own bed and Angeline was still here beside her. She hadn't had a nightmare in so long, it must have been the fear of losing Angeline.

"Mother, you can't send Angeline away," Thea blurted out.

"Dorothea…" her mother began.

"No," Thea interrupted, "you have to promise me."

Her mother's bottom lip trembled and she could sense how Angeline had frozen uncomfortably beside her. Her mother seemed hesitant, glancing between the two.

"Mother, I forgive you."

"Oh, Thea," she sobbed.

"But you must listen to me," Thea said, "she means a lot to me. More than you can ever know. I need her here to get me through this."

Her mother nodded slowly, taking Thea's hand from her cheek before looking at Angeline.

"I cannot express to you how sorry I am," her mother admitted.

"Oh, Mrs Miller, you don't have to…" Angie said.

"I do," Thea's mother interrupted, "the responsibility I placed on you was unfair. The friendship you two have is special, I'd always feared Dorothea wouldn't have a best friend but she does, I'd have to be evil to take that away from you."

Thea could feel her heart pounding right out of her chest.

"Thank—"

Thea cut Angeline off with a forceful hug, unable to hold back her tears of joy as they dampened Angeline's nightie. Thea heard her mother let out a little laugh. This was everything she'd had prayed for: Angeline right beside her with no threat of her leaving. She hadn't been lying to her mother when she'd claimed she forgiven her; it hadn't been a ploy to ensure Angeline would stay at the farm. She truly did forgive her mother. She'd come to realise that love makes people do strange things.

"I think that's enough theatrics for one night, don't you think ladies?" Thea's mother joked.

Angeline and Thea both hummed in agreement.

"Off to bed then," her mother stood and smiled once more, "I love you, Dorothea."

Thea swallowed, she couldn't remember the last time she'd heard her mother say that. Perhaps it would take a while to rebuild what they'd had, but the reassurance that her mother loved her made her feel that it would be possible.

"I love you too," Thea said, her mother looked like she was about to cry.

Angeline sat with her eyes wide once Thea's mother had left the room.

"Well that was a development," Angeline swallowed.

Thea chuckled and lay back against her headboard, looking at Angeline with a smile. She always looked so beautiful, even in the dull light of her bed lamp. Thea reached out to tuck a piece of golden hair behind her ear.

"You have nightmares too?" Thea tilted her head.

Angie shrugged.

"They're never that bad," she said.

"Sorry," Thea smiled sadly.

"Don't you apologise", Angie tutted and put their foreheads together, "if only Scary Mary would leave us alone, then it would be totally perfect."

Thea had been so tangled up in grief, she'd barely even thought about that threat.

"As long as we have each other," Thea said.

"Well I don't plan on going anywhere," Angeline chuckled, heading back to her room.

Thea closed her eyes and rolled onto her side. Even though her father was not there, she'd felt his presence stronger than ever. She understood now that the dead live in the memories of those living.

CHAPTER THIRTY-FIVE

<u>Angeline</u>

Time was a peculiar concept. Some moments moved tortuously slowly but recently it had been moving too fast to even begin to contemplate. It felt like hours ago since Angie had learnt of the deaths of Dorothea's brother and father. So much had changed since then.

"Angeline?" Mrs Miller called from the kitchen.

"Yes?"

"Could you help me put away the groceries?" the woman asked.

Angie entered the kitchen with a smile, taking a brown paper bag from Mrs Miller. At first, assisting around the cottage had been a challenge but now she was as familiar with the cottage as she was her home back in London.

"There are far more tins than usual," Angie noted as she reached up to place some in the top cupboard, balancing herself on a wooden stool.

"We tend to buy food that keeps well as the weather gets cooler," Mrs Miller said, "I don't like Dorothea going out to the village during winter, we get some terrible ice."

The idea of colder weather made Angie's skin crawl. It was hard enough keep warm in the winter in London, the Carters spent most of their time indoors and were lucky enough to have afforded a hot water boiler before the war started. The cottage on the Miller's farm didn't boast this luxury and was far too miniscule for seven people to comfortably spend all day indoors, Angie had grown accustomed to spending most of her days outside in the warmth of the summer sun.

"The shopkeeper must like you," Angie said, "to let you buy all this food at once during times like this."

"Well, Henry knows we struggle to get into the village when the snow falls," Mrs Miller replied, "and most of his fresh produce comes directly from us. We're lucky to live here where so much food is home grown. I can't imagine what rationing is like in the city."

Angie's memories of London were distant now, it seemed she'd pushed her previous life far back in her mind and entirely embraced life on the farm.

"I don't think it was too bad," Angie said. "But the food here is much nicer."

Mrs Miller grinned and it was strangely familiar; the way one side of her mouth raised slightly higher than the other and her subtle dimples showed. It was much like Dorothea's smile.

"I have spent many years practising my cooking on my family," Mrs Miller explained. "There wasn't much else for me to do."

Angie tilted her head, "What do you mean?"

"Well, you know," Mrs Miller shrugged, beginning to slice a carrot with practiced ease. "Beyond tending house and raising children, there isn't an awful lot for a woman to do on a farm."

"Dorothea does far more than that," Angie said. "You could work on the farm, like the Land Girls."

"I'm not quite as active as them anymore," Mrs Miller chuckled sadly, "but I don't mind being a housewife."

Her voice cracked on the word 'wife'. Angie could tell that the reality had struck her again; she wasn't a wife anymore, she was a widow.

"I can cut up the vegetables, Mrs Miller," she offered, reaching out for the vegetable knife.

Mrs Miller didn't bother protesting as she passed it over and sat on one of the creaky kitchen chairs. There were times when Dorothea's face would fall at the memory of those she had lost as well and she'd stop whatever she was doing. Angie came to realise that in those moments, all they needed was a moment to sit down and gather their thoughts.

"He was such a wonderful man," Mrs Miller whispered.

Angie smiled sadly as she dropped the chunks of carrot into a pan, starting to peel an onion.

"I wish I'd met him, Mrs Miller," Angie replied.

"Please call me Maggie," Mrs Miller– Maggie– said.

"Of course," Angie nodded.

"Does Dorothea talk about him?" Maggie asked, her eyes glossy.

"Yes," Angie smiled, slicing an onion into smaller pieces. "All the time, she remembers how much he adored you."

"He adored all of us, he truly did. It's a reminder, isn't it? To tell everyone we love that we love them, before it's too late."

Angie swallowed hard but nodded in agreement, Peggy had said the same a while back. It also reminded Angie that she hadn't written to her mother in so long.

"I better go and hang the washing out before it rains this evening," Maggie said. "You should go and see Dorothea."

Angie desperately wanted to but would wait until it was dark, when Scary Mary was asleep, to seek her out.

"She's busy out on the fields," Angie replied, throwing the onions in after the carrots. "I'll go and write to my mother, I think."

Maggie picked up the basket of washing.

"I'll see you later then, love," she said, "oh, and check on your brothers for me please."

"Of course," Angie replied.

She made her way to the front of the house after chopping up the remainder of the vegetables and setting them to simmer. Angie grinned at her brothers who were playing some sort of ball game, undoubtedly rowing over who had won.

She jogged upstairs to her bedroom, thinking of all she would have to tell her mother.

*

Dearest Mother,

I sincerely apologise for how long it has taken me to respond to your last letter. There have been plenty of reasons for my slow reply that I shall discuss with you now. Firstly, I should reassure you that William, Michael, Peter, Charles and I are all well and safe. We've grown used to the place and I cannot speak for them, but I have learnt to love it.

It pains me to say that Mr Miller and his son have sadly passed away. Mrs Miller is obviously devastated as is her daughter, Dorothea. They've had a few disagreements that I won't share in detail, but everything seems to have settled down now and I am trying my best to support them as they grieve.

It may surprise you to know that Dorothea and I are now friends. Yes, Dorothea is the same girl I wrote four paragraphs complaining about to you a few months ago. I wish I'd given her a chance during those first few weeks, rather than instantly deciding to dislike her. We are very different, practically opposites but she is the most wonderful friend I have ever had. Do not misunderstand me, Charity Smith was my very best friend in London, but it seems that the time we spent together cannot begin to compare to the time spent with Dorothea. She's so interesting, Mother. She puts everybody else before herself and is so passionate about working on the farm. I miss you more than anything, yet the idea of leaving ~~Thea~~ Dorothea brings me great sadness. I want to know she is alright when I return home. Of course, we can exchange letters but that will not be the same.

I'm so glad to know that father is safe, especially after witnessing how news of a death can affect a family. But I trust that we will stick together if anything bad happens. I miss you more than I can express, but I'm so happy here, Mother. I know it's strange; I should despise being away from home. In a way it has begun to feel like home. I feel safe but most of all; loved.

*I love you so much and look forward to hearing from you
soon.*

All our love,

Angeline, William, Peter, Michael and Charles.

*PS: Charles says "I'm going to play ball games in the
Olympics when I'm big." Michael says, "I've won five
games of hide and seek in a row." Peter says, "I miss you,
can you send us another picture of father?" And William
says, "I love you lots, mother."*

Angie folded up the letter, inserting it into the
envelope.

"We should post it now!" Charles exclaimed from
behind her.

"We can post it tomorrow, we'll be heading into
the village with Peggy again," Angie said.

"But we're meant to be having a football
tournament!" Peter groaned.

"No, we're playing hide and seek with Dorothea
again!" Michael argued.

Angie placed the envelope on the cabinet by the
front door where she wouldn't forget it.

"We can't play hide and seek with Thea," Angie
said.

Not with Mary's spiteful eyes looking out for them.

"But why?" Michael pouted.

"Because she's busy," Angie replied, her tone final.

The boys headed to the dining room, she didn't mistake seeing the way Michael had rolled his eyes.

"Hello you," Angie jumped at the unexpected voice, very close to her ear.

She span to meet Dorothea's gaze, her mouth pulled into a wide grin.

"You scared me."

"That was the point," Dorothea teased, "what was Michael complaining about now?"

"He wants to play hide and seek," Angie muttered, "with both of us."

Dorothea's face fell.

"Ah," she sighed. "well, we can't do that with Scary Mary around."

"I know," Angie replied.

Dorothea didn't look too upset, however, she was grinning at her.

"What?" Angie asked.

"It's funny when you get grumpy," Dorothea whispered under her breath.

Angie whacked her shoulder.

*

When night had finally fallen, Angie didn't waste a moment longer. Once she'd seen the moon bright in the black sky, she headed to Dorothea's bedroom. She was already leaning against her door, arms folded with that familiar grin on her face.

Without any discussion, they snuck through the back door of the cottage and ran beside each other in the silence of the night, only slowing when they eventually reached their field. Angeline glanced up at the stars as they lay beside each other on the damp grass.

It was a little cold but feeling the warmth of Dorothea's fingers lacing her own, Angie couldn't bring herself to care.

CHAPTER THIRTY-SIX

<u>Dorothea</u>

Thea's good mood never seemed to last long when she had to work up close with the cows. Her favourite jobs were in the fields, where she could enjoy the feel of fresh air on her cheeks and the earthy scent of nature, or in the stables as she chatted away to the horses. Kneeling under an uncooperative cow was not Thea's ideal task.

"Stay still, will you!" Thea groaned as the cow knocked over what little milk she had already collected in the bucket.

The animal mooed and knocked it over again as Thea was about to continue milking. This was a job that she'd always leave to her father. He'd been patient and gentle with them. Thea didn't think there was a single animal on Earth her father didn't adore.

She found herself reliving memories of him, not dwelling on thoughts long enough to become upset, but enough to make sure he remained living on in her memories... She'd been thinking about her brother this morning as she watched the Carters playing a ball game in the courtyard through the kitchen window. Seeing the way Angeline played with her brothers always brought back memories; like playing cricket the previous summer and how James would always win, Thea would claim it was because of his longer legs.

Thea sometimes wondered if James and Angeline would have been friends. James was much like Thea; stubborn but sensitive beneath his thick skin. Thea considered that, if James had stayed on the farm, everything could have been very different. Maybe Angeline would have taken a liking to James and they may have even got married. After all, James looked like a male version of Thea. *Perhaps that's what Angeline would have preferred anyway*.

She had to remind herself that that wasn't how things were. Angeline was with her and she wouldn't spend every night in a flower field, dozing off on Thea's chest, if she didn't like her. Angeline always chided Thea about how much she doubted her self-worth and encouraged her to be kinder to herself. It was undeniable that Thea was a better person with Angeline Carter.

She smiled at the thought as she stood up, picking up the still empty bucket.

"I give up with you," she informed the cow.

Just as Thea began to lead the cow back to her stall, she came face to face with Mary. She gasped in surprise, startled she'd snuck in so quietly.

"Dorothea," Mary said, her voice harsh.

"M-Mary," Thea stuttered, cursing the way her cheeks reddened as she grew more nervous.

"I'll assist you," Mary suggested, although her tone brooked no argument.

Mary snatched the bucket from Thea's hand and dragged a stool across the ground, sitting on it as she began to milk the cow with ease. Thea wondered for a moment whether Mary was secretly a witch that had cursed the cow to only produce milk for her. Her imagination seemed to run wild when she was frightened.

"Why aren't you out playing with the Carters? You should be making most of this warm weather before winter comes," Mary remarked.

"You told me if you saw Angeline and I together, you'd tell my mother what you saw," Thea whispered, glancing around to ensure no other Land Girls were about.

"But it doesn't seem to stop you being together when night falls, now does it?" Mary didn't look up; her threatening tone was enough to send shivers down Thea's spine.

"I don't know what you…"

"Don't lie to me, Dorothea," Mary interrupted, "you sin enough. Let's not add more to the list."

Thea heart was beating out of her chest, her mind racing as she tried to think of when Mary could have possibly seen them together.

"I know you're grieving," Mary continued, "but we made a deal."

Tears welled up in Thea's eyes, closer to spilling at every word Mary spoke.

"I need her. I care about her…"

Mary let out a laugh that was nothing short of evil, she stood up from the wooden stood and glared at Thea.

"You don't care for her. You just desire her, in the most sickening way and your distorted desires are a sign that you have turned away from God," Mary said.

"It isn't like that," Thea protested weakly. Her relationship with Angeline stretched far beyond desire. Their connection was magical; it made romance from books feel real, it made the beauty of touch far better, it made them feel as if they had a purpose. That the universe had designed them to fit together like puzzle pieces.

"That's all it is," Mary hissed. "'If a man lies with a male as with a woman, both of them have committed an abomination; they shall surely be put to death; their blood is upon them.' I am certain the same applies to you and your abnormal ways. It is not what God intended and I won't work for the mother of a sinner."

Thea stumbled back, mouth falling open.

"I gave you a warning; this is your final one."

Perhaps a slap on the cheek should have been expected. The force of it knocked her to the ground. Thea cupped her face in pain and shock. She tried to scramble back, looking up at the cow as if it would save her or call for help. She was so overwhelmed with shock, her mouth felt as though it had been sewn shut.

Mary had a tight grip on her wrist, nails digging into her skin made her cry out. The woman was close to her face, Thea could smell her bitter breath.

"What on Earth is going on?"

Thea let out a cry of relief when she saw Florence in the doorway.

Mary loosened her grip, only slightly.

"Florence," Mary said, "thank goodness you're here."

"I don't want to hear it," Florence snapped, pointing a finger at Mary.

Thea was still too afraid to meet Mary's gaze even though she'd took a step away from Thea.

"I don't suppose you've heard of homosexuality," Mary continued, seemingly ignoring what Flo had said.

There was that word Thea had been too scared to say.

Florence hissed through her teeth, "what of it?"

Mary tilted her chin up, as if she was proud of herself for defending God's word.

"Man shall not lie with man, so surely woman shall not lie with woman."

"What are you talking about?" Flo spat.

Mary's wrinkles around her eyes crinkled further as she narrowed her eyes at Thea.

"Miss Miller here seems to be keeping a secret from us, more specifically her mother. I'm sure she'd be disappointed to know the truth. I can't even imagine how her father would've reacted…"

"You didn't know my father! You know nothing about him!" Thea argued, she couldn't stop tears trickling down her cheeks.

Florence seemed mostly calm and content as she took a step closer to Mary.

"If I were you, Mary," She began, "I'd stop talking. Or I fear I may need to mention to Mrs Miller that you just physically assaulted her daughter."

Mary and Florence didn't take their eyes off one another; Mary's face was burning red as the devil. Lost for words, Mary retried the bucket of milk on the floor as she looked back briefly.

"You shouldn't defend the sinner, Florence. Then you are just as bad yourself."

With that, Mary left.

Thea finally let out the breath she'd been holding in. She slumped against the wall and threw her head back against the wood.

"I..." Thea didn't even know where to start.

"You don't have to explain," Florence said. "I've never liked that woman."

Thea nodded jerkily and wiped her damp cheeks.

"She won't stay away from me."

"I'll make sure she will," Florence said firmly, lips in a straight line.

Thea had missed Florence, she'd seen her occasionally when she'd eaten lunch at the guesthouse with Peggy but they hadn't had a heart to heart since she'd discovered that her brother and father had passed away.

"How did she know? You haven't been spending much time with Angeline at all."

Thea rubbed her arm.

"I know, I'm busy during the day," she said.

"It seems like it's more than that," Florence raised a brow, lowering herself down to sit beside Thea.

"Mary doesn't like me being around Angeline," Thea replied, "she thinks I'm a bad influence."

"Well I don't think that is any of her business," Florence remarked.

Thea let out a sad huff of a laugh.

"I know how happy she makes you," Florence smiled, tucking a piece of Thea's dark hair behind her ear in a motherly gesture. It warmed Thea from the inside out to be accepted, even if it was just by one person.

"She does."

"I'll keep Mary and her bible quotes away from you," Flo promised.

Thea looked at her, blue eyes wide and hopeful "You will?"

Florence nodded as Thea let out a breathless laugh at the wonderful feeling Flo's protection provided.

"And Dorothea, your father would be proud of you no matter what."

Thea smiled to herself, she knew that deep down but the reminder felt good to hear.

Sharing the news with Angeline would be the first thing she'd do. Being slapped was entirely worth it if it meant Scary Mary would leave them alone for good.

Angeline's joyous smile would be the cherry on top.

*

Thea would never tire of listening to Angeline's gentle breaths beside her. The stars always shone brighter when Thea was with Angeline, the sky was putting on a display just for them.

Thea had been planning this all day; she'd snuck out of the back of the cottage with Angie when it was dark, as if they still had to hide. Thea couldn't wait a moment longer to tell her the news.

"This might be the last time we spend a night together here," Thea said, breaking the peaceful quiet.

"What are you talking about?"

Thea turned on her side to meet her eyes.

"I'm serious," she said.

"W-what?" Angeline stuttered, sitting up straight, "why?"

379

"Because," Thea smirked, resting her chin on her elbow. "Why sneak around at night when we can spend all day together?"

"Don't be absurd, Thea," Angeline sighed, "you know we can't do that."

"Not unless we somehow got Mary to leave us alone, right?" Thea asked.

She tilted Angeline's chin up with two fingers so she could meet her eyes.

"I should tell you about my day," Thea said, confusing Angeline with the sudden conversation change. "Mary came to see me when I was milking the cows. She slapped me just as Flo walked in. Flo didn't even ask for the story; she just promised to keep Scary Mary away from us."

Angeline's lips parted and Thea waited for the smile of relief she'd anticipated all day, yet she was met with a frown.

"She slapped you?"

Thea chuckled, cupping her cheek.

"I tell you we're safe together now and you're worried about the slap?" Thea asked.

Angeline nodded as she nuzzled into Thea's touch.

"I'm fine," Thea rested their foreheads together, "it was a weak slap as well."

Angeline let out a giggle.

Thea felt like she was floating, every single time she heard that beautiful laugh.

"But for your information," Angeline said, "I still want to spend nights with you."

Thea brushed their noses together, a silent promise.

CHAPTER THIRTY-SEVEN

Angeline

It would embarrass Angie to admit that she was as upset at missing family Christmas as she was leaving her parents. The homemade biscuits flavoured with warming spices (though Mrs Miller's shortbread was just as enjoyable) the calming crackle of the fire as it roasted chestnuts and the scent of pine from the tree in its rightful place beside the piano. Angie knew it was unreasonable to expect things to be exactly the same, but the way Christmas was celebrated at the Miller farm was entirely unfamiliar.

The build up to Christmas had always been Angie's favourite part of the winter months, her favourite carols would be sung at church and her favourite readings would be read. Everybody seemed to walk with a skip in their step and had a smile on their faces. Other than the excited squeals from Peter and Charles when they'd woken up to a thick blanket of snow, there seemed to be a distinct lack of festive cheer.

"Let us stand for a hymn," the priest announced with a smile.

It had taken a while for her to grow used to the Sunday morning services in the countryside. The seats were practically empty in comparison to the filled pews back in London.

Dorothea was looking down at Angie in confusion as the song in Latin began. Angie stood up swiftly and began to sing. Dorothea had been looking at her that way a lot since summer had ended. It had been a difficult adjustment for Angie; she'd spent months in summer dresses, playing ball games with her brothers during the day and warm evenings running through cornfields or dozing beside Dorothea on the roof until the sun came up. Having to stay inside more gave her far too much time to think, especially about her relationship with Thea.

Attending church seemed to put Angie in a terrible mood. She'd always been so dedicated to her religion; there hadn't been a single year in her memory when she wasn't in the church choir or assisting the church in raising money for charities. It was a significant part of her life. Questioning her standing with God now became a common occurrence; a woman in a relationship with another woman was not strictly written about in the bible, but that didn't mean it wasn't a sin.

"Angeline," Dorothea whispered.

Angie looked up at her with wide eyes.

"You seem distracted," Dorothea said, a few people turning around to frown at her as she spoke during a hymn.

Angie held a finger to her lips, picking up her hymn book to find where they were up to. It was pointless bothering Dorothea with her concerns when she had enough on her plate and she certainly wasn't discussing them in church.

"Angie," Dorothea whispered again.

"Leave it, Thea," Angie snapped, surprising herself at how loud she'd been.

Dorothea's face dropped. Her hands clenched into fists by her sides and she nodded.

Angie's stomach knotted painfully at the sight but she didn't say another word.

*

The walk back to the cottage was eerily quiet, the only sound the crunch of snow beneath their boots. Dorothea had marched ahead, leaving Angie with Mrs Miller, the Land Girls and her brothers. The boys stopped walking every now and then to launch a snowball at one another.

"What was that little disagreement about?" Florence nudged Angie in the side gently as she pointed to Dorothea, who was storming ahead.

"You heard that?" she mumbled.

"We all did," Mary scoffed behind her.

Florence gave her a scowl.

Angie hadn't believed Florence at first, how she alone could prevent Mary from telling Mrs Miller what she'd seen. However, now she felt entirely protected and safe.

"She's probably a little upset about spending Christmas without Arthur and James," Maggie smiled sadly.

Angie swallowed, that was undoubtedly true and yet Angie was the one in the bad mood. *Pathetic*.

"Actually, it was me. I snapped at her," Angie admitted.

"What an Earth for?" Heather, the only Land Girl besides Mary that Angie hadn't gotten to know, asked.

"Well… I suppose I'm struggling to adapt to the colder weather," Angie shrugged dismissively, "I think it has put me in a bad mood."

"You and I both," Maggie smiled.

Angie was grateful to end the conversation but it didn't make the situation any better as one thing was extremely evident; Dorothea was now unhappy with her.

"Would you help me hang the Christmas decorations?" Angie asked.

"Busy," Thea replied tersely, turning a page in the book she was reading.

It was *The Wonderful Wizard of Oz* and Angie could tell from the battered book that it was a well-loved edition. Angie decided to leave her alone, despite how tempted she was to tell Dorothea that decorating the tree had always been one of her favourite things about Christmas.

When evening finally came, Angie was becoming impatient. Dorothea 's short answers grew more frustrating and it ached to spend precious time helping Maggie in the kitchen or playing hide and seek around the cottage with her brothers, when she could spend it out in the snow with Dorothea. They didn't know how long they had left before Angie would be miles away from Dorothea.

"Dinner!" Mrs Miller called from the kitchen.

Angie came out from her hiding spot under the stairs.

"Found you!" Charles pointed at her excitedly.

"The game is over, dinner's ready," she said.

"Oh," Charles pouted. "I still found you."

"You absolutely did," Angie smiled as she took her seat at the dining table, praying Dorothea would sit beside her as she usually did.

All of the Carters had settled at the table and Maggie had brought all the plates through and served up the vegetables by the time Dorothea joined them.

"I was finishing my chapter," she grumbled, slouching in the chair beside Angie.

Maggie rolled her eyes, serving Dorothea some carrots.

"You've read that book a million times over," Maggie said.

"Well that's because I like it."

"It's her book for when she's being a grump," Maggie chuckled to the Carters.

"I'm not being a grump!"

"That's what somebody being a grump would say," William remarked matter of factly.

Mrs Miller laughed, taking a seat at the head of the table. She said a prayer before they all tucked into their meals, which were increasingly smaller as food became scarcer.

Dorothea kept her head ducked, pushing the food around with her fork rather than actually eating it.

"The temperature seems to have dropped quite a lot so I've just washed some blankets," Maggie smiled.

"Thank you," the boys and Angie replied, practically in synchronisation.

"I imagine you'll need some help shovelling snow tomorrow, Thea?" Maggie asked.

"The Land Girls can help," Thea muttered.

"Well, they could but perhaps it would give Angeline something to do."

Angie smiled at the idea, thankful to Maggie for bringing it up.

"Sure, whatever," Dorothea replied with disinterest.

The rest of dinner was uncomfortably quiet; Mrs Miller seemed to be the only one willing to start a conversation. Thea barely ate anything and retreated to her bedroom rather than offering to help with the dishes. Maggie didn't complain, she'd been awfully lenient and thoughtful since the telegram incident, trying to make amends.

This attitude from Dorothea made Angie feel like she had done something wrong, as if she was responsible for pushing her away again, it had taken so long to get this far. The uncertainty of the future nagged at her; just a few days before, Angie had received a letter from her mother, claiming she was certain the children would be called upon to return to London soon. Her mother wouldn't give her false hope if she didn't believe that the war was soon to be over.

One day soon, she knew she would hear the announcement "*War is over*".

That knowledge should have made Angie's heart race with excitement, but it made her heart pound out of her chest with fear. How would she survive without Dorothea? Would she return home, only to grow older, marry a man and have many children? Her stomach tied itself into agonising knots.

As fast as a lightning bolt, she opened her bedroom door, knocking on Dorothea's.

She heard shuffling behind the door, but Dorothea didn't make a move to open it.

"Come on, Thea," Angie whispered, mostly to herself.

This had happened so many times before; Angie waiting outside Dorothea's door to apologise after a disagreement. It was petty. They didn't have time for this, not when all Angie could hear was a deafeningly clock, ticking away the seconds until they would be parted. Every moment she wasn't with Dorothea felt like a stab in her heart.

Angie would normally never open somebody's door without permission, but in that moment she could not care less.

The first thing she noticed was Dorothea's red rimmed eyes.

The ticking of the clock grew more insistent.

Angie took a stride towards her and hugged her arms around her neck.

The ticking stopped when her lips met Thea's.

It was as if the universe was calm again; as if nothing else mattered. Dorothea wrapped her arms around Angie's waist. They'd kissed before, of course, but not like this. For the first time there wasn't a single moment of hesitation. They both knew that wasting time was not an option when they could be together like this.

Angie's knees practically gave way, the surging tide of warmth left her limp in Dorothea's arms. Dorothea leant away with a soft laugh against her cheek and her arms tightened around Angie's waist.

With her bottom lip trembling, Angie managed to speak.

"We should probably close the door," she croaked.

"Probably," Dorothea agreed.

Her arms tightened around Dorothea's neck, as if she was her anchor while the rest of her world span on its axis. Dorothea ducked her head to capture Angie's lips again. She smiled into the kiss, lowering one arm from Dorothea's neck to reach behind her for the door. She finally managed to find it, wincing when it slammed shut as Dorothea pressed Angie against it. They both pulled away with wide eyes, waiting to hear if the sound had woken anybody up. After a few moments, hearing only the sound of their shaking breaths, Angie kissed Dorothea again.

Hands travelled to Angie's lower back, Dorothea brushed her fingertips lightly against the bumps of her spine. Angie's lips parted at the touch, that was when she kissed her deeper. And... *Oh.*

Angie had never understood the concept of kissing before Dorothea. But now, it was so much more than lips touching and wandering hands. It opened the door to a world of desire, her feelings could finally be expressed, in touch rather than words. Dorothea cupped her face, thumb brushing against her cheekbone.

"You kiss me like you're saying goodbye," she whispered.

Angie swallowed.

"Angie," Dorothea met her eyes.

"What happens when I go back?" Angie asked, "when I have to go back to London?"

Dorothea bit her bottom lip, shaking her head.

"We don't have to worry about that now."

"I *always* worry about it," Ange whispered.

Dorothea pressed their foreheads together, her fingers threading through Angie's golden hair.

"No more disagreements," Thea insisted, "we will be together as often as we can."

Angie smiled, closing her eyes as she relaxed into her loving touch.

"Together," Angie breathed out.

"Together," Dorothea breathed with her.

CHAPTER THIRTY-EIGHT

<u>Dorothea</u>

31ˢᵗ December, 1943

The air in her bedroom was crisp in the early hours of the morning. Not that Thea knew it was morning yet, the blacked out windows didn't let in any light.

Despite walls as thin as paper, Thea remained comfortably warm. The pain of loss and the sting of grief were miles away from her. As if a tall fence had been built up around her; a fence that was impossible for other people to climb. Nothing could harm Thea if she remained inside that fence guarded by Peggy, Florence, Angeline and to her own surprise; her mother.

She'd always been jealous of other girls with close relationships with their mothers but she was happy that she was now finding common ground with her own. Maybe Thea and her mother would never understand one another entirely, but just having her there for her was enough.

Florence had taken care of her too, supporting her in her usual motherly fashion. Thea didn't mind filling the space in her heart reserved for the children she could never have, alongside Angeline. Then there was Peggy, who had been like an older sister to her; relentless teasing and snowball fights that went on until both of them were drenched from head to toe. Florence was the protector, Peggy the trouble maker, and it worked out perfectly.

If Thea had been told a year ago how much her family would change; she wouldn't believe it. But then, neither would she have believed how much she herself would change. Angeline Carter the cause.

She had been Thea's first experience of fate; she'd learnt so much from her and she saw the world in a different light now. Every bad thing that happened, every pain she had endured throughout her seventeen years of life was worth it. Thea didn't know what she'd done to deserve Angeline's company or the way she made her feel about herself. Thea had heard it said that it took great effort to love the world and all its unpleasant features. Thea would disagree; it took a lover that could provide a light on even the darkest days.

Longing for Angeline's company, Thea got up and strolled across the landing. The cardboard had been taken down from the small window beside the bathroom. Her eyes adjusted to the light, her brows furrowing in contemplation as she noticed an unfamiliar frame placed on the window sill. Her mother's treasured photographs were still hidden after she had removed them all once the men had been drafted.

Despite the black and white photograph, Thea could tell her mother was wearing her sky blue dress; her lips red and her hair styled in elegant waves. Thea sat beside her on the bench outside their cottage. She was smiling at her father, who grinned right back. They both wore their favourite muddied overalls. James stood beside the bench, his mop of brown curls lopsided as he smiled at the camera.

Despite years teaching herself to cry was to admit defeat, Thea did not fight her bottom lip as it wobbled. Lifting the frame up, she held it to her chest.

"Do you remember how furious I was when that photograph was taken?"

Thea smiled, nodding as she lowered the frame to look at it again.

"You and your father weren't looking at the camera," she chuckled, "it cost a lot of money to get that."

"And you would never frame it," Thea recalled.

Her mother took the picture gently from her daughter's hands.

"How didn't I see before?" her mother mumbled, mostly to herself.

"See what?" Thea asked.

"That this photograph is perfect," she explained, "that this is exactly our family."

"Well, of course it is."

"No, silly," her mother said as she pointed to her father and Thea at the centre of the image. "You two, smiling at each other and the fact you were still in those muddy clothes."

Thea looked down at it.

"It's honest, it's real and pure," her mother said, "I was a fool to never frame it."

Thea pressed her lips together to prevent a sob; it was barely muffled by the action.

"Oh, my darling," her mother whispered.

She blinked her tears into the material of her mother's dress as she hugged her tightly. She smelt like tea and baking. There, in her mother's arms with the photograph pressed between them, Thea felt like a daughter again.

"He'd be proud of us," Thea whispered as she leant away from the embrace.

"I know he would be," her mother cupped her face, pressing a kiss to Thea's forehead.

She put the photograph down and took her daughter's hand.

"But we must prepare to start 1944 the right way," her mother smiled, "not in mourning but in celebration."

"I know," Thea nodded, "but it won't be the same."

"No," the pair began to walk down the stairs together, "but they're still here with us."

As they passed her father's office, Thea glanced at the piano stool. She was sure she could see the figure of her father sat there, he turned around and he smiled. It was a cheeky grin as he pressed a finger to his lips, before spinning back around on the creaky stool to face the instrument, playing once again. However, Thea could hear no sound from the piano as he seemed to fade away, he was nothing but a spirit.

"Are you alright, Thea?" her mother asked.

Thea faced her, feeling light as a feather.

"I'm just fine," Thea replied.

As they approached the dining room, Thea let go of her mother's hand. Her heart was in her mouth when she saw golden hair, glowing in the morning sun, hazel eyes bright with joy. Thea didn't imagine there was anything in the universe that could match the perfection that was Angeline Carter.

Until she smiled.

*

The day went smoothly, only disrupted by the Carter boys arguing over whose turn it was to hide when playing a game of hide and seek, which they'd somehow encouraged Florence, Peggy and Heather to join.

The Land Girls didn't spend many days in the cottage, it had only been on Christmas day and New Year when they'd be missing their families the most it only seemed fair to provide them with some company. Scary Mary sat with her usual cold expression, but after Florence's promise to keep Mary away from Angeline and Thea; the hateful gaze wasn't directed at them.

Angeline and Thea spent time only in each other's company, rejecting the multiple requests from William to join in with their games. However, it wasn't like most days when their conversation flowed like a stream in the Welsh mountains. It was simply quiet, as quiet as it was sitting on Thea's roof during the summer nights. Just the two of them and the comfort they felt in one another's company.

"Play me something," Thea whispered, breaking the silence.

The pair had found themselves in her father's office, both of them squeezed onto the creaky old piano stool.

There wasn't a moment of hesitation as Angeline placed her hands on the keys, beginning with a few gentle chords with her left hand. Her right hand began to move along the piano, fingers dancing as they made a melody like no other that Thea had heard. It was light-hearted and playful yet with unexpected turns as the music suddenly slowed. Angeline's hands stopped as she took an intake a breath before pressing down on the keys again, moving her hands calmly. The music became slow, melancholy as the melody became quieter, fading away with the final chords her left hand played.

It was them. It was Angeline and Thea as music. It was the arguing, the petty disagreements, the kiss, the fear of Mary telling someone about them, James and Arthur's death, flower fields in the summer, placing violets in Angeline's hair, it was *love*.

"Why did it end like that?"

"End like what?" Angeline looked at her hands in her lap, her face one of guilt.

"Sadly," Thea replied.

Angeline looked at her with glossy eyes.

"Because I'm terrified," she whispered. "What on Earth will happen?"

"We don't have to talk about that now," Thea muttered.

"But when?" Angeline stammered, "when are we going to stop pretending this will all be alright?"

"Angeline..."

"Don't say it will be."

Thea put her hand on Angeline's cheek without hesitation; she'd promised herself she'd never again be the reason Angeline cried.

"But it will be," Thea said.

"How?" Angie croaked, leaning into her touch.

"I'll write to you," Thea said, "you can come back and see me."

Angeline wept.

"Please don't cry," Thea whispered, "we'll find a way. London isn't that far away. And I'm not going anywhere. When you get lonely you can just think of me, because I'll always be right here. Even when you grow up and forget about me..."

"I will *never* forget about you," Angeline blurted out.

Thea smiled softly, not wanting to argue further. The image of Angeline married, happy with her children was burned into her brain, keeping her awake at night.

"Well then," Thea continued, "there isn't a thing for us to worry about."

Angeline nodded, closing her eyes.

"Attlee's making the speech!" Heather called from the kitchen.

Thea pressed a quick kiss to Angeline's forehead and smiled.

"Come on."

The family gathered in the living room, as The Deputy Prime Minister Clement Richard Attlee broadcast a New Year message to the nation.

"I suppose that most of us, on New Year's Eve, look back on the old year and count our blessings, and look forward to the New Year with hope," the man on the radio said.

"Count our blessings," Michael scoffed under his breath.

Thea watched Angeline nudge him in the side. Perhaps a year ago, Thea would have scoffed too. It was a war; she had no reason to be grateful. But whilst sat

403

beside Angeline, their legs brushing secretly under the table, it felt she had everything to be thankful for.

"Every one of us has had his or her particular losses and gains in 1943, but as a nation we can say thanks to the old year as it departs," Deputy Attlee continued.

"Thanks for sending me away from my family," Mary muttered under her breath.

It seemed she'd always be responsible for ruining the mood.

"Cold and dark is the outlook for Hitler and the Nazis. The passing year has been for their forces one of continued retreat and of failure by land, sea and air. The Germans have felt the weight of a bombing weapon which they used so ruthlessly and so light-heartedly against defenceless victims in the day of their strength. The hour of reckoning has come, and they know that 1944 will mean for them only heavier attacks," the voice on the radio said. "We can therefore close this year in a spirit of thankfulness for the past and of hope and confidence for the future, but we must not translate hope into relaxation or confidence into complacency.

We cannot tell what unsuspected trials may lie ahead of us: a war is full of surprises."

Angeline looked to Thea, her lashes brushing the tops of her freckled cheeks as she met Thea's eyes.

Whatever Attlee was saying after that went unregistered in Thea's mind, every one of her senses distracted by Angeline.

"May I wish you all health, happiness and victory in the New Year," Thea heard as the speech ended.

She couldn't care less about what a man on the radio had to say; Thea had all the happiness and victory she required right beside her.

EPILOGUE

<u>Angeline</u>

It was past midnight. The merry songs had been sung, the New Year kisses across the country were kissed. It was then that the celebrations seemed to die down and the reality set in; war wasn't over.

Florence, Mary, Heather and Peggy were quick to return to the guesthouse once the grandfather clock in the downstairs hallway chimed midnight. William, Michael, Peter and Charles all went to their rooms, rubbing their tired eyes. Mrs Miller headed to her lonely bed with no kisses or lover beside her.

It was then, when everybody else was asleep, that Thea and Angie felt most awake.

"Put your bloody boots on!" Thea whispered with a giggle, pointing to Angie's pumps. "Your toes will fall off if you wear those."

"You're insane to be dragging me out in the first place," Angie replied.

"Don't be so boring," Thea said, wrapping her scarf around Angie's neck. "You love our midnight walks."

Angie kept it to herself, but she knew it was not only the walks that she loved.

"Alright, alright!" she laughed and swatted Thea's hands away as she fussed over her. "I can dress myself."

Thea smirked.

The smirk that had lured her in from the start.

Angie fastened her boots with ease and stood up.

"It had better be somewhere amazing you're taking me," Angie commented, "because I would much rather be in bed right now."

Thea raised a brow as she did her coat up.

"Somebody's eager."

Angie whacked her arm.

"I meant asleep! Not in bed with you!"

Thea pouted playfully before unlocking the door.

She held her hand out expectantly, her dark hair framing her porcelain skin in the dim light of the moon.

"Coming, Princess?"

Angie took her hand.

*

The cornfields always looked so much larger at night. The whole world seemed that much vaster, as if the only two people in existence were the golden haired princess from the middle-class family in London, and the farmer's stubborn daughter.

They walked their usual route; the one Angie imagined she could walk blindfolded now. Oh, how things had changed.

The pair came to a stop beside a fence.

Angie knew exactly where they were. It was here that Thea had first kissed her. Angie wished she'd just recalled that memory instead of the hurricane of events that followed.

"I'd like to tell you a story," Thea said after a while.

"It's… about a girl," she began, "who introduced me to new levels of frustration that I did not know were humanly possible. Despite the fact she did nothing wrong."

"I wonder who that could be," Angie chuckled.

Thea held a finger to her lips. That gesture would always leave Angie silent.

"She frustrated me because I'd never felt so much admiration and adoration for somebody in my entire life," Thea continued.

"I'm not good at... words..." Thea whispered, "but... what I want to say... well I mean... I already feel it so this shouldn't be so difficult I..."

"I love you," Angie blurted out, "that is what you were going to say, wasn't it? Or..."

Thea cut her off with a kiss.

It wasn't gentle, it was firm and confident, as if Thea was sealing a promise. Angie wrapped her arms around her neck and Thea placed her arms around her waist, lifting her up off the ground.

Angie yelped in surprise as Thea smiled against her lips.

"I love you," Thea said, testing the words on her tongue.

"I love you," she repeated, placing kisses all over Angie's face.

Angie giggled and wriggled out of her grasp.

Thea seemed to be staring into the distance, her lips pursed.

"But I would like to make a compromise," Thea said, "if we spend every day together, I mean every single day until you go home."

Angie's heart raced, it sounded like paradise. She wouldn't want it any other way.

"Anything at all," Angie replied, taking Thea's hand.

Thea face changed, already begging with her wide eyes.

"Get married," Thea whispered, "when you get the chance, marry Albert or Joshua or Matthew or whoever he ends up being, just marry him."

Angie frowned, snatching her hand from Thea's grasp.

"What?" Angie scoffed, "why would you ask that of me?"

"Because I don't want to hold you back," Thea said, her voice remained calm.

"Hold me back?" Angie let out a laugh, a full-on belly laugh.

"If you spend your life alone then..."

"Well I won't be alone!" Angie protested. "I'll be with you– just like you said! I'll write to you and..."

"Come on... you can't live your life through letters," Thea said.

"But, it..." Angie could feel her cheeks burning red with frustration.

"If you don't get married, you'll have no way to get money."

"Stop it," Angie interrupted.

Hadn't Thea been the one, all those months ago, to tell her that there was so much more to a woman's life than marriage?

"You won't have children or..."

"Stop it!" Angie shouted. "I don't care!"

Thea looked down for a moment, chewing her bottom lip as she contemplated what to say next.

"If you promise me," Thea said, "I'll stop talking about it."

"I don't want to admit that there's a chance," Angie whispered, "a chance that I have to live a life without you in it."

Thea's fingers carded through Angie's hair as she pressed kisses across her forehead.

"It isn't a life without me in it," Thea said, "I'll always be there in your memory. The beautiful thing is that nobody can erase the past. "

Angie replayed that sentence in her mind.

"I promise then, for you." Angie finally said, defeated.

Thea cupped her cheeks, her thumbs brushing over her cheekbones like they had done so many times before and she put their foreheads together. The pair didn't move for a while, only shifting from their position when their teeth began chattering.

"We should go home," Thea said.

"I suppose," Angie frowned, "I don't want to be apart from you."

Thea looked up at the night sky, at the moon and her eyes were blue and bright.

"The longer the time we spend apart, the more wonderful we will feel when we are finally together again," Thea smiled.

She looked up at the moon too as her heart ached in her chest. Thea brushed the backs of their hands and Angie linked their fingers.

They continued blissfully, ignoring the inevitable. Moments like this made Angie wish she could stop time. So she could lie next to Thea, close her eyes, feel the beat of her heart and forget about the rest of the things they would leave behind.

"Love is like a war; easy to start but hard to end and you never know where it might take you."

-Oscar Wilde

Dorothea and Angeline will return.

Printed in Great Britain
by Amazon